SCREAMS OF SHADOWS

ASPEN SHERWOOD

ISBN: 978-1-7382714-7-4

ISBN:978-1-7382714-8-1

Book Cover by MiblArt

Map by Cartographybird

aspensherwood.com

For my dog, the inspiration behind Yugar, may you live forever within these pages

WOLFMIRE

WALLGROVE
BASIN

TEMPLEMERE
THICKET

LIGHT CLIFF

WILDMERE

BONEGLEN

PINE BAY

HATBROOK
WOOD

RIVERMAW

THORNVALE

STORM
HOLLOW

THE ISLAND NATION OF

DRYSDEN

MAPPED

IN THE PRESENT AGE

LUNENSOR MOUNTAINS

THE MUMBLING FJORDS

NORTHHOLD

FAIRGUARD

GRAYTHORN

THE BONE PASS

EBONWELL

NEWTIDE

LEMNORA FOREST

HAZELPEAK

COBALT LOCH

DIRT TOWN

GOLDHELM

◉ CAPITAL CITY
◉ MAJOR SETTLEMENTS
◯ MINOR SETTLEMENTS
◇ KNOWN RUINS

THE AGATE SEA

ALSO BY ASPEN SHERWOOD

NIGHTMARES OF NIGHTFALL SERIES

ASPEN SHERWOOD

SCREAMS OF SHADOWS

CHAPTER
ONE
BRYN

The War Chamber was a cold room. Not in terms of heat, with the absence of windows on the walls and a fire roaring in the corner, there was no lack of warmth. But in terms of the chills that the conversation sent racing down my spine, the decisions that spun my stomach in knots.

In this room, we held people's lives in our hands—our choices determined who survived and who didn't. Who had a chance to see the war's end, and who didn't.

A map of Drysden was laid out atop the large circular table in the centre of the room. The true map that showed every inch of the realm including the land that had once been hidden in plain sight: the mountain fortress that served as the prison for the exiled commanding family behind a barrier that no longer stood.

Wooden pieces dotted the map, showing the locations of warriors, reports of Skolli attacks, and key locations. A collection of metal pieces was waiting by the side to mark the decisions we settled upon. It looked almost like a game board, except the pieces were armies, and we gambled with people's homes. With their lives.

Ragna, the daughter of the King Commander and Chieftain of the Striking Shadows, placed the final wooden marker on the map and stepped back around the table. "Currently, things stand largely as we expected." She gestured to the table. "Since the barrier fell a week ago, the number of attacks has not increased. If anything, they have slightly decreased in number. They have, however, concentrated their attention in areas close to where the barrier once stood."

I scanned the map as she spoke, my eyes catching on the pieces marking reports of Skolli attacks. They were clustered in small villages and towns close to the mountain fortress. A few were even placed in locations a little further from the mountains, isolated from the rest of Drysden. Maybe even forgotten like many in my village, Ebonwell, had felt.

"They are preparing themselves. Every piece of evidence we've found, every note I've read, shows that the exiled commanding family are intelligent. Not to mention that many believed they were some of the best tacticians of their time. They would have been trying to sway people to their side from the moment that Pétur first weakened the barrier, if not earlier," Georg said, his deep voice rumbling through the room. The trainer of the Verndari had spent a lot of time studying the history of Drysden when he had won his position decades ago. Yet, I knew that he had re-read every book, studied every note and journal with fresh eyes once we had learned the truth.

Once we had learned that the exiled commanding family still lived.

"They need to see who will bite," Jarl Marik agreed. He had arrived at the fortress only a day before, his warriors and healers in tow. He had left enough behind to protect Pine Bay and brought everything he could spare to join our defence. "Any allies they have are undoubtedly making their way towards the mountain fortress now. And if they are not, it is for a reason. An assignment."

While the War Chamber had not changed, the people around the table had. Aron had filled Pétur's spot, and Sigrún's had been empty since she fled the fortress to finish what Pétur had started. When the barrier fell, and it became clear that war was no longer a probability but a certainty, further changes were made. Jarl Ottó and anyone else on the council who had not yet pledged their support and warriors to the King Commander had been barred from the room. Jarl Marik and other powerful or respected Jarls and Warlords had begun to be added to fill the spaces left by the others.

Some chairs remained carefully tucked under the table, empty and unneeded, but it was better to eliminate the risk of betrayers in the room than to ensure every seat was filled.

"This lull allows us to prepare," Ragna continued after nodding in agreement to Georg and Jarl Marik. "As tempting as it is to strike them during this time, it is too risky. Their fortress is too hard to breach in its location. Not without more information, that is. We would lose numerous warriors just in the attempt."

"And the odds of success of the attack?" Baldur asked. The Commanding Son's question could be taken two ways. Either he was dismissive of the cost as long as the attack succeeded, or he was trying to see if the likelihood of victory was high enough to justify the deaths it would bring.

Surprisingly, I couldn't tell which way he had meant the question.

Gier cleared his throat. "When the exiled commanding family were sent to their prison, the need for future attacks on their position was not considered. They were sent to die—it is clear that no one suspected that they would have allies to ensure that they didn't. The exiled commanding family are in a mountainous area, which is difficult for large numbers of warriors to traverse. The fortress is on high ground with minimal tree cover close to it, leaving any attacking armies exposed. Even if we attacked during the day when the monsters can't be exposed to the sun, they would be on us as soon as we breached the doors. And they would know the terrain in ways that we wouldn't. I wouldn't be surprised if one of the first things they did when the barrier fell was cataloguing every nook and cranny around their fortress." Gier took a moment to gather his thoughts. "The odds of success are low at best."

"Then we prepare for their next move instead," the King Commander decided, bracing his arms on the table as he studied the map. "We establish our military strongholds and the front line now, so they are ready when they strike."

"While an all-out attack on the mountain fortress may not be in our best interest, that does not mean that there isn't something else that we can do to weaken them rather than just sitting back on our haunches for their attacks," Jarl Marik said, his brows furrowed.

"We have suspicions where the exiled commanding family may turn for support. If we target them, we may be able to weaken their forces," Gier suggested, his long hair tied back from his face with a leather band. After Ragna, Gier would be the most informed. If he thought that was a good option, then I believed him.

And, honestly, it would be better than sitting around and waiting for the war to come to us.

The King Commander shook his head, not bothering to look at the people around him. "No."

"It's a good idea," Hákon agreed. As not just a son of the King Commander but also Hersir of the Royal Regiment and leader of the healers of the fortress, Hákon was almost as comfortable on the battlefield as we were.

"We could go," Georg said, his eyes alight at the possibilities. "We'll be more subtle than—"

The King Commander slammed his hands on the table, silence immediately filling the room. "Did I, or did I not, already say no to the suggestion?" The King Commander's words were quiet but threaded with venom. My body tensed, my muscles going rigid at the tone of his voice. "We will proceed with preparing for the battles to come."

No one said anything as the King Commander began to place the metal markers on the map. One was set atop Wolfmire, another on Newtide, and a number in a line connecting the two. "This shall be the focus of our military."

My hands shook as I took in what lay before the line. "There are settlements, there are people, in front of that line that you are condemning, like Northhold and Fairguard."

"Fairguard will receive a small contingent of military support, enough to protect the mines," the King Commander said, brushing aside my words and placing a much smaller marker there. It was so small compared to the others that it was almost pitiful.

Gil pressed the back of his hand to my side, steadying me. "What about Northhold? And the other small villages and settlements in the area?"

"They will need to protect themselves."

I came from one of those small villages. I knew exactly

what kind of military power and bloodrites were typically housed in those areas.

And it would not be enough to survive any true attack.

If they stayed in their homes, they were going to die.

"You're abandoning them," Rúna accused quietly from her place beside Baldur. Regardless of how feisty and courageous she was, she had learned to hold her tongue when she was by his side. The fact that she was speaking up—*calling out*—the King Commander, meant she felt the same way as me.

This was wrong.

No one spoke. No one dared to break the oppressive silence that now weighed heavily in the room.

Finally, the Queen pasted a small, fake smile on her face. "We will warn them, though, so that they are not unprepared."

"Yes, we will do that," The King Commander said dismissively. "One team will be dispatched to Northhold while another will travel to the smaller settlements to inform them of my decision."

"The teams will inform the people of your decision and leave?" Gil asked, his eyes searching the faces of those around the table. He was no doubt trying to see if they were as disturbed by the idea as we were.

The King Commander nodded. "Exactly."

"You're not even going to offer safe transport to the closest protected city?" Óskar's voice was incredulous.

"Perhaps for the people of Northhold, that may be an option, but for the smaller settlements, it would require more warriors than I am willing to spare," the King Commander said. I pursed my lips together, trying not to say anything that could worsen this situation. It felt like we were standing upon dry kindling, one spark away from a fire. "After all, these villages and outposts should expect this to happen."

"They should expect their King Commander to deem them unworthy of protection? For them to be evaluated and ultimately labelled as unimportant?" I snapped, unable to hide the fury that flickered through my body as he brushed away hundreds—thousands—of lives.

The King Commander rapped his knuckles on the tabletop, his eyes piercing my own. "Watch your tone with me, girl."

Gil shifted by my side as though he would step forward to react to the King Commander's tone. I intertwined my fingers with his with a squeeze. A silent plea to not do anything. Things were rapidly spiralling out of control. I refused to let him bear the brunt of the King Commander's anger over something I could easily deal with.

"If I may," Aron started hesitantly. "There is already some... discontent in some of the settlements north of Newtide. They already feel as though the Commanding Family has forgotten them. I would tread carefully in presenting this information, or you risk igniting something there."

"Is that a threat?" the King Commander growled, his eyes flashing.

Georg stepped forward. "There is no threat, King Commander. Aron was bringing it to your attention to warn you. Is that not what this council is for? To advise and to share information so that we can make the best-informed decision."

"A decision has been made, so there is no need for further *counsel*," the King Commander spat, venom oozing from his words. "Should your team be one of the ones chosen for this role, you will be informed. Now get out—the council's guidance is no longer wanted."

TWO

BRYN

T he courtyard was full of people. Stable hands awaited the opportunity to care for the horses as the servants lingered nearby, ready to care for the items the arrivals inevitably brought with them. Ottó was there likely to evaluate the support we would receive while the King Commander waited to welcome them and accept their promises of service.

I didn't know who would arrive this afternoon; we had been pulled out for Warlord after Warlord, Jarl after Jarl and lined up alongside the Commanding Family. Whether it was to provide us the opportunity to survey the troops that we would lead or to serve as a reminder of just how powerful the King Commander was, I was unsure.

We were either a weapon to wield or a jewel to show off to the King Commander, nothing more.

Once again, Rúna didn't stand in her rightful place by Gil's side. Instead, she stood beside Baldur, her arm linked to his.

"I wish they would hurry this up," Óskar muttered by my

side, shifting his weight between his feet. "The waiting is boring."

Georg narrowed his eyes at him, forcing me to smother my smile, not about to get wrapped up in whatever Georg would have Óskar do. Although he was fond of assigning Óskar hand-to-hand sparring with Gil, which I found I tended to enjoy much more than he did.

Horns sounded in the distance and were echoed by the ones on the walls. The gates creaked open as the people in the courtyard quickly shifted to ensure the path to where the King Commander stood was clear.

Jarl Einar entered first, flanked by his generals. I grinned, knowing that somewhere in the steady stream of warriors, healers, and War Camp supporters was Sofie, the heir to his healing centre, and Luck, an incredible warrior who had ended up fighting by my side as we held the line at Wolfmire.

Jarl Einar rode his horse most of the way across the court-yard before dismounting and crossing the rest of the distance to the King Commander on foot. The stable hands rushed forward as the rest of his party began to dismount.

The King Commander stepped to the edge of the platform he stood on, prompting Jarl Einar to bow towards him.

"Rise," the King Commander said. Once Jarl Einar stood tall once again, he continued. "Have you come to pledge your support to me?"

"I have come to support the cause." Jarl Einar chose his words very carefully. Before we left Wolfmire, he made it very clear that the King Commander had not earned his support.

I had.

"To support the cause is to support me, Jarl Einar," the King Commander pointed out, his face not showing any concern over the fact that Jarl Einar didn't immediately bend his knee to him.

"Be that as it may, King Commander, you will not be the person to whom I pledge my allegiance," Jarl Einar announced, his shoulders back and his chin high. Not intimidated, not nervous about the declaration he was making. About the divide that he was drawing through the already fractured court. "You have not earned it."

I had been the one to hold the line when nothing awaited me but death. I had been the one, alongside my comrades, that stood between the Skolli and his city. Not the man demanding his allegiance.

The King Commander didn't have his support—I did. With every drop of blood I spilled, with every bruise and cut that marred my body, I had won it.

While I knew that it might cause a problem, I hadn't expected the reveal to the King Commander to happen in such a public setting. It would have been bad enough happening in private, with one of the most powerful Jarls declaring his support to a Verndari rather than the Commanding family. But in public like this?

I grimaced, my fingers shaking by my side. Not only was he choosing me over the King Commander, but he was also painting me as more worthy.

Gil had warned me of the threats that the King Commander had made against his sisters; I had seen the disregard he had for the safety and wellbeing of his people in the War Chamber. He was teetering on a dagger's edge between calculating and cruel, and I had no idea how he would fall in this situation.

The King Commander was silent for a moment.

"And who, pray tell, has earned your allegiance?" His words were colder than ice.

"Jarl Brynja," Jarl Einar said, his eyes landing on me. "She is the only one that I will pledge my support to."

The King Commander turned his attention to me, his face emotionless, but his eyes blazed with fury. "Jarl Brynja," he barked. "To me."

I tucked my hands behind my back, holding my wrists to hide my nerves before I stepped forward to accept my summons. No one said a word, the silence a heavy weight on the courtyard, allowing the click of my boots against the stone to ring out across the space.

When I was close enough, the King Commander reached out, his fingers encircling my arm. He turned his back to the crowd, shielding his whitening knuckles from the onlookers. The King Commander squeezed tighter, leaning towards me until his breath brushed my face. I bit my tongue, the metallic tang of blood filling my mouth, refusing to show a hint of the pain that he was causing me.

"You will accept his allegiance and end this spectacle without drawing more attention to yourself, girl. Am I clear?" he hissed, his words so quiet that I doubted the other people on the platform would have heard him.

"As crystal, King Commander," I answered, equally quiet.

He squeezed me again, my fingers going numb, before he finally released me. The feeling rushed back, causing pinpricks of pain to race down my arm from bicep to fingernail.

I refused to let any discomfort show, turning towards Jarl Einar with a small smile.

"Jarl Einar," I said, my words ringing throughout the court-yard. "Have you come to pledge your support to me?" I echoed the King Commander's words from earlier, about to succeed where he had failed.

Jarl Einar bowed his head, sinking to a knee. "My sword, coin, and grain are yours, Jarl Brynja. My warriors will fight for you; my healers will support you."

"Then rise, Jarl Einar. And welcome to the cause."

THE KING COMMANDER had quickly ended the gathering in the courtyard after Jarl Einar had sworn his allegiance to me.

He had assigned some new recruits from the Striking Shadows to show Jarl Einar to his rooms and his people where they would stay in the fortress. It was a slight, and everyone in the courtyard knew it. We had been showing people to their places since the forces had started to arrive. A gesture of the King Commander's appreciation to have the Verndari, who outranked everyone who walked through those gates, taking the time to guide them.

But Jarl Einar did not receive that gesture.

And we had been very clearly dismissed, making it clear that we were not to interfere.

I kept my head high, my hands neatly tucked behind my back, ignoring the impulse to cover the bruises the King Commander had left behind. Gil and Óskar fell into step with me, Georg and Aron not far behind.

I didn't relax until we were again safely behind the doors to our wing, Gil a steady presence by my side.

"Jarl Einar really should have thought that through," Óskar pointed out, flopping on a couch. "He singled you out over the King Commander in front of everyone. With the power trip he's on, I'm surprised that the King Commander didn't smite you right there."

Georg clipped him behind the head. "Careful of your words, even here," he told him before turning towards me. "What did he say to you?"

"That I was to accept Jarl Einar's allegiance and not draw more attention to myself," I sighed, resting a hand on my forehead, overwhelmed by the last several moments.

"That's it? I saw the look in his eyes, Bryn. He was pissed," Aron asked, his brows furrowed in confusion.

Gil was quiet, his attention focused on me.

I swallowed. "That's all he said. He showed his...displeasure in other ways," I said, carefully choosing my words at the small chance I was overheard.

Gil's eyes immediately locked on my arm where the King Commander had grabbed me. He stepped forward, his fingers gentle as they landed on my wrist. Gil gave me a moment to pull away, to stop what I knew he would do, but I made no such move.

I needed to see just as much as they did what the King Commander had done to me.

Gil's calloused hands were soft as feathers as he rolled up my sleeve to reveal the bruises the King Commander had left behind. One for each of his fingers.

"Bastard," Gil breathed, his words barely loud enough for me to hear as Aron cursed.

Georg's mouth was tight, the faint lines around his mouth deepening as he avoided voicing his thoughts at the darkening marks on my arm.

"At least we know where Baldur gets it from," Óskar muttered angrily. Where he got his abusive tendencies. Where he got the belief that it was acceptable to brutally beat Rúna when she had already lost their spar.

"Even before this, I think we all knew it wasn't from his mother," I disagreed.

The Queen had always been the complimentary opposite of the King Commander. Soft where he was rough. Quiet where he was loud. A calm tactician to his erratic strategist.

"I should get some bruise paste on this before it gets any worse," Gil said, his healing instincts shining through more by the day.

I studied him for a moment, debating whether to point out that it was something that I could do for myself. Something that I had done for myself multiple times whenever he wasn't near to help me. But I knew it was important to him to help me where he could, as it was for me when it came to him.

"Alright," I agreed. He interlaced his fingers with mine and led me to my rooms.

I sat on the edge of my bunk as he went to grab my healing supplies. He returned with the tin of bruise paste and knelt before me. He easily opened the container and began to cover the handprint on my arm.

"What's he going to do?" I asked, voicing the fears that had taken root in me since Jarl Einar's declaration.

"What is he going to do about what?" Gil finished what he was doing, closing the tin and giving me his full attention.

"About what just happened. He is not going to forget that, Gil. He was talking about leaving people to die like discussing sailing conditions; he threatened your sisters. The King Commander is going to retaliate. He's going to blame me for what just happened."

Gil was silent for a moment. "He will," he agreed, never one to soothe my worries with false platitudes. "But you are a

Verndari, a well-respected one, with the backing of Hákon, Ragna, and Jarl Einar. He cannot target you like he has my sisters. You are more protected than them."

"Ma and Fannar—"

"Are also protected. By us and the Royal Regiment," Gil cut off my spiral before it could begin. "We will not let them be harmed. I will not let you be harmed."

I slipped off my bunk, sinking to my knees before him, bringing our faces closer together. His eyes were locked on mine, following each of my movements with an intensity that rang with love. I looped my arms around his neck, my fingers stroking through the hair at the base of his head.

"We can't know what he will do," I said softly with a sigh. "He's unpredictable at the best of times, volatile at the worst of them."

"We cannot change him. We plan for him; we react to his actions as needed." Gil's hands came to rest on my hips. "Until then, we do our best to ignore him. We focus on other things until we have no other choice."

I moved closer to him, the front of my body pressed to his, his heartbeat thumping against my chest. "And if I was having trouble focusing on other things—would you be willing to help?"

"It seems like you have something in mind," Gil pointed out, the corner of his lips quirking as his fingers tightened on my hips.

"What gave it away?" I breathed.

Gil lifted a brow before grinning at me. "I like how you think," he said softly before pressing his lips to mine.

His lips were gentle as if he savoured each movement and sound he pulled from me. Gil pressed a kiss to the corner of my mouth, to my cheek, before tracing down my throat.

"I thought you were going to distract me," I pointed out as Gil nibbled at the crook of my neck.

"Is this not working for you?" he asked against my skin.

"Oh, it's working," I told him with a gasp as his teeth found a sensitive spot. "But I want to forget my name, I'm so distracted."

He pressed kisses up my throat and nipped at my ear. "Your wish is my command," he said, his breath fanning against me.

Gil shifted his hands to the very top of my thighs before he stood, lifting me with him. I wrapped my legs around his waist, interlocking my ankles with a gasp as he strode across the room. Gil cupped the back of my head, his fingers tangling in my curls just before my back met the wall.

He pressed against me, making it clear just how much he was enjoying this, pinning me between his warm body and the cool, hard wall at my back.

The wall supporting some of my weight freed his hands for other purposes. Immediately, they were skimming my body, finding all the places that made me moan; all the places that he knew made me gasp. As familiar with my body as his own, Gil could play it like an instrument, strumming all the right parts to make me lose my mind.

One hand found my chest, the other settling between my legs, causing me to squirm against him as pleasure flared through my body. "Gil," I breathed, tilting my head back and causing it to thump against the wall. "Gil. Please."

"Is this what you wanted, darling?" His lips were warm against my skin as they nipped along my throat before soothing the slight pain with his tongue.

"*Yes.*" I bucked against him. "Please," I begged.

If I had thought his movements had been feverish before, they were nothing compared to what they turned into. His hands were everywhere on my body: his lips, his teeth, his tongue, on my skin. The pleasure ratcheted up higher and higher until it finally burst, my toes curling, my fingers tightening in his hair, pulling a hiss from him.

He released me, my body sliding down every inch of his until my feet rested on the floor. My legs quivered slightly as he pulled my shirt over my head, tossing it unceremoniously across the room before doing the same with my pants. Gil shed his own clothes even faster, as though he couldn't wait to put his hands back on me again.

Gil's hands reached for me, sliding on my skin before effortlessly lifting me back into his arms. I hissed at the cold wall against my back as Gil settled against me. "Still what you wanted, darling?"

"Yes, Gods, yes," I said against his lips as he sank into me. He cursed, his head dropping to my shoulder as he paused for a moment. I shifted against him, urging him to move, causing him to lift his head to lock eyes on me.

His eyes were dark, his cheeks flushed, as one of his hands shifted to my waist. "Hold on," he muttered, giving me just enough time to loop my arms around his neck before he began to move.

Before he began to pound into me, his movements bordering on erratic, as if he wasn't in absolute control of every one of his body's movements.

Every one of mine.

The pleasure flared again, low in my stomach, coiling through my body tighter and tighter until it burst. Gil stilling moments later, lazily pressing kisses to my head and my temple as we allowed our heartbeats to slow. My eyes fell shut as I relaxed in his hold.

"Did that work?" he asked me.

I opened my heavy eyelids to look at him. "What had we been talking about again?" I asked.

Gil chuckled as he pulled us away from the wall and walked over to my bunk. He set me down gently on the furs. "I will take that as a yes," he said, his eyes dancing.

THREE

BRYN

I looked forward to dinners with the Verndari whenever we were in the fortress. Georg always insisted that we eat together almost every night like a family rather than just an elite fighting force.

And that was exactly what we were—each other's family. The ties between us flowed just as deep between us as they did our blood. We were the family we chose, the people we laughed, ate, trained, and bled beside. We entrusted each other with our well-being every time we stepped on the battlefield.

That level of closeness, that level of trust, bonded people more deeply than almost anything else.

But since the barrier fell and war loomed closer every day, it was no longer just family dinners. It was one of the only times we let go of the responsibilities that weighed heavily on our shoulders. When we could laugh freely, joking, singing, and teasing each other without feeling guilty for not prioritizing something else.

A time when we could just be ourselves—not warriors, not commanders, but just an average person. When we could let go of our stresses and anxieties and enjoy each other's company.

Ever since we had held the line at Wolfmire, Hákon, Gier, Fannar, and Lúdvík had had a standing invitation to our dinners. They could join us whenever they liked; some took us up on the invitation more than others. And I suspected that with Sofie and Luck now in the fortress, they would receive their own invitations sooner rather than later.

Tonight, Gil and I entered the common rooms to find all the other Verndari already there, along with Fannar. With Fannar being my adoptive brother and Aron's blood brother, along with one of the people leading our stand at Wolfmire, he was practically considered an honorary member of our group.

He sat by Aron's side, his head thrown back in laughter at something his brother said. I sank into the open seat beside him, and Gil took the one by my side. Across from us, Rúna, Óskar, and Georg were locked in a loud debate, the smiles on their faces showing that it was good-natured.

"Did you hear the story about Aron deciding to climb up the mast of his ship to fix the sail without noticing the large wave approaching?" Fannar asked me; a faint pink dusted Aron's cheeks at his words.

I snorted, picturing what had probably happened. "No, I haven't." I leaned forward to speak directly to Aron. "Have you heard the story of Fannar climbing a tree when he was fourteen years old and the girl he—"

Fannar cut me off by covering my mouth with his hand. "He doesn't want to hear that story."

"Oh yes, I do." Aron's eyes were bright. "Do tell, Bryn."

Fannar groaned, knowing I wouldn't hesitate to tell the story, emphasizing every embarrassing detail. I raised an eyebrow, giving him the choice. He could tell it, or I could.

He sighed, begrudgingly launching into the story. Aron's eyes were fixed on him, happily drinking every detail he could about his little brother. He had even joined Fannar and me on some of our visits with Ma, engraining himself in our family even as he welcomed Fannar back into his own.

I chimed in throughout Fannar's story, adding my side of the events, causing Aron to smile and Fannar to roll his eyes playfully.

When I felt I had fulfilled my role as little sister in embarrassing Fannar, I turned my attention to the debate happening on the other side of the table.

"I'm telling you there is no way that Ragna and Svanna will officially announce their relationship anytime soon," Óskar argued. Svanna was one of Jarl Ottó's daughters and a member of the Striking Shadows. Ragna and Svanna's relationship was obvious to their friends, but it was kept largely secret from the fortress as a whole. "It's more likely that Gil and Talon announce their engagement than that happening anytime soon. I'm willing to put money on it."

"Hold your horses there, Óskar," Georg laughed. "Let Gil and Bryn get through the war ahead before they have to worry about all that."

Gil's hand found my own under the table, interlacing our fingers.

"I think Fannar and Sofie courting will happen before both of those things," I pointed out.

Fannar perked up. "Did you say my name?"

"Bryn was talking about you and Sofie—" Rúna cut herself off with a chuckle as Fannar's face turned pink.

"There is no me and Sofie."

"Not yet," I teased, causing his face to darken further. He

21

returned to his conversation with Aron, whose eyes were dancing in humour.

Gil turned his attention to Rúna. "If you are not careful, the King Commander is going to expect the announcement of your and Baldur's engagement before any of the others."

Rúna shudders in her chair. "There is no way that I am going to marry Baldur."

"We all know that he is not the traitor now, Rúna, you can drop the act with him," Óskar pointed out. Rúna had gone through with the sham of a relationship with Baldur to find evidence that he was the traitor among the Commanding Family. But it had turned out that it had been Sigrún, which meant her role was done.

She could be free of him.

"I can't. Not yet," Rúna said, her shoulders slumping.

"He still has something on you," Georg gathered, leaning back in his chair and crossing his arms. "Tell us, and we can help you. You don't have to keep doing this, Rúna."

Rúna shook her head. "I won't put you all in danger like that. Not over me."

"Then do not put us all in danger; just tell me." Gil's words were practically a plea. He was as close to Rúna as I was to Fannar, her brother in everything but blood. His protective instincts had been screaming at him the whole time that Rúna had been with Baldur, desperate to help her. And now that we knew that he was not the traitor, there was no reason for her to put herself through this.

"I can't," she whispered. "I won't put you and your sisters at risk over me."

Gil's eyes widened slightly. "The only way my sisters would be at risk is if I was involved with something treasonous."

"If I told you what Baldur has on me, then you would be." Rúna's words were no louder than a whisper, but what she said thundered through the room.

It wasn't just some secret that Baldur knew about her.

She was involved in treason, and the Commanding Son knew about it.

THE KING COMMANDER'S summons arrived the next day.

And it wasn't just for me like I had expected; it was for all of us. For the Verndari as a unit. To report to his office and bear the consequences of Jarl Einar's actions together. As one.

Rúna was meeting us there, having to come straight from a commitment with Baldur, so Gil was free to walk by my side. With Óskar on one side and Gil on the other, I almost felt strong enough to face what lay ahead. As much as Gil had reassured me that there was nothing that the King Commander could do to me or my loved ones, I knew there would be some consequence for what had happened.

Jarl Einar had publicly undermined the King Commander, and he used me to do it.

The King Commander couldn't risk losing Jarl Einar's support, which meant that I would bear the brunt of whatever consequence was coming.

When we reached the closed door to the King Commander's office, Georg hesitated, looking back to ensure we were ready for what lay beyond. A second later, he knocked.

"Enter," the King Commander ordered.

Rúna joined us as Georg opened the door, and we filed into the room. We settled into a line across the room by pairing, leaving me between Gil and Óskar.

The King Commander ignored our presence, writing on the parchment before him. He finished, signing his name with a flourish before carefully folding it and sealing it with wax. Finally, his attention landed on us.

His eyes slid down the line from Georg on one end to Rúna on the other before returning to me.

"I thought that your role as Verndari was quite clear," the King Commander said, his voice like ice. "You are a representation of the Commanding Family. An extension of me—my sword arm."

"Of course, King Commander. It is an honour to play such an important role for the realm." Georg bowed his head in a gesture of respect.

The King Commander's eyes flashed angrily before he slammed a fist on his desk. "Then why the *fuck* do I send you to Wolfmire to earn me the support of Jarl Einar, and you return with his support of *you*?"

"It was not intentional, King Commander. We never sought out his support for ourselves," Gil said, trying to keep the King Commander's attention from me. And as much as I appreciated what he was doing, I didn't want the King Commander's attention on him either, especially with how his family was treated.

"I don't want your attempt to protect that bint beside you," the King Commander hissed before he swung his focus to me. "I want to hear from her own treasonous lips."

I swallowed before I stepped forward and locked my shaking hands behind my back.

"I assure you, King Commander, that we—that I—only ever advocated for the Commanding Family. We never tried to gain his support for ourselves." I spoke carefully, aware of every word that came out of my mouth and how they might be interpreted.

"Then how did that spectacle in the courtyard come to be?"

I took a deep breath. "Jarl Einar had said, from the moment we arrived in Wolfmire, that he would only give his support to whoever he thought deserved it. After we held the line for his city, he deemed that the Verndari, that I, in particular, had been the ones to earn it."

"I had a son there with you both times. First, there was Baldur and then Hákon. Are you saying that you were more deserving than them? That Jarl Einar had deemed you so?" I didn't answer his question, didn't react to his words. He had already used the word treasonous to describe me; I wasn't about to give him another reason to dislike me. "Did you plan what happened in the courtyard?"

"No, King Commander. I had no idea that would happen," I told him honestly.

I would have preferred if it hadn't happened.

The King Commander drummed his fingers on his desk, eyes narrowing on me. I locked my knees, refusing to show any nerves to the man.

"But it did happen. You usurped me before everyone there. That news will spread through the fortress and Goldhelm faster than sickness on a raiding ship, Jarl Brynja."

"I apologize, King Commander. That was never my intention." His profound silence prompted me to add. "How do you want me to fix this?"

His lips curled into a cruel smirk. "If you are so set on pulling my armies from me, you can execute my other wartime duties. Such as informing Northhold that we will not be providing them with any support in the coming conflict."

Rúna gasped. "You will have us bear the brunt of their anger."

The King Commander ignored her, his focus still locked on me. "You may want to be their hero, but I will sooner make you their villain."

He was threatened by the support that I had, that the Verndari had as a group. With one of the most powerful Jarls in the realm declaring their support to me rather than the King Commander. It opened the door for others to do the same. It showed that there was an alternative to supporting the Commanding Family.

It undercut his power. It made the King Commander look weak.

So he would strike first. He would tear me down before the realm, paint me as evil, and make me his villain.

Before they had the chance to do it to him.

He would be the face of additional resources, of reinforced military outposts while I represented his decisions to leave people to die, of deeming his people unworthy.

And I had no choice but to nod. "I am here to serve, King Commander," I said mechanically. Void of any emotion.

"The Verndari will ride for Northhold within the coming days and share the War Council's decision regarding their fate. You are dismissed." I turned immediately for the door, not wanting to linger a moment longer with the King Commander. The Verndari around me doing the same.

Georg had just reached the door when the King Commander spoke again. "You will all remember your place, or I will be forced to express my discontent with other, less prevalent members of your houses."

FOUR

GIL

Violet and Klara shared a suite of rooms not too far from where Bryn's mother lived. Óskar's twin sister occupied the rooms across the hall from them, while Rúna's family should have been across from Bryn's mother. It was smart on behalf of the original Verndari to group their families together like this.

They were far enough apart that they felt some semblance of independence but close enough that they would be easy for us to defend should anything happen.

As far as I knew, no one had been stupid enough to attack the family of a Verndari at the fortress. That was asking for your head to end up on a pike. Even if the Verndari were away, their families were often just as lethal.

My sisters' rooms were a perfect blend of both of them. Violet's healing items were neatly prepared by the door for easy access, while Klara's various weapon memorabilia were scattered throughout the room, with only her swords neatly tucked by the door should she need them.

I knew that if I were to peek into their rooms, Violet's bunk would be neatly made, and Klara's furs would likely lie wherever she kicked them. Regardless of the opposite natures of my younger siblings, they lived together harmoniously.

Violet beamed at me as I shut the door behind me. "Hi, Gil," she said softly as Klara slid into the room, her eyes bright.

"It's good to see you, brother," Klara told me, settling onto the couch beside Violet.

I took the chair beside them, stretching my legs out in front of me and relaxing into the soft fabric. "It is good to see the both of you as well. It has been too long."

"Don't blame us for that," Violet rolled her eyes. "We're always in the fortress. You're the one that is constantly away lately."

"Or tangled up in Bryn," Klara muttered, her lips quirking up in a smirk, betraying the humour she could see in the situation.

I knocked the tip of my boot against her. "Say something there?"

"I was just asking when we get to meet Bryn," Klara said, blinking innocently over at me.

It was my turn to roll my eyes with a soft chuckle. "I am sure that she would love to meet you as long as you promise not to scare her away."

"Would we do that?" Klara gasped, placing a hand on her chest.

Violet giggled. "If your big broody walls didn't scare her away, I doubt that we would be able to, even if we tried."

"Not that we would try," Klara added softly, all traces of humour gone. "She's good for you, Gil, and you are happier than I can ever remember you being. I am more likely to trap her with us than scare her away."

Violet nodded in agreement.

I shifted in my seat. I loved my sisters desperately, but they were one of the few that could see through me. Only Bryn could read me better, and Rúna wasn't far behind them. And for them to describe me that way, for them to describe my happiness when I had prepared myself to be content in life at best, made me blatantly aware of just how profound of an impact Bryn has had on me.

Just how deeply she has woven herself into my very being.

As if sensing my desire to change the subject away from myself, Violet launched into filling me in on everything that had happened at the healing centre since we last sat down together. With Hákon as their leader, they had been preparing for war before we were actively voicing that that was what we were doing.

But since the barrier had fallen, he hadn't made any more effort to disguise their efforts. They had been stockpiling supplies and giving anyone who showed any potential rapid training in the basics of healing. Even those without a blood-rite would be needed in the healers' tents in the War Camps, and if they could take on the more basic cases, the other healers would be left to focus on the more dire cases.

It allowed them to save their bloodrites for the people who needed it most.

"Hákon said that he would be announcing his leadership team in the coming weeks," Violet's eyes were so bright they were almost glowing. "He's hinted that I have a good chance of being on it."

My nerves tangled in my stomach like a leaded weight had settled there. I cleared my throat. "His team here at the fortress?" I asked, desperately hoping that my sister would be spared the horrors that awaited us on the battlefield.

She shook her head. "No. In the War Camps."

"I am proud of you," I told her softly after a few moments of silence. "Have you worked anymore on your defence skills?"

"I don't want to kill anyone," Violet winced. "I want to go to save lives, not take them."

Klara whistled and settled back into the couch to watch the battle of wills about to happen. She had witnessed a variation of this argument between us multiple times, but it had always been hypothetical.

Now, it wasn't.

And I wasn't about to send my sister out to war without faith that she could, at the very least, defend herself should the worst happen.

"You have to," I said, holding up a hand to hold off her arguments until I finished. "I am not saying that you have to train on your front lines. I need to know that you are prepared and that you can defend yourself should those lines fail. And they can fail; they *have* failed. I will never forget the sight of the War Camp at Wolfmire—the tents trampled, poles snapped, the fabrics singed and ripped and dangling. Bryn was able to evacuate the healers behind the city walls, but there will not always be that option. I need to know that if my lines crumble, if I or the other Verndari fall and the enemy breaks through, you have a fighting chance."

Violet and Klara just blinked at me, stunned by my speech. I had always been more open with my sisters than the others, but it was hard to shake the need to carefully assess each word I said, to watch every movement I made, and to hold myself back from the people around me.

My sisters could probably count on one hand the number of times I said that many words in one go.

"I don't want to use a sword," Violet finally whispered. "I don't think I could bear that. But if there were something else, something that wouldn't impact my healing or remind me of such bloodshed, I would be willing to learn."

My shoulders relaxed. "Thank you. I have an idea if you trust me."

Violet threw a pillow at my head. "Of course, I trust you, you idiot."

"Wait just a moment." Klara leaned forward in her seat. "You're going to let her go? You won't let me go!"

I sighed. "I'm not letting her do anything right now; we will cross that bridge when Hákon announces his team. But if he names Violet, and she wants to go, I will let her go." The words threatened to crack my heart. I couldn't stand the thought of my sisters at risk. "If you prove to me that you can hold your own, I will let you go too, Klara. But you won't have the relative protection of the War Camp—you are a warrior. You will be out there in the thick of it with the rest of us. I need to know that you can handle that before I let you join the rest of the forces."

Klara was quiet for a moment, considering my words. "And how do I prove that to you? What do I have to do?"

"I do not know," I told her honestly. "But if you accept more training, if you both do, I would feel better."

She grinned at me as Violet tipped back her head with a groan. "When do we start?"

FIVE

BRYN

G il wasn't at breakfast the next morning.

I looked to Rúna for an explanation, but she just shrugged. She had no more idea of where he was than I did. Georg didn't mention it when he sat down to the table, much less of a stickler for our attendance at breakfast and lunch than he was for dinner.

As long as Gil was on time for training, he would not face any of Georg's ire.

I grabbed an apple when we stood to leave for the training hall in case Gil hadn't had a chance to eat before he went to do whatever he was doing that morning. The apple wouldn't do much, and he would surely be ravenous after training, but at least he would have something in his stomach.

Gil stood just inside the training hall with two girls by his side. They had to be his sisters, the similarities between them were striking.

"Klara! Violet!" Rúna greeted them enthusiastically, throwing her arms around them in turn.

Gil turned to Georg. "After we are done training for the day,

I was hoping some of us could work with Klara and Violet. They both will be dragged into this conflict, and with the King Commander already threatening them—" he cut himself off to gather his thoughts. "I may not be able to protect them from the war ahead, but I must ensure they face it as prepared as possible."

"Of course," Georg agreed with a nod. "They are more than welcome to train here whenever they have the time."

"Thank you," Gil said as he turned back to his sisters. "They will watch our training, and I will work with them afterwards."

I stepped up towards his sisters, curiosity lighting their eyes as they watched me approach them. One of them stood with confidence in her training clothes, a pair of swords clasped between her hands. The ease that seemed to radiate from her told me that it was Klara, his warrior sister.

The other seemed much more uncertain, pulling at her clothes with unease. She didn't hold any weapons, meaning she didn't have her own blades like her sister. Which meant that she was the healer. That she was Violet.

I introduced myself to the girls. "I'm Bryn," I said, prompting a smirk to curl up Klara's face.

"Oh, we know. We've heard plenty about you," she teased me.

"Only good things, I hope." I gestured to her swords. "You take after your brother, I see."

Gil joined us, drawing Klara's attention for a moment before she focused on me again. "He taught me himself." Her words were threaded with pride.

She was proud of her brother in a way that so few people in the fortress were.

It immediately made me like her more.

I turned to Violet. "Did he teach you as well?"

"I didn't like the swords." Violet's voice was soft. "And they are too bulky; they could get in the way of my healing."

Gil's face creased with worry, his lips pursed. Violet needed a weapon if she was healing in the War Camps, but it was clear that it made her uncomfortable. Her primary concern was her ability to heal, not ensuring she had the means to protect herself should something go wrong.

I was quiet for a moment, debating if I was about to over-step, before ultimately deciding it was worth it. "I can teach you how to use daggers," I offered, Gil's face immediately relaxing at my words. "They are small enough that you will barely notice them when healing. Not to mention that you will always have a knife nearby in the healers' tents should you not have your daggers on you."

Violet considered my words for several moments. "I would appreciate that. Thank you. I don't have any daggers, though."

"You can use some of mine for now." I smiled at her. "And then we will look into getting your own."

I turned away to rejoin the others when Gil's hand gently wrapped around my wrist. Stopping me. "Thank you," he said softly. "I thought that would be the best option, but I did not want to pressure you into anything you are not comfortable with."

"Of course. They're your family, Gil," I whispered, my words just for him to hear. "I would be happy to help them with anything they need."

Violet and Klara watched from the sidelines as we trained. Klara was enraptured with the spars, leaning forward in her seat and cheering from the sidelines. Violet was the opposite. She winced whenever someone landed a blow, her fingers twitching by her side as though she were reaching for her healing supplies.

When we were done training, I joined Gil as he approached his sisters. Klara immediately stood up, eager to join her brother in one of the sparring circles. From the small smile on Gil's face, he had been expecting nothing less.

I led Violet to my weapons rack and began to choose a couple of knives and daggers for her to start with.

"I don't want to learn to fight. I don't want to shed blood," Violet admitted. "But Gil said that things can still happen in the War Camp. That they have been overrun before."

"They have. When we were in Wolfmire for the attack, we protected the healers' tents as much as we could, but they still ended up crushed by the Skolli when we were almost overrun one of the nights." I told her. "Gil knows you will be in the safest place in the War Camps, but nowhere is truly safe on a battlefield."

"I save lives. I don't take them."

I led her to the throwing targets where Georg had stood not too long ago, teaching me. I wrapped her fingers around the dagger's hilt, showing her the proper grip. "The warriors in your tents will be wounded, dying, and utterly defenceless to any attack. By taking the life of the person attacking your tent, you will be saving their lives. That is what I remind myself when it gets hard. For every life I will take on the battlefield, I have saved countless others."

Violet watched me throw one of my daggers, her observant gaze evaluating every movement I made.

"You're good for him, you know," she said, nodding towards the ring where her siblings sparred, their blades a blur.

"We're good for each other," I corrected. "Now let's see you try throwing one."

WE HAD ARRANGED for Hákon and Ragna to meet us in one of the meeting rooms in the Verndari wing. We seemed to rotate through meeting in Hákon's office and Ragna's office in the Striking Shadows buildings. But we had gotten them to agree to come to us this time.

For once, we were all around the table when they arrived. Even Rúna.

More often than not, Baldur kept her by his side until the very last moment, not able to prevent her from attending an official Verndari meeting but keeping her with him long enough to make her late.

We had pulled two chairs up to the table, shifting the others to make them fit.

Ragna sank into her chair with a sigh, dark circles marring her eyes.

"Did you get any sleep last night?" Georg asked her softly. We all felt the pressure and impact of the war, but as Chieftain of the Striking Shadows, as the person responsible for gathering as much information as she could, Ragna had been stretching herself to the limits for weeks.

"A bit," she said. "I was up late going through all my reports regarding Northhold and the lands around it. I found nothing of note. Perhaps some evidence of Ógn, but that is unconfirmed."

While the Skolli were hard to miss, the massive beasts with sharp fangs, long talons, and claws on the tips of their wings, the Ógn could pass undetected. The shadowy creatures took on the persona of someone's loved one, allowing them to pass through crowded areas without arousing any attention and leaving nightmares in their wake.

"We all know where Northhold is located and exactly how close it is to where the exiled commanding family was banished. There is going to be a high risk regardless of whether you knew what we were walking into or not," Aron pointed out, trying to reassure Ragna.

"It's not the first time that we have been dispatched with very little information, and I doubt it will be our last," Georg said quietly. "You can't be everywhere, can't see everything, can't hear everything, even with your Striking Shadows, Ragna."

She sighed. "I can try," she muttered before turning to each of us. Evaluating us. "It's too dangerous to send just the six of you out, but with the barrier down, the risk of an attack is too high. We can't send a large force with you because that may leave us open elsewhere."

Hákon leaned forward, resting his arms on the table, his gloved hands neatly folded. "I suggest that we use a team similar to the response teams from before and have a line from the Royal Regiment and a member of the Striking Shadows join you."

"It is a good idea," Gil agreed. "Any larger of a force, and it will slow our travel."

"Who do you have available to send with us?" Rúna asked, brushing her hair out of her face.

"Tell me who you want, and I'll tell you if they are available," he countered.

We turned to Georg, deep in thought, his fingers drumming on the table. Evaluating our choices and what each would mean not just for us, but for the forces we would be leaving behind.

"The easiest grouping would be Lúdvík's line from the Royal Regiment and Gier from the Striking Shadows, as they have the most experience fighting by our side should it come to that," Georg finally said.

"I can't give you Gier; he will have a different posting from which I can't pull him away," Ragna bit her lip as she considered her options. "I could give you Svanna."

"How likely is she to be on Ottó's side?" Gil asked, not hesitating to ask the question regardless of how awkward it may make the room.

It had to be asked, especially considering the likelihood that we would be facing an attack. To have someone working against us, to not be able to trust them to have our back, would be dangerous.

"She is mine as much as she is his," Ragna said, defending her choice.

As much of Ottó's, her father, as she was Ragna's, her lover. She carefully maintained her neutral stance until the time came for her to pick a side. Until she had to decide between her blood and her heart.

Her family or her morals.

I only hoped that time didn't come while we were on the road.

"I had Lúdvík's line assigned to something else, but I can shift things around. They will go with you. This is more important. You're going to need strong warriors that you can trust. The people of Northhold will not be happy with the news you share with them."

"You can't mean that they will attack us." Rúna arched an eyebrow.

"People attacked the response teams simply out of the fear of the unknown," I said quietly, remembering exactly how a spot had opened up on the Royal Regiment for Fannar. "They will know that we are abandoning them. Condemning them. I wouldn't blame them for doing something similar to us."

"Let's hope it doesn't come to that." Aron's voice was grim.

Footsteps carried down the hallway, growing closer and closer to the room. There was no knock before the door was pushed open to reveal Baldur. He tensed at the sight of his siblings at the front of the room and made his way to the opposite side of the table.

"I hope you weren't done with your planning. I'm planning to go with you as well." Baldur leaned against the wall and crossed his arms over his chest.

"What's with him lately?" Óskar muttered, only loud enough for me to hear.

I shrugged, not knowing how to answer his question. I hadn't expected Baldur to volunteer to join us when we went to Wolfmire to try and earn Jarl Einar's support, and I certainly didn't expect it now. Especially when the King Commander was trying to make us look bad.

"You shouldn't go," Hákon said after a moment.

Baldur sneered. "Are you trying to change my role within the fortress now, brother dearest? The rest wasn't enough for you?"

Hákon's jaw clenched at his brother's hissed words, his gloved hand forming a fist briefly on the table before relaxing again. "I would never intentionally do anything to hurt you or impact you like that, Baldur."

"Then it's settled. I will be joining them."

GIER SWEPT into the room with dark circles under his eyes and heavily creased clothes. The Striking Shadows, the Royal Regiment, and the Verndari had equally borne the weight of the increased attacks while the barrier still stood. But in this quiet in-between period, where both sides were holding their cards close to their chest, the demand had heavily shifted to the Striking Shadows. We needed their information more than ever, and the strain was already starting to show on Gier.

Just as I was sure that it would show on us when the expectations inevitably skewed in our direction.

"The Chieftain is not able to join us, so you just get me," Gier said, tying his hair back into a messy horsetail before shrugging off his cloak.

"I heard that you just arrived from the field; your information is going to be the best that we have." Georg gestured to the space at the head of the table. "The floor is yours."

Gier glanced around, his brows furrowed. More than likely confused by the phrase Georg had used, he still took his spot at the front of the table and laid out a map.

"I have spent the most time near Northhold out of all the Striking Shadows. Regardless of their position by the water, it is isolated because of the mountains along the city's west side. And the very mountains that cut them off from the rest of Drysden are also the perfect grounds to house Skolli." Gier's finger traced the mountain ridge on the map.

Aron leaned forward in his seat to study the map closer. "Have there been any Skolli attacks?"

"Nothing of any scale, and they may be able to escape without anything of note."

"Why do you say that?" Rúna asked.

"When it becomes clear that we are making no move to defend Northhold, the exiled commanding family will certainly set their sights on it. Its isolated nature makes it easy to defend; it is a sizeable city with the resources and warriors to match, and it has its own set of docks. Northhold would make a good ally to them."

Baldur crossed his arms over his chest. "And their healing centre, how is that?"

"Good, but it does not compare to Jarl Einar's or Hákon's," Gier answered matter-of-factly, causing Baldur to tense. "But it is still one of the best centres in the realm and certainly better than what the exiled commanding family currently has."

"Is there anything else that we need to know?" Georg asked, running a hand over his bald head.

"There have been reports of nightmares in the area. It is hard to decipher if they are triggered by what is happening around them or if they are true nightmares from the Ógn."

Óskar sighed. "And I'm guessing there have been no reports of the Ógn?"

"Correct." Gier nodded.

"What is your opinion? Do you think the Ógn are responsible for the nightmares?" Gil asked, pushing Gier slightly.

Gier was quiet momentarily, his eyes locked on the map as he worked through his answer. "They haven't seen enough, experienced enough, to explain the level of nightmares. It is more than likely the Ógn."

I had been a victim to the Ógn's manipulations as they turned my dreams into things dripping in blood, saturated in screams, back when the exiled commanding family had still been carefully hiding their existence.

But I hadn't experienced them since.

And I hadn't had to fight them head-on.

"Do you have any advice for facing them on the battle-field?" I asked, curious if perhaps Gier had gained some knowledge that we may not have.

"Do not die. And be absolutely certain that it is a monster before you kill an innocent person."

CHAPTER
SIX
BRYN

The courtyard was filled with people, but it wasn't like when we had left for Wolfmire, when they had been curious about the Verndari being sent out into the field. Instead, it was more reserved, clearly divided, no longer driven by intrigue but by ulterior motives.

Ottó and Emilía lingered on the courtyard's edges, carefully observing us as though they could determine where we were going simply by how we looked. With Ottó barred from the War Chamber until he declared allegiance to the King Commander, they lost their font of information. They had lost access to the confidential information we discussed and the decisions that went along with it.

While it was a relief not to have to worry about censoring our conversation, that meant that they no longer had an impact on our decisions. Which would make them more desperate to try and get the information.

I just hoped that we would see the move coming before it happened, but I also knew that that was more than likely hopeful thinking. We hadn't seen their two previous moves; why would we suddenly be able to predict this one?

The courtyard edges were ringed with the people in the fortress who had not declared their loyalty to the King Commander. They lurked, watching us, judging us. Trying to determine whether we were worthy of their support or what we were doing so they could share the information with the exiled commanding family.

Either way, it was unsettling; the weight of the eyes on me caused my skin to prickle.

Within the courtyard mingled our supporters as they offered us words of encouragement or reached out to brush their fingers along our furs. Desperate to touch the warriors that stood between them and the monsters. The commanders that would lead them to the battle. Who they ultimately thought would take them to the hellscape that was the battle-field and ensure that they walked off of it again.

I couldn't decide what lay heavier upon my shoulders, the piranhas on the edges waiting for us to slip or the people who looked at us as though we were their guiding light.

The Royal Regiment warriors we brought were preparing their horses behind our own, Lúdvík and Fannar the pair closest to us.

After the death of his second at the battle at Wolfmire, Lúdvík promoted Fannar to the position. And as concerning as it was, the responsibilities that he was accepting, how fast he was rising through the ranks, I had fought alongside Fannar. Had held the line with him, had both saved and been saved by him. Fannar could hold his own on the battlefield, of that much I was certain.

Sofie's horse was stationed safely in the line beside Svanna, behind Gil and Rúna and in front of Lúdvík and Fannar to ensure that she was adequately protected from any attack we may face. She trotted around the corner of the fortress and towards us, her saddle bags so full that they looked like they would burst. Fannar was the first person to meet her, reaching a hesitant hand to take her items and secure them to her horse for her.

People moved out of the way of the King Commander as he made his way down the steps of the fortress and towards us. While he looked perfectly coifed and dressed, there was an air around him, a glint in his eye that made me hesitate. The smallest crack that revealed the nastiness beneath his skin threatening to break free.

A hesitant tap fell on my shoulder, different from the touches of the other people in the courtyard.

I turned to find Ma, her eyes darting nervously around us, her hands twisted in the skirts of her dress.

"Ma," I said, shocked, drawing Fannar's attention. His eyebrows lifted before he quickly made his way over to us. "I didn't expect to see you here."

Her smile was wobbly, overwhelmed by the controlled chaos of the courtyard. She reached out to Fannar and me, gently squeezing our hands.

"Did you come to see us off?" Fannar asked, his voice showing he was just as shocked as I was. This was her first time leaving her rooms alone without our encouragement or accompaniment.

She smiled again, easier this time, as she nodded. Ma released me to rest her hand on Fannar's shoulder, her eyes scanning him from his head to his toes and back again.

Taking in Fannar in his Royal Regiment armour for the first time.

"I know; I look quite dashing, don't I?" Fannar asked, his lips quirking as he fished for a compliment.

Ma patted him gently on the cheek, her hand lingering there for a moment before turning to me.

She scanned me just as she had Fannar, her eyes not missing a single detail. My hair was braided, just as it had always been on my runs with Da; the leather armour, reinforced with metal rings, that clung to my body like a second skin. The hilts of the many daggers sheathed in special slots in my armour or hung from my weapons belt. Then her eyes landed on the necklace around my neck that had freed itself from beneath the collar of my shirt where it normally lay.

Two pendants hung from the fine metal chain. One, the crest of the Verndari that I received when I swore my oaths to the King Commander, the other the family crest that Gil had made for me with metal from Ebonwell.

Ma's fingers shook slightly as they reached our family crest, her eyes sad as though she were reaching out to Da.

She released it after a moment and rested her hand over my heart. Silently telling me what she couldn't bring herself to voice out loud.

"I love you too," I said quietly, knowing exactly what she had meant. "I will come see you when we get back."

"Jarl Brynja." I hid how I wanted to tense at the King Commander's voice. I turned to find him watching us closely, his eyes darting from me to Fannar to finally rest on Ma.

I shifted, subtly shielding her from his gaze. Fannar mirrored my actions naturally, not knowing why I did what I did but trusting me without question.

"I haven't had the pleasure of meeting who you are speaking to. Am I right in assuming that she is your mother?"

he asked, his voice pleasant, but his words reminding me of the threat he had laid against her.

With no other choice, I shifted just enough to reveal her to the King Commander. "King Commander, please meet my mother, Cora. Ma, this is the King Commander."

Ma bobbed into a curtsy, her single hand ensuring she didn't trip over the hem of the dress.

"Oh yes, I remember the tragic injuries she sustained in your village and the unfortunate loss of her voice." He smiled at Ma, but there was no light in his eyes. "You must be very proud of the skilled warriors that your daughter has surrounded herself and yourself, by extension, with," he said to her.

Ma's eyes shifted from the King Commander to me and back again before she finally nodded her agreement.

The King Commander turned to me. "I would mount up, Jarl Brynja. You and your comrades have an important job to carry out." He smiled that wicked smile once again. "Don't fret; I will keep a close eye on your mother until you return."

To the onlookers, it was the act of a kind King Commander, but I knew exactly what his words were. A threat of what may happen if I failed to carry out my orders.

A promise of retribution if I failed to become the villain to the people he wanted me to be.

I nodded, gritting my teeth to keep myself from saying something I shouldn't and mounted up. Fannar followed my lead silently, trusting I would fill him in on what had just happened. The King Commander offered his arm to Ma, guiding her towards the platform he would use to officially dispatch us into the field.

I settled into my place beside Óskar, my eyes never leaving Ma.

"Are you alright?" he asked me, his words carefully pitched so that only I could hear him.

"No," I answered equally as quietly.

The King Commander raised the ancient horn to his lips, officially dispatching us into the field. I nodded in respect to him as we passed, my words forming the traditional words easily. *Strike hard, strike fast.*

The picture of a perfectly obedient Verndari.

But the words coiled inside me, desperate to take on another meaning. One that the King Commander should fear.

THE INITIAL JOURNEY from the fortress was subdued; no one was happy with what we were leaving to do. Even Baldur was quiet, not speaking up once from his place beside me. Not even to debate that Georg and Aron led our group rather than him.

Perhaps he was under orders from the King Commander to downplay his role in our group.

Or, perhaps, he was quiet for a different reason. Maybe he was just as upset with what we were doing as we were.

Seeing as the last time Baldur joined us, he had fought with Óskar and me, Georg grouped him with us again, figuring there would be some familiarity.

It concerned me that I could no longer fit Baldur into the box I had him in since my arrival at the fortress. He was still cold and often cruel in the fortress. But when he was outside of it and away from his family, Baldur seemed like he was almost a decent person. Then I remembered how he treated Rúna, how he was blackmailing her into a relationship with him, and it confused me even further.

Baldur was a conundrum—one that we could do without.

We stopped for the night before the sun began to sink beyond the horizon to ensure we had enough time to set up our camp and establish our watch schedule before the threat of the Skolli truly began. They would die in the light of day, which meant that the darkness of night was their territory.

I easily settled into the typical routine of the Verndari, assisting Óskar with caring for the horses as the others began to set up the tents.

I made my way towards Svanna and Sofie to take the reins of their horses, but Fannar beat me there. His fingers fidgeted with the edge of his cloak.

"Hello, Sofie," he said.

"Hello, Fannar," she giggled. When I took the reins of her horse, she gave me a smile of thanks before she turned her attention back to Fannar. "That's rather formal, don't you think?"

Fannar's cheeks reddened. I lingered longer than I needed to grab Svanna's horse interested in how the interaction would play out. It was a rare thing for me to see him blush.

"I was wondering if you would like any help with your tent. Not that I don't think you can do it—" Sofie cut him off with a finger over his lips.

"I would like that," she said with a smile.

I finally made my way over to Óskar. He lifted a brow at me as I approached with the two horses. In the time it had taken me, he had already gathered all the others with his bloodrite.

"What took you so long, Talon? Get lost?" he teased as he wiped down one of the horses.

"I was distracted by Fannar approaching Sofie." I removed the saddle from Sofie's horse.

Óskar snorted. "Figured that would only take a matter of

time; he's seemed taken by her since the moment he met her. How did he do?"

"He stumbled through it, but Sofie seemed endeared by it more than anything."

Óskar snorted again.

We made our way through the horses quickly, ensuring they were all brushed, fed, and watered before rejoining the others.

The tents were already set up, and the others were mingling in the space in the centre.

Rúna was reclined against Baldur's chest, her body slightly tensing as he gently ran his fingers up and down her arm. They were chatting with Aron, Lúdvík, and some other members of the Royal Regiment as they ate their rations for the night.

Fannar and Sofie sat off to the side of everyone, their cheeks pink as they chatted.

I was about to duck into the tent I would share with Sofie and Svanna when a hand wrapped around my wrist. Gil gently led me back into the shadowy area behind my tent. He spun me to face him, one hand resting on my hip and the other on my cheek.

"How are you?" he asked softly.

"After that display that the King Commander made with my ma? I feel sick to be leaving her in the fortress without us there. While the King Commander may have been vaguely aware of how vulnerable she was, I don't think it was widely known, but now everyone will know." I swallowed thickly. "I can't let anything happen to her, Gil."

"I will see if Óskar can track down a bird for me to send a note to my sisters. Klara and Violet will not let anything happen to her."

I released a sigh, some of the tension in my body loosening.

"Thank you," I breathed, resting my forehead against his shoulder. "I didn't even think of that."

"I will write to them now," he said, pulling away.

I wrapped a hand around the back of his neck, pulling him back to me and pressing my lips to his. His hand tightened on my hip, pulling me closer so that I was flush against his chest.

I traced my lips from his, to the corner of his mouth to his cheek before tucking my head into the crook of his neck and simply hugging him close to myself.

"Thank you," I whispered again.

"You do not need to thank me, darling. She is important to you, so she is important to me. I also want her to be safe, and there are very few people that I trust more than my sisters. Your mother will be just fine under their care."

CHAPTER

SEVEN

BRYN

Northhold reminded me of the coastal towns and villages near Ebonwell, where I had grown up, just on a slightly larger scale. The walls, while not very high, were made of solid stone, and the gates were well-maintained. The docks were not far from the city's boundary and were calm and orderly, only a single ship braving the still-tepid waters of the waning winter.

The gates were closed even in the middle of the day, a sign that the people of Northhold were not just aware of the dangerous times we lived in but that they were potential targets.

Were more than likely a target.

And we were here to abandon them to that fate.

A warrior paced the length of the wall and, spotting us, called down to someone within Northhold. As we approached the town, the gate opened silently on well-oiled hinges. A pair of women stood there, their armour well-polished.

"Good tidings," one greeted us as she bowed her head in respect to our group. "How can we assist the Verndari?"

"We are here to speak to the Warlord," Georg said. "Is he available?"

She snorted. "For the Verndari? Of course, he is. He'll be in the stronghold at this time of day."

Georg and Aron led us through Northhold to the stronghold, the large building easy to spot over the single-story buildings that made up the vast majority of the town. When we reached the stronghold, we all dismounted and handed our horses over to the various stable hands that came forward to meet us.

"You all should wait out here for us. We will need to figure out lodgings after we meet with the Warlord," Georg told Lúdvík, who agreed with a nod. He turned to Baldur. "Are you with us?"

Baldur pursed his lips, his eyes staring at the stronghold with an emotion I couldn't quite place. It almost bordered on longing. "No. I'm not to join you for this meeting. I've been forbidden."

There was one reason that the King Commander had determined that we were to be the ones that delivered the news to the Warlord of Northhold—for us to be the target of their anger. If he allowed his son to be in that room, there was a chance that he, and by extension, the King Commander, would bear some of that.

There was no way that the King Commander would allow him to risk that.

Georg simply nodded; it was too dangerous to draw any more attention to what was going on, especially with our loved ones back at the fortress within easy reach of the King Commander. And he had made it clear that he was willing to target them.

We turned to the stronghold doors as they opened to reveal

the Warlord. He was younger, perhaps only thirty or so, with a head of black curls. A large smile was on his face as he made his way over to us.

"Well met," he said with a grin, holding his hand to Georg. "Boy, are we happy to see you.""

Georg clasped his hand. "Well met, Warlord. Do you have somewhere we can speak privately?"

The Warlord tilted his head slightly, confused, but recovered quickly. "Of course, please follow me. I will have someone show the warriors with you to your lodgings."

"I appreciate that," Georg nodded in respect before following the Warlord into the stronghold. The rest of us filed behind them in our typical formation. Everyone we passed turned to stare, their eyes lighting up with happiness. I could imagine exactly what they were thinking. They thought that we were there to help them.

Little did they know we were here to do the exact opposite.

The Warlord led us to his study, taking up a place behind his desk and gesturing to the seats in front for us to use. Gil shut the door as we settled in before joining us.

"I cannot tell you how happy I am to see you all here. We need support more than you know," the Warlord said, echoing his words from earlier.

"Have you been getting attacked?" Aron asked.

The Warlord shook his head. "We faced some, but the attacks have largely backed off. It's the isolation we're facing. Instead of attacking us, the merchant caravans have been targeted in our place. It is hard for us to get supplies or information into the city."

His words weighed on me, settling in my stomach like a stone. How long would Northhold be able to last without our support?

Georg took a deep breath. "We are here to inform you that it has been decided that Drysden will focus its military support elsewhere in the coming conflict."

The Warlord tensed. "And that means what exactly for Northhold and my people?"

"There will be no military support given to Northhold to supplement your forces."

The Warlord was quiet for several moments. "And who, exactly, made this decision?" His words were like ice.

"The War Council made the decision," Aron joined the conversation, his words carefully neutral. "We are just here to deliver the information."

"And what do you expect me to tell my people? That we are being abandoned? That we do not deserve our country's protection? That we have been deemed *lesser than* others and left to die?"

I swallowed thickly, his words striking at my heart. They came close to echoing the dissent that was threatening in Wolfmire, the bubbling undercurrent that had been growing in Ebonwell.

"You tell them we are here to guide them to safety in Newtide," I said softly. "Anyone that would like our protection as they travel behind the military line being established is welcome. We will leave in two days."

The Warlord laughed, but the sound held no humour. "I will share the news with my people tomorrow. I am sure they will all be excited to learn that their best chance at survival is to abandon their homes."

"We will support your forces while we are here; provide what little respite we can," Georg said as he stood.

"What a relief," the Warlord scoffed. "I will provide you

lodgings, but I cannot guarantee you will receive any pleasant hospitality."

No one in the fortress treated us any differently than we had when we arrived. But when the Warlord called people into his office as we left, I knew it was only a matter of time. And as soon as the stronghold knew, the people of Northhold wouldn't be far behind.

News and whispers travelled fast in northern, isolated cities. It travelled even faster when war was nipping at your heels.

And as soon as everyone knew, they would no longer look at us with joy. With relief.

No—instead, their eyes will be filled with hatred. Betrayal.

Whether Georg was making a preventative move to counter their anger or he was using one of our last opportunities to try and help these people, we took charge of the walls that night. The Royal Regiment was evenly spaced out along the walls, and we were making our rounds in our pairs. Svanna had taken up her own spot, her training with the Striking Shadows more than qualifying her to fight alongside us.

Sofie was set up in Northhold's healing centre, ready to treat any injuries that would arise if we were attacked.

The healers and warriors were more than happy to accept the night off and spend time with their friends and families, not knowing that it would be one of their last restful nights.

Óskar and I checked in with the Royal Regiment members that we passed as we circled the walls, Yugar, Óskar's dog, safely tucked away with Sofie for the night. Yugar had been trained to fight, had been trained to be effective on the battlefield. He had yet to set a paw on one, but when he eventually did, I knew that my attention would be partially focused on keeping him safe.

"To the north!" one of the warriors yelled. Óskar and I spun on our heels, charging towards the yell. Gil and Rúna met us there.

I scanned the sky, only to see a handful of Skolli approaching the city.

"Bows!" Óskar bellowed.

While none of us outranked each other, we yielded to whoever had the most expertise in times like this. And Óskar, the archer among the Verndari, was best suited to take the lead in this situation.

I palmed a pair of my throwing daggers. If the Skolli managed to get past the arrows, I could take down a couple on my own. Rúna uncoiled her whip by my side, undoubtedly thinking the same thing I was. With her light bloodrite, she could extend the reach of the leather and attack them before they breached the walls.

Gil slid two swords from their sheaths and slid to take his place at mine and Rúna's back, prepared to launch a closer defence if they were able to evade all of us.

"Nock!" Óskar stepped closest to the wall, his bowstring drawn to his ear as he picked his shot. "Fire!"

His bow twanged, echoed by the Royal Regiment warriors around us. Every arrow found its mark, and five of the Skolli fell from the skies. Dead.

But that still left three of the monsters, their sights set on Northhold.

"Again!" Óskar roared. He fired again, taking out the lead Skolli. The bows around us were fired at the warriors' own pace, and it didn't take long for the remaining monsters to fall to the ground.

Rúna and I stepped up to the edges of the walls, studying the creatures on the ground below, looking for any sign of movement.

But there were none.

They were truly dead.

I scanned the skies again, looking for the next round of attacks. But there wasn't a single dark speck in the sky, brightly lit by the full moon.

"What was the point of that?" Rúna asked, her brows furrowed.

"Even without us here, any decent archers could have taken them out before they reached the walls," Óskar said.

Gil shook his head. "It makes no sense. It did nothing but remind the city that the monsters are out there."

I re-sheathed my daggers, finally convinced there wouldn't be another round of attacks to follow. "Unless that was the point. Maybe they wanted to remind them of what they were capable of."

"You think they are playing with their food," Óskar pointed out, slinging his bow over his shoulder.

"Or going easy on them," I countered, crossing my arms over my chest, the possibility settling like lead in the pit of my stomach.

We were quiet for a moment. "You think that the exiled commanding family is trying to convince Northhold to join them," Gil finally said.

"We discussed the possibility of losing Northhold to them back at the fortress."

Rúna brushed her hair over her shoulder. "You think they

are going easy on them as a threat of what would happen if they don't side with them."

I nodded, glancing out to the town safely ensconced behind the walls, merriment in the streets and houses as they relaxed for the night. Confident that the Verndari and Royal Regiment would protect them as they enjoyed the time with their friends and family on a rare night off.

"That means that they are currently in the process of convincing them, and our arrival and the news that we shared will only push them closer to the exiled commanding family," Gil said with a curse.

"I think we are about to witness Northhold declare their support, but I don't think it will be for us." My voice was grim as I watched a group of townspeople begin a dance in a nearby square, braving the cold in their happiness. "I would be willing to bet we are about to watch Drysden lose this town entirely."

CHAPTER
EIGHT

BRYN

R aised voices roused me from my bed the next morning. Sofie sat up beside me, glancing around as though trying to identify the source of the noise. Svanna rolled over, pulling the pillow over her head to block it out. The words were indistinguishable, but the mixture of voices was coming from outside the boarding house where we had been granted lodging for the next few days.

I rose, dressing quickly, before turning to Sofie. "Let the others know that something is happening. I'm going to go and see if I can work out what it is."

I left our room, bumping into Fannar and Lúdvík in the hallway. Lúdvík steadied me with a chuckle before I fell into step with them.

"Did they wake you up too?" Fannar asked as we made our way down to the main floor of the building.

"They did. They woke Sofie, too. Svanna is doing what she can to sleep through it. Could you hear what they were saying?" I asked as I clumsily braided my hair. I hadn't taken the time to tie it back before leaving the room, but I wanted it out of the way in case we walked into a heated scenario. Hair was a wonderful thing for an opponent to grab.

"No, we couldn't. I guess we will find out together," Fannar said as he opened the boarding house door.

A crowd marched down the streets, homemade signs of parchment and fabric held above their heads.

We don't matter!

Verndari: friend or enemy?

Exiled or misunderstood?

I swallowed. News had clearly spread about the King Commander's decision and the truth about why we were here. And it was clear that the people of Northhold didn't agree with what had been decided.

We exchanged a wary glance with each other but were quickly swept up into the crowd, the surge of people too powerful for us to stand against. We stayed to the edges, ready to risk an escape from the masses if needed.

Their chanting surrounded us as their bodies pressed against us, people bumping up against us and knocking into our shoulders. The crowd was so thick that it stretched almost from building to building across the entire street. This wasn't just a crowd; it was a protest.

A protest that was one altercation away from becoming a mob.

They ripped every banner holding the symbol of the King Commander down, and people with torches set it alight. They left the banners on the ground to burn, the smoke coiling up among the edges of the crowd.

"Down with the King Commander! Down with the Verndari! Down with the Royal Regiment and Striking Shadows! Down with the King Commander!"

Some people's breath smelled of mead, the alcohol fuelling

their movements. They would be dangerous—unpredictable. But the ones that didn't, the ones that carried weapons in their hands with crystal clear eyes—they would be the biggest threat.

They were well aware of what they were doing; no alcohol clouded their judgement or fuelled their movements.

Only anger and hatred did.

I clasped hands with Fannar as Lúdvík's fingers encircled my wrist. We couldn't risk being separated in the crowd, especially with us being the target of their anger. I glanced back to see the boarding house but couldn't spot it.

Luckily, we had gone unspotted so far, the crowd unaware of who was in their midst.

A window of a government-run shop shattered nearby, another stone sailing through the glass panes beside it. People streamed through the doorway and broken windows to wreak further havoc. Some ran out with the stolen merchandise in their arms, while others threw it to the mob outside.

It didn't take long for smoke to stream through the windows—for the flickering light of flames to climb up the walls of the building.

There was nothing we could do as the mob continued to surge around us, propelling us down the street like a strong current. They were destroying any trace of the King Commander, not knowing that a Verndari was among them.

That one of the targets of their anger stumbled along beside them.

But I stumbled, my necklace with my family crest and the Verndari crest slipping out from under my shirt, the metal glinting in the sunlight. I immediately reached for the chain, hoping to tuck it away before anyone caught sight of it. But the metal gleamed in the light around us, drawing the attention of the marchers nearest to us, who pointed to us with a yell.

"There's a Verndari!"

"Gods' bones," Fannar said with a curse as he and Lúdvík tried to hide me from sight, but it was too late, and they were a target too. They were as much of a symbol of the Commanding Family as I was.

"There are Royal Regiment members too!"

The people around us stopped marching, encircling us and cutting off our exit. They pushed closer; their fingers ripped my shirt, they pulled Fannar's cloak from his shoulders, and they scratched Lúdvík's skin.

"We need to get out of here," Fannar panted, pushing the crowd back with an arm, trying not to harm anyone.

"Tell us something we don't know, lad," Lúdvík answered with a wince as another scratch marked his face.

Regardless of the hits they took, they kept me between them. We were all trained warriors, but even with my bloodrite and our skill, we were far too outnumbered. They had all three of us bleeding and bruised within moments.

We wouldn't win in a fight.

We had to get out of the mob, and we had to do it quickly. I scanned the crowd for an exit but couldn't spot one. A man managed to grab a fistful of my shirt, tearing it from my body as I pulled back out of his reach.

Shouts sounded down the road, but I couldn't understand what they said.

"Take this!" yelled a lady from above, prompting the crowd around us to disperse. We didn't have a chance to move before she heaved the contents of a pot onto us. It landed primarily on me, but Fannar and Lúdvík got covered in their share. The smell and texture told me exactly what the lady had tossed on us.

The contents of her chamberpot.

"Verndari trash," someone yelled, trying to hit me, but I ducked out of the way. Another person lay in wait, their punch landing on my temple.

"That's it," Fannar hissed, his eyes alight with anger. He pulled the war axe from his back, brandishing it at the crowd. Lúdvík drew his blade, each of them securing an arm around my waist to guide me as my vision was mostly blocked by the chamberpot contents. They guided me through the crowd towards the yells coming down the street.

Some people were smart enough to back away from their weapons, but others were aware of the advantage they had over us and tried to break through our defences.

Others simply threw whatever they could reach at us.

Food. Bits of wood.

Stones.

We finally broke free of the back of the mob—even the sight of us wasn't enough to stop their forward march for revenge.

"Bryn!" Gil's voice was easier for me to hear now. His hands found my waist, taking the place of Fannar and Lúdvík. "Gods, darling."

"They aren't our biggest fans right now," I said, stating the obvious.

A snort came from near us. "You don't say, Talon." Óskar. Óskar was here, too. "Let's return to the boarding house and regroup with the others."

We stopped at a well, Gil giving up his handkerchief so that I could clean the scummer from my face and see again. None of us were comfortable with me being impaired when the whole city appeared to be against us.

Gil took his shirt off and pulled it over my head, covering me much better than the ripped tatters of what had once been my shirt.

The others were stumbling out of the boarding house as we arrived, our belongings in their hands.

Georg cursed at the sight of us and turned back towards the owner. "Please reconsider. At least let them clean up before you make us leave," he asked, gesturing to Fannar, Lúdvík and I.

The owner turned to look at us with a scoff. "It looks like your rotten cores are finally revealing themselves to the world."

"We are here to offer protection to anyone that wants to travel to Newtide. If you have heard of the military decision, you must have also heard about that."

"You want us to abandon our homes, our livelihoods, for the chance of survival in a different city rather than protecting us here?" The owner crossed his arms over his chest. "We have been offered protection here in exchange for our support, and your decision has made ours that much easier." He spat at Georg's feet. "You have five minutes to vacate my premises before I report you to the Warlord."

Georg was quiet for a moment before he finally straightened his shoulders. "We understand. We will not trespass upon your hospitality any longer."

We gathered our items and left the boarding house behind.

"Guess we were right about the reasoning behind the attack," Rúna said quietly. "The exiled commanding family is recruiting, and we just handed them Northhold on a silver platter."

WE WALKED STRAIGHT to the stronghold, not even pausing for Fannar, Lúdvík, and I to clean ourselves up. Georg had asked if we wanted to, and Gil had encouraged me to. But I had denied the option, and Fannar and Lúdvík had followed my lead. If we were going to confront the Warlord and show the state that his people were in and how we were treated, I wanted him to see it —*smell it*—for himself.

And if he was also going to refuse to house us, then I wanted him to do so, having seen exactly how we were being treated in the streets.

We barely saw any other people on our way to the stronghold; most of the people of Northhold were involved in the protest. Only servants remained, no warriors to be seen. We retraced our steps from the day before to the Warlord's office. The door was open to show the Warlord standing at the window with his arms crossed, observing his city.

Georg knocked on the door.

"I was wondering how long it would take you to make your way here," he said without turning around. "When I informed them of the decision, I didn't tell them where you were staying, but I couldn't guarantee that those that did know didn't reveal it themselves." He finally turned to look at us, his eyes landing on me. "Yet it seems as though they found you anyways."

Georg stepped into the room, and we followed his lead. The Royal Regiment members waited in the hall. We hadn't been comfortable leaving them in the courtyard with the heightened tensions, but it would come across as a threat if they entered the room with us.

"Bryn and two members of the Royal Regiment had a rather unpleasant run-in with the mob this morning," Georg said, his voice gruff. "The people of your city have taken offence to the King Commander's decision."

The Warlord scoffed. "Do you blame them? They thought, we all thought, that you had come here to save them. Instead, you have delivered their death warrant."

"We are going to provide safe transport to Newtide in the morning to anyone that wants it."

"You want to uproot them from their lives and make them live in a strange place with only what they can carry. I can't say I don't understand how unappealing that option is to them."

Aron stepped forward. "They would live."

"In a strange place with no employment, no resources. You save them to make them paupers," the Warlord hissed, his eyes sparking in anger.

"They can rebuild their lives. They are not the first people displaced by this war, and they will not be the last," I said softly but firmly. We weren't sentencing these people to a life without hope; we were giving them the chance to live. To shape their life how they wanted.

"With all due respect, my people don't have the benefit of a title or a valuable bloodrite to ease their rebuilding."

I stepped back as though he had slapped me.

"Bryn did not have an easy time because she is a Verndari," Gil said, his hand resting on my lower back. "She has had to work to get where she is; she has had to sacrifice for it. She has had to bleed for it."

Georg raised a hand, quieting us, before refocusing on the Warlord. "Regardless, the matter at hand is that we have provided the opportunity to your people, and we are not about to renege on that. However, we have lost our lodging. Do you have anywhere that we can stay for the night?"

The Warlord was quiet for a moment. "I believe that my

people have made it quite clear how they feel, and I will not go against them. I have no other lodging to provide for you."

Georg took a deep breath, no doubt weighing his options. How much should we throw around our title of Verndari, and how much of this situation may be repaired? "We will camp outside the walls tonight, but because of the location of our camp, we will not be able to support any efforts on the walls."

My fingers shook, forcing me to intertwine my hands behind my back. Gil noticed, his thumb rubbing circles on my back to soothe me.

Georg wasn't going to debate the Warlord's decision not to provide us lodging, but he was making it clear that if he continued down this road, he would have no more support from us.

He was drawing a line in the sand and leaving it up to the Warlord to decide.

"I understand," the Warlord said with a nod. "I will tell my warriors to resume their regular rotations."

"Then I believe that there is nothing more for us to discuss. We will return at midday tomorrow if anyone would like to take us up on the offer for safe transport to Newtide."

Georg started towards the door, and we followed. But I froze, remembering what I had heard in the mob. I turned back towards the Warlord, stepping forward, away from Gil, to stand on my own.

"Your people spoke of aligning with the exiled commanding family. Is that what you have decided to do?" I asked him bluntly. The Warlord had made his stance regarding us very clear, so I risked nothing by accusing him of such a thing. He couldn't lose respect for us if there were nothing left for him to lose.

The Warlord pursed his lips. "I believe it is a bad leader

who doesn't listen to their people. Especially when others have already deemed them dispensable. Does that answer your question?"

Yes. It did.

Northhold had just fallen into enemy hands.

CHAPTER
NINE
GIL

We made our way out of the town as fast as we could. None of us wanted to risk another run-in with the mob that had done their best to make Bryn, Fannar, and Lúdvík pay for the King Commander's decision with their blood. They had suffered enough this morning, and none of them wanted to stop and clean up until we were safely outside the city walls.

The mob was big enough and angry enough that they were easy to hear, allowing us to avoid their path as we made our way out of the town.

At least one thing had gone right this morning. We dismounted, the others being quick to grab the reins from Bryn, Fannar, and Lúdvík.

Bryn stepped forward to grab the reins of her horse back from Óskar, but he simply tucked them behind his back. "Go and clean up—you smell awful," he told her.

Bryn wrinkled her nose but slowly made her way towards the creek that we had passed on the way to our campsite.

I pulled her soaps and a change of clothes from her saddlebags before falling into step with her, Fannar and Lúdvík leading the way ahead of us. Bryn looked up at me with a wince. "You don't have to come. I'm sure I'm not the most pleasant to be around right now."

"I wanted to bring you these," I told her, holding up her items in my hand. "And those two can watch each other's backs; I assumed that you would not want them watching you as you bathed."

She smiled softly at me before moving further down around the bend of the creek so that she wasn't within the others' sight. "Thank you. I didn't even think of something new to wear before coming down here. I just wanted to be clean." She toed off her boots as she stared at the water in front of her. "This is going to be really cold, isn't it?"

I knelt by the bank and dipped my fingers in the water. I quickly pulled them back out with a wince. "It will not be pleasant," I told her as a yelp sounded further down the creek.

Bryn dropped her clothes on the bank and studied the water in front of her for a moment before taking off for it at a run. She charged a few steps into it with a curse before submerging herself below the frigid surface. She must have been scrubbing at her body as the water darkened around her as she cleaned herself off.

She burst back out of the water with a curse. "This is awful," she hissed through her teeth. I tossed her the soap, and she quickly got to scrub the rest of herself off. The part that took the longest was her hair, which required her to dunk her head multiple times, leaving her spluttering when she came back up.

When she was finally clean, she hurried back towards where I stood holding a towel open. I wrapped it tightly around her before doing my best to dry her off and get her warm. Bryn dressed quickly, holding her cloak close to her body and the hood covering her wet curls.

I wrapped my arm around her shoulder and tucked her close to my body as we slowly made our way back to the camp.

"I guess he got what he wanted," Bryn said softly. "I'm nothing more than a villain to them."

"They are scared, and they are hurt. They need someone to blame, and you were the easiest one—you were there."

Bryn sighed, kicking at a loose stone on the ground in front of her. "After tomorrow, the next time they see me will be on the battlefield. And they will likely be on the other side. I'll definitely be the villain then."

I pulled her to a stop, my hands finding her cheeks. "We cannot control the King Commander, and we cannot change what is going to happen. The only thing that is within our control is how we react, the choices that we make when it matters." I dropped a hand through the opening of her cloak to rest over her heart. "We will show what really lies here, and darling, your heart is the purest thing I have seen. You cannot be a villain with that goodness inside of you."

"You say that as though you aren't just as good of a person as I am, Gil," she sniffled, her words curling around my heart. "You are not a monster."

"You taught me to believe that," I told her softly. "What a pair we make."

She chuckled as we continued back to the campsite. "That we do."

Sofie was the first person to meet us, her hands landing on Bryn in an instant. "Letting that scummer sit on you when you had open cuts was a stupid decision. I had to burn the infection out of Fannar and Lúdvík, and now I have to do it for you."

"Thank you, Sofie," Bryn smiled at her. "What would I do without you?"

"Die, apparently," she snarked back.

I left Bryn in Sofie's very capable hands and joined the others. Fannar and Lúdvík had thick furs wrapped around their shoulders, and I ducked into Bryn's tent to grab her one to use. When I returned, I took a seat beside Aron. Óskar and Svanna joined us a second later.

Svanna had been quieter than she typically was, but she had been like that since the barrier fell. While some people jumped to declare their support for either side, others bided their time.

But none of them were sitting so carefully in the middle as she was.

"How can you support him?" I asked her quietly. Aron tensed slightly by my side, but Óskar just focused his attention on Svanna.

She was quiet for a moment, staring at the food in her hands. "They are my family. I have loved them my whole life. I have done everything I could to make him proud for as long as I can remember. It is hard to throw that away."

"A time will come when you have to make a choice. How will you decide?" Aron asked her softly.

"I already know what I will choose," she whispered, slumping as though weighed down. "I know what the right thing to do is, even if my father and sister don't. I have sworn oaths, and I will stand by them. But I will not lose my family a second before I must."

Óskar clasped her shoulder in silent support as the rest finally joined us. Sofie settled against Fannar, who had opened his arms so that she could settle under the furs with him. I draped Bryn's furs around her shoulders as she settled beside me, leaning her weight against my side.

Baldur crossed his arms over his chest as Rúna sat down. "I'm sorry that you had to experience that. You had no choice, and you bore their anger over their options being ripped from them."

I studied him closely, trying to find any minute clue that would clue me into what he was thinking. I didn't believe he was the type of person who would apologize, not without significant coercion, at least.

Bryn was silent by my side, leaving Fannar to speak. "You don't have to apologize. Not for that."

Because he certainly did have things to apologize for, but Fannar was right. Baldur had played no part in what had happened and had no need to apologize.

"You sound like you really understand them," Rúna said softly, her words drawing Baldur's attention. He took a seat beside her. "You understand what they are feeling."

"They are not the only ones that have had their options, their choices, ripped from them." Baldur's words were lined with anger but also something quieter.

Something that seemed a lot like regret.

TEN

BRYN

We kept our distance from Northhold the following morning, taking our time to pack up the camp. Sofie had shyly asked Fannar to accompany her to gather some plants that only grew in the north that would be beneficial for healing. I don't think that she had even finished her question before Fannar stood from his seat with a shy grin.

Finally, when the sun hung high in the sky, we finished loading our supplies and rode for the gates.

The gates stood open, but when we approached, the only group on the road, the gates were pulled shut.

My shoulders tensed. The Warlord had made it quite clear that they hadn't seen much traffic since the barrier had fallen. This meant that, more than likely, we were the only ones they were expecting. When we approached, they had deliberately had the gates open to pull them shut.

They were making a point.

We weren't welcome.

Georg pursed his lips, his face grim. "Keep your eyes open," he told us softly; his words echoed down the line to ensure that all of us heard them. "I think that made it very clear how they feel about us. But we have a job to do and will ensure that that is carried out."

He made his way to the gate, pounding his fist against it three times.

There was no response from inside the walls. No sounds of movement to indicate that they were coming to open it.

"So that's how they want to play it," Óskar muttered by my side, his horse shifting on its hooves as though echoing the unease of its rider.

"What will happen?" I asked, my voice quiet.

"We promised these people safe passage if they wanted it. Georg will ensure we uphold our end of the deal, even if we must force our way in," Óskar said as his fingers tensed around his bow.

One of my hands rested on the hilt of my dagger.

Baldur moved up beside Georg. "How far do we want to push this?" Baldur asked him.

"I am getting inside those walls regardless of what it takes," Georg said. "We gave those people a chance at survival; we will not pull it away from them like this."

Baldur was quiet for a moment; his eyes on Georg were steady. Searching. Evaluating. "Alright then. Do what you need to do, and if you need me to step in, let me know."

I blinked in surprise as Baldur retook his place in our group. This was a Verndari mission. We had the lead, we made the calls, we issued the commands. And the King Commander had made it quite clear that we were to bear the brunt of the people's anger.

But for Baldur to offer his support, his status as Commanding Son, should we need it, was a shock. He would gain nothing from it except for his father's displeasure should word reach him that he was involved. It was a move that confused me as much as it relieved me.

Much like his apology last night.

Georg banged on the door again. "In the name of the King Commander, you will allow the Verndari admittance to your city."

His words were devoid of any emotion. He knew what we needed to do and what was at stake, but that didn't make it easier for us to pull rank like this, especially when we knew that their actions were fuelled by fear. Fear that had only grown when we had condemned them to die.

Still no movement beyond the gates.

"The Verndari demand entry," Georg bellowed, ensuring his voice carried as far into Northhold as possible. "You have five minutes to open these doors."

The five minutes that passed felt like five hours.

But still no movement.

Georg turned back towards Baldur. "It seems as though they have decided not to listen to me. Maybe you will have better luck."

"They will open those gates," Baldur said grimly as he dismounted his horse and stalked to Georg's side. "Or I will ensure they no longer have gates to close.

"In the name of the Commanding Son, you will open these gates before I reach the count of ten," Baldur demanded, his voice carrying easily through the space. "Or I will burn them to the ground and leave you to defend yourselves without them. One. Two. Three."

The sounds of a scuffle carried over the walls, indistin-guishable shouts along with them.

"Four. Five. Six."

"Open the damn door," someone cried from beyond the walls as another person shouted, "Leave them shut and call the archers."

Óskar casually nocked an arrow on his bow as Rúna loosened her whip. We would not be the ones to fire the first shot, but we would not hesitate to defend ourselves.

"Seven. Eight. Nine."

The scrape of the gates came a second before the doors slammed open to reveal the Warlord. His hand rested casually against the hilt of his weapon, but I didn't doubt that he could draw it faster than I could blink if he wanted.

"Commanding Son Baldur, what a rude way to demand entrance to my city." The Warlord's words were like ice.

Georg stepped up to Baldur's side. "I tried asking nicely, and it didn't seem to get us anywhere."

The Warlord ignored him, not bothering to even look at Georg.

"You would dare to threaten your loyal citizens like that?" he hissed at Baldur. His eyes alight with anger.

"You forget yourself, Warlord," Baldur warned him as he hooked his thumbs into his weapons belt. "You and your people have made it quite clear where your allegiance lies with the Verndari. The Verndari are an extension of the Commanding Family; my own intended serves among them. You condemn them; you condemn us." Baldur cocked his head. "I wonder what my father would think of where your allegiance now lies. I'm sure burning down your gate would be the least of his actions."

The Warlord spat at their feet. "Northhold declares that we no longer support the King Commander." He pressed a letter to Georg's chest. "Now get the hell out of my city."

Georg grabbed the Warlord by the bicep, pulling him closer

to him. "We are here to grant safe passage to anyone that wishes to leave to Newtide. You will still provide them the choice."

One of the warriors nearby started to draw his weapon, but Baldur pressed the edge of his axe to his throat. "Don't even think about it."

We slid from our horses, taking positions at Baldur and Georg's backs, ready to defend them if needed.

"I would like to go," a middle-aged man called from the crowd. A woman similar to his age was by his side, and two young children were in front of them. Four horses stood near them, one carrying what looked like their possessions.

Rúna stepped forward with a smile. "I'm happy to hear that. Allow me to get you situated." She led the family out of the gates and to where the rest of our group was gathered.

"Anyone else?" Georg called, not releasing the Warlord.

A man close my age stepped forward, the reins of his horse in his hands. "I will join you as well."

We lingered for another few minutes, but no one else stepped forward.

Georg finally released the Warlord, whose face was red with anger.

"I will see you on the battlefield," he hissed, spit flying from his mouth.

Baldur scoffed as he backed away from the gates and towards the rest of us. "If you are against us, they are the last people you want to see on a battlefield. You will not be the one to walk away."

CHAPTER

ELEVEN

BRYN

We eased our pace of travel to ensure that it wasn't too strenuous for our companions. We had always planned to, but with the children that had joined us, we had slowed even further to ensure that they could maintain their pace throughout the journey.

I had expected the children to be upset about leaving Northhold, but they were in good spirits. The youngest, a six-year-old named Greta, was thrilled to be riding a horse and would speak to anyone around her about the adventure they were going on.

The oldest, a ten-year-old boy named Vallum, watched everything around him with wide eyes. Starstruck, his mother had told us, by the warriors around him. A talented boy with a strong bloodrite who dreamed of being a member of one of the most elite fighting teams in Drysden. The Royal Regiment or the Striking Shadows.

Or, his ultimate dream, being the next trainer of the Verndari.

When we stopped for the night and the camp had been set

up, Rúna pulled the boy aside. When she handed him one of her spare staffs and started to walk him through a few basic moves, I swear that his eyes were brighter than the stars.

I watched on with a soft smile. At our pace, we had a few more nights on the road before we reached Newtide. I would pull him aside tomorrow to show him what I could with the daggers. There was something so pure about the joy and dreams in his eyes when surrounded by so much fear and uncertainty.

I would do my part to ensure that that light wasn't extinguished.

Baldur lingered by my side, his eyes on Rúna. A strange expression drifted across his face as her laugh meshed with Vallum's, their smiles bright.

"It's nice to see her so happy," I said softly. I knew it was reckless—we had been careful around Baldur for good reason. We had all seen what he was capable of when he beat her ruthlessly, when he blackmailed her into this relationship with him.

But he had been an enigma since we had been in Wolfmire. Showing a softer side to himself. Showing an interest in healing. Showing an unwavering dedication to protecting his people.

I couldn't quite pin him down, making me nervous about heading into the war ahead of us, especially when it seemed more and more likely that he would be joining us on the battlefield. Or, at the very least, desired to.

"It is." His words were barely above a whisper, but they still sent a shock of surprise across my face. "I know you think me a monster."

"I—" I stammered, caught off guard by the bluntness of his words.

"I fear that I am too. After all, I was raised—trained—from the time I started walking by the one on the throne." He turned his attention from Rúna to me. I gaped at him, unprepared for his candour. "Both of us had our choices taken from us." He nodded in Rúna's direction. "She has done better with it than I have."

I took a moment to consider what to say to him. But with how open he was being, I finally decided to be honest with him, consequences be damned. "I don't know if I can forgive you for what you have put her through."

"I don't know if I can forgive myself," he whispered, taking one last look at Rúna before walking away.

Gil joined me a second later, the warmth of his body seeping into mine from his closeness. "What was that about?"

"Another layer to the puzzle that is Baldur," I told him. "A further complexity to unravelling who exactly he is inside."

Gil wrapped an arm around me, pulling me closer to him. He tucked his chin on the top of my head as we watched Vallum run through another set of moves with Rúna.

"Excuse me, Jarl Brynja?" The man around our age, Luka, approached us hesitantly, a piece of parchment in his hand.

I turned to him with a smile. "Yes?"

His eyes darted from me to Gil and back again, but I couldn't see any judgment. No, it appeared as though he were evaluating his surroundings. "You're from up north, right?"

"I wasn't as northern as you, but I am from this area, yes," I told him reassuringly. He was nervous about something, and I would be willing to bet money on the fact that it had to do with the parchment in his hand.

"Did the people from your village ever—" he paused as though trying to find the right words. "Complain about the King Commander?"

It was my turn to consider my words carefully. "Complain feels harsher than it was, but some were starting to be displeased."

"I fear that displeasure has spread further than you think, and I think it's grown." He handed me the parchment. I shared a look with Gil and unrolled it to reveal the title Criers of Justice. It was an advertisement of some sort for a gathering. "They call themselves the Criers of Justice and have travelled from town to town, village to village, city to city. And they gather a loyal group of followers in each place they visit."

"What do they want?" Gil asked. "What is their purpose?"

Luka swallowed. "They are angry with how the King Commander treats people and call for a drastic change."

"They want to be rid of him," Gil said bluntly. Luka nodded, causing Gil to purse his lips and study the parchment again. "This flyer was for the date we reached your city. Were they in Northhold when we arrived?"

"I believe so. I found the flyer this morning on my way to the gates." Luka's words were soft. "But I fear that what happened just fuelled them further."

I cursed. "We just provided them with the spark they needed to start their revolution. And gave them a whole town of people willing to support them."

I stood by Fannar's side with only the moon to light the ground around us. Georg had paired each of the Verndari with a member of the Royal Regiment for our watches to ensure everyone was as rested as possible. Aron and I had fought over Fannar, resorting to him alternating between us each night, not wanting to hurt either of our feelings. On the nights that

Fannar was with Aron, I paired up with Svanna. She may not be on the Royal Regiment, but her role on the Striking Shadows more than qualified her for watches.

I glanced up to the sky, our watch halfway done.

"So, Sofie, then?" I asked him quietly, my voice teasing. It was nice to give him a hard time about something so normal and light as the girl he liked.

I was just able to make out Fannar's blush. "So, Sofie, what?" He tried to deflect my line of questioning half-heartedly, knowing that I would find out eventually.

Even if he didn't tell me, sisters had a way of learning these things.

And how Fannar felt about Sofie was written all over his face whenever he was around her. Or talking about her.

"I've seen what you're like around her." I gently bumped my shoulder against his.

He smiled softly, his fingers fiddling with the hem of his sleeve. "She's...special."

"I'm happy for you," I told him, resting my head on his shoulder.

A whisper of movement came from behind us. The slightest of sounds. My hands dropped to the hilts of my daggers as I casually turned around, not wanting to alert them that I heard them.

Gil was approaching a tent; his hair dishevelled from sleep, his loose clothing creased.

I relaxed and moved closer to him, Fannar by my side.

"What are you doing up?" I asked him. He stopped walking and turned in my direction. "Couldn't sleep?"

"No, I went for a walk to clear my head."

My brows furrowed as I stepped closer to him. "By yourself? Gil, you should have brought someone with you. Do you want to talk about it?"

"No," he said, his eyes drifting from Fannar to me. "I don't think you would understand."

I gestured to Fannar to stay where he was and stepped closer to Gil, close enough to touch him. My hand rested on my belt. "I love you," I said softly.

"I love you too, Bryn."

My eyes fell shut for the briefest of moments as I sent up a prayer to the gods. Praying that my instincts about this were right, that I knew Gil as well as I felt I did.

Before I drew my dagger and stabbed him through the heart.

Gil's eyes widened as he slumped to his knees before falling to the ground.

"Gods' bones, Bryn. What the *fuck*," Fannar cursed as he knelt by Gil's body, already reaching for the dagger.

I reached out and wrapped my fingers around his wrist to stop him. "Don't." I knelt by the body and brushed Gil's hair out of his face. "It's not him. It *can't* be him." My voice broke.

I had to be right. *I had to.*

"What do you mean? That's—" Fannar cut himself off, his eyes darting from Gil to me and back again. "You don't think it's an Ógn, do you?"

"That's absolutely what I think it is." My fingers shook as I watched the fake Gil, desperately waiting for it to revert to its original form. Whatever that may be. "Wake the others and be aware. I wouldn't be surprised if there is another one around."

And their disguises were just as good as everyone said. It was in what it said that gave it away. Hopefully. And only because I knew Gil as well as I did—the other half of my heart.

85

But if I had gotten it wrong, if I had indeed stabbed my love, that would break me.

Fannar stumbled back from the body as he followed my orders, but I didn't dare look at him. I didn't dare remove my eyes from the body before me, still wearing the face I had come to love so much.

And the longer it took for that face to melt away to reveal what was truly underneath, the more I doubted myself. Maybe I had been wrong. Maybe an Ógn didn't lay in front of me; maybe it was Gil.

Dead, with my dagger buried through his heart.

A ripple across his face carried throughout his body as it slowly began to melt Gil's visage. A humanoid made of shadow and darkness lay on the ground before me, scraps of clothing where Gil's sleep clothes had been. Long claws cloaked in shadows dominated its hands; its head was nothing but a plume of darkness.

My shoulders slumped, and I allowed myself the briefest of moments to bask in my relief before I stood and pulled a fresh dagger from my belt. Burning pooled in my eyes as I shifted them to those of a Skolli. Their unparalleled night vision allowed me to see that the others were beginning to stumble from their tents, their eyes drifting throughout the space as though trying to make out the enemy in the darkness.

I stepped forward and began systematically going through the camp, searching every nook and cranny for another Ógn.

I would not allow them to harvest our fear.

CHAPTER

TWELVE

BRYN

I stayed close to Fannar for the rest of the watch, not speaking to anyone else. He had summarized it for the others—that there had been an Ógn, that I had been the one to defeat it. He had shown them its body, dead on the ground, but didn't elaborate on who it had been.

On whom I saw in my mind as I stabbed him in the heart over and over.

I hadn't missed the looks that the others had sent Fannar or the reassuring gestures that he sent back to them as I stayed close to him. He had walked me to the tent I shared with Sofie, squeezing my hand before I climbed inside and closed the flap behind me. I lay in my bedroll, staring at the top of the tent.

I knew that the Ógn wasn't Gil; I knew that I had killed a monster and not my love.

But it was hard to remind myself of that fact when all my mind focused on was the look on his face when I stabbed him in the heart. The utter stillness of his body as it lay on the ground. Dead.

By my hand.

Sofie stayed by my side the next morning as we prepared to leave, walking me to where Óskar stood waiting with our horses. I mounted automatically, my body knowing the motions even when my mind was elsewhere. Even Baldur seemed aware of every movement I made as he and Óskar slotted me between them. I could see Georg pull aside the others from the corner of my eye, but I made no move to join them, and he made no move to make me.

When we left for the final portion of our journey to Newtide, I allowed myself to settle into the rhythmic motion of the horse and the familiar scenery from my childhood around us. I slowly pulled myself together, piece by broken piece, as we travelled.

And by the time we reached Newtide, I felt mostly myself again. I still hadn't spoken a word, but I no longer felt one breath away from shattering.

Our large group waited by the gates as a guard left to fetch the Warlady that ran Newtide. We were a large group, and it would be harder to navigate the busy streets of Newtide without the direction of where she wanted us to go. Frightened residents of the smaller towns around the area had already sought shelter in the city, limiting our options for housing for the people from Northhold.

The Warlady arrived moments later, clasping hands with Georg with a smile. "Good tidings," she told him before surveying us all. "To all of you," she added.

Georg repeated the greeting before gesturing to the people of Northhold. "These five people were brave enough to set aside their lives in Northhold for the promise of safety and a better future here in Newtide."

"I am honoured to have you put your faith in myself and my people that way," she told them as she approached them.

Vallum looked at the Warlady as though she were a hero. The lady's keen eyes didn't miss it. "Do you have dreams of being a warrior, lad?" she asked him.

"I do!" Vallum nodded, a big grin across his face. "I want to be the best of them."

"We can work with that," the Warlady told him, her eyes sparkling. She turned to survey the others. "For your bravery and trust in me and mine, you have my word that I will do everything possible to ensure you have good lives here. Whether you are only here until the war ends or if you are here for longer, that is my promise to you."

The mother's eyes glittered with unshed tears as she dismounted her horse to clasp hands with the Warlady. "Thank you."

The Warlady patted her hand and waved to the guard that had fetched her. "Please show these people to the lodging house on Wayfinders Way. Ensure they get as many sets of rooms as needed and tell the landlord that the city funds will take care of the bill."

They began to say their goodbyes to us and well wishes for what was ahead when Luka made his way to me. He pulled a letter from his saddle bag and passed it to me. "My sister is a member of the Royal Regiment. Can you please ensure that she gets that?"

I cleared my throat, swallowing once before answering. "Of course."

"Thank you. For what you have done and will have to do in the times ahead."

I gave him a weak smile. "It's my honour."

The guard guided the five of them into the city, Vallum and Greta waving to us until they could no longer see us.

Georg turned to the Warlady. "That was kind of you. You didn't have to do that."

"That is one of the reasons I started the city fund: to be able to help those who needed it. From what I have heard, it took a great deal of courage for them to make the decision that they did. It was the least I could do to soften the fallout from it." Her eyes scanned the rest of us before turning towards Georg. "Are you on your way, or would you like some lodging for the night?"

"We would appreciate rooms. We could use the time to replenish our supplies and recover from our journey before we are on our way in the morning."

My cheeks warmed at the mention of recovery, embarrassed that he may be referring to me. That he may be referring to how I struggled to deal with the night before.

"Of course, you are more than welcome. There should be plenty of rooms at the taverns; we haven't had many travellers since the barrier fell."

GEORG LED us to the tavern where I had first met Gil, where I had first laid eyes on the man who had become my comrade. My confidant. My love.

Most of the Royal Regiment members were happy for the afternoon and night off and disappeared into groups to the city once they had dropped their items off in their rooms.

I settled at the table with the others. Gil took a seat on my one side, Fannar on my other. Their quiet, steady presence further pulled me out of the state I had been in, allowing me to enjoy the brief moment of freedom. Bowls of stew and tankards of mint water and ale were distributed around the table. My eyes danced around the people I sat with, relishing in the lightness that had settled over all of us.

Even Baldur seemed to have loosened up, joking with Rúna, Aron and Svanna, their laughter almost overpowering the noise from Óskar's antics. Fannar quietly chatted with Sofie, the tips of his ears red but his smile bright. Lúdvík and Georg alternated between chatting and joining in conversations around the table.

Gil had his chair pressed against mine, the warmth of his body seeping into me as he reassured me of his presence without a word. He occasionally chimed in with the others, but he seemed more than happy to observe, to bask in the happiness around us like I was.

Eventually, the cheerfulness around the table thawed the last lingering chills in my body, and I began to chuckle at their jokes and even threw a roll at Óskar when he reached a new level of absurdity. I still didn't actively participate, but no one forced me to, allowing me to re-find my centre at my own pace.

The sky finally darkened outside the windows, and we began to split off. Some went to the bar for another round while others made their way to their rooms, determined to make the best of a night without watches.

Gil stood from his seat and held out his hand to me.

I took it with a small smile, waving to the others still at the table, and followed him up the stairs. He led us to a room, opening the door and allowing me to enter first before shutting it behind him. With more than enough rooms available at the tavern, we had the freedom to change up the sleeping arrangements from the road, and Gil had seemed to take full advantage of this as I spied both of our saddlebags tucked neatly against one of the doors.

I sat on the edge of the bed, my fingers drifting over the

furs that covered it. Gil stood, watching me for a moment, his eyes dim, before he took the chair from the small desk and placed it in front of me. He took a seat, his knees pressing into mine, and intertwined our fingers.

"Please, Bryn," his words were soft, drawing my attention to him. "Talk to me, darling. Please."

I took a shaky breath. "Did Fannar tell you about the Ógn?" I knew he had avoided the full details last night, but I didn't know if that had changed today.

"He only said that you killed one." Gil paused for a moment. "Who did you see? Was it your ma?"

"No." My lips wobbled, forcing me to push them together for a moment. "It was you."

Gil's eyes softened. "How did you know it was an Ógn?"

"There were two things." Gil squeezed my hands, encouraging me to continue but not rushing me. Allowing me to tell the story at my own pace. "It told me that I wouldn't understand. We have never claimed that about each other. Then, when it told me that it loved me, it called me Bryn; it didn't call me darling." I took a shaky breath, my head dropping to stare at our joined hands. "So, I stabbed it through the heart," I whispered.

Gil released one of my hands, his fingers finding my chin and gently lifting my face. He brushed a thumb across my cheek, wiping away a tear. "That was not me." He gave me a soft smile. "I am right here. I am okay."

Of course, he knew exactly what having to do that did to me. Why I hadn't been myself since it had happened.

"But it was you. When its eyes flared with pain and surprise, they were your eyes. And when it lay there not moving—" my voice broke. I took a deep breath and tried again. "And when it lay there not moving, it was you who lay there dead. It felt like it took forever for it to finally reveal its true self."

Gil gently rested my hand on his chest, right above where his heart beat, his own resting on top of it. "I am okay. I am alive. You did not hurt me; you did not kill me."

That final reassurance, proof that he was alive, healed the final crack from the night before.

I threw myself forward at him, causing the chair to rock back slightly. My arms wrapped tightly around him as I tucked my head into the crook of his neck and breathed in the smell of him. The tears that had been threatening and building since the night before finally broke free. I sobbed into him, soaking his shirt with my tears.

His hand stroked up and down my back as the other gently wrapped my curls around his fingers.

It provided me the safety to feel everything and break down so that I could build myself back up stronger than before.

Eventually, my sobs slowed, and I found the strength to pull back from him enough so that I could see his vivid green eyes. "I am proud of you for having the strength to do what had to be done, and I pray to the gods that should I face the Ógn, I have a shred of that same strength. Because I already know I will see you, darling, I can only hope to survive like you."

I pressed a gentle kiss to his lips. "You will. You already do." I pressed my forehead to his. "Do you dream of what comes after this? When there is no more war, when there are no more of the monsters?"

"Every day."

"What do you dream about?" I asked him in a whisper,

wanting to have happy visions dancing in my head rather than the ones from last night.

Gil gave me a soft smile. "Of exploring Drysden with you. At our own pace. Of holidays with my sisters and your ma and Fannar."

"And Aron," I giggled, tacking on my quasi-brother.

He resisted the urge to roll his eyes. "And Aron," he echoed. "Of having the time to make a home together."

I pulled Gil towards me, laying back on the bed. I looped my arms around his neck as he braced himself on his elbows.

I pressed my lips to his, our pace slow, savouring.

Until that wasn't enough.

I pushed up on his shoulders, rolling us over and straddling his lap. Gil raised a brow at me. "Let me explore you this time," I murmured, my hands landing on the hem of his shirt.

Let me explore him.

Let me reassure myself that he was indeed alive and well beneath me.

He studied me for a moment, reading every thought and feeling behind my eyes before nodding. I lifted his shirt, and he raised his body with rippling muscles to help me. I tossed it to the side and pressed a kiss to his mouth. Gently nipped his ear lobe before tracing my lips down his neck.

Across his chest.

Down his stomach, the muscles quivering under my touch. My fingers followed my lips, tracing shapes and lines across his skin.

My lips met the waistband of his pants, prompting me to look up at him through my lashes as my fingers fiddled with it. At his nod, I unfastened his pants, pulling them down his legs before continuing my exploration.

94

My mouth traced lower until he was cursing, a mixture of my name and the gods' spilling from his lips.

THIRTEEN

BRYN

Our journey back to the fortress passed easily without other attacks. But as we drew closer to returning, we also drew nearer to having to inform the King Commander exactly what happened. The fact that not only did our journey not go well, but the Warlord had withdrawn his support and ordered his forces to return to him.

As much as he wanted to make me the villain of the war, the figure to direct all the hate and anger towards, I could not imagine him being happy that he lost the support of Northhold.

I couldn't imagine that Ragna would be happy either. Every warrior on the field mattered at this point, and we had just ripped numbers from her plans. Added more work to her over-flowing load as she figured out how to accommodate the changes.

There was no welcoming party awaiting us when we entered the courtyard. While the Verndari alone may not have warranted it, Baldur certainly did. And from his pursed lips, he had realized the same thing I had.

A maid scurried down the stairs towards us as the stable hands stepped forward to relieve us of our horses. She dropped into a curtsy before Georg. "The King Commander has asked that the Verndari and Commanding Son Baldur visit his office as soon as possible."

Georg nodded. "Thank you. We will be there as soon as we have a chance to clean up."

"I don't think you understand." The maid fidgeted with her fingers, her feet shuffling uncomfortably on the ground. "He wants to see you as soon as possible."

Georg's jaw clenched. "He wants to see us immediately." He sighed, dismissing Lúdvík with a clap on his shoulder. "We will make our way there now."

We naturally settled into our typical order. Baldur surprisingly conceded the lead of our group to Georg and settled into Georg's typical place beside Aron. I glanced over my shoulder towards Gil for some reassurance, but there was nothing that he could offer me. Óskar drifted closer to me as we walked through the halls, as though sensing my anxiety, but there was nothing that he could do without drawing attention to me.

And the last thing we wanted to do was show the fortress that the Verndari did not want to see the King Commander. The fortress was already fractured, with nothing more than cobwebs and whispered promises keeping it from falling apart. If the Verndari, who were going to be the commanders in the coming war, the warriors wherever the fighting was thickest, were withdrawing from the King Commander, everyone else would do the same.

We couldn't risk that.

The door to the King Commander's office was shut when we arrived. Georg knocked, and the King Commander took his time, allowing us to enter the room. Another one of his fucking power games. He knew that after our time on the road, we would be ready to return to our rooms to relax, but he was deliberately preventing us from doing that. Or, perhaps, he was proving that he had the power to control our time. The power to control our lives. He held our strings and knew how to pull them to make us dance to his tune.

When we were finally allowed to enter, we silently filed into the room and sank into a bow. Even Baldur.

And he left us in our bow until he was ready to allow us to stand. Long enough, the muscles in my legs were starting to quiver, already taxed by time in the saddle.

"Report," the King Commander demanded.

Georg stepped slightly forward and cleared his throat. "Our initial arrival at Northhold was met with enthusiasm by the townspeople. We informed the Warlord of the decision of the War Council and offered our support while we were there, as well as the safe transport of his people to Newtide should they choose to leave."

"Why?" The King Commander's face was unreadable.

"I'm sorry, but I don't understand, King Commander. Why what?" Georg's brows furrowed.

"Why did you offer your support? Northhold was to no longer receive our military support—which also extends to the Verndari."

I blinked. Did he expect us to do nothing while we were there? Let Skolli tear the town apart should they choose to?

"There was a Skolli attack, and we reacted appropriately," Baldur said; his eyes were pinned on his father, but his voice was carefully level.

The King Commander's eyes flared with anger. "This was the Verndari's mission; you are lucky that you were allowed to go, son. Allow them to face the consequences of their actions."

"I participated alongside them; if you punish them, then you punish me." Baldur's body was the perfect image of the Commanding Son, head high, shoulders back, not an ounce of regret or fear marking his face.

I glanced at Rúna out of the corner of my eye. She had done a good job of schooling her face to hide her reaction, but her eyes still flared slightly with surprise.

Surprised that he would side with us over his father?

Or surprised that he would be willing to face whatever punishment the King Commander was considering? Was he trying to lessen the impact of his father's actions or was it a sign of solidarity to us?

The King Commander's hand tightened to a fist on his desk, his knuckles whitening. With every moment he was silent, the nerves in my stomach knotted further.

Finally, he turned his attention from his son back to Georg. "And how did the townspeople react when they learned of the true reason that you were there?"

"They were not pleased. They were marching through the streets, bordering on a riot, making it quite clear that they believed that we were their enemy. Some of our party got discovered within their masses and were the targets of their anger until they could escape."

"And who was targeted? Not my son, surely."

Georg shook his head. "No, King Commander. It was Bryn and two members of the Royal Regiment."

The King Commander's grin bordered on feral as he turned to me. "Not their shiny new saviour anymore, are you?"

"I'm not trying to be a hero; I'm just trying to do the right thing," I said softly.

"The right thing is what I tell you." The King Commander turned back to Georg. "What else happened?"

Georg took a deep breath, which I echoed. That we likely all echoed. We all knew what was coming next, and we all knew just how well that tidbit of news would be taken.

We were about to be the messenger that was punished for the contents of their delivery.

"The Warlord has given us a letter to deliver to his troops stationed at the fortress. He is withdrawing his support, and we believe that the exiled commanding family will receive it instead," Georg said, his voice carefully level.

The King Commander leaned forward in his seat. "Burn it."

Georg blinked, clearly caught off guard by the order.

"I will ensure that it is burned as soon as it is read to ensure that no one else learns of the decision," he promised.

"No, you misunderstand me. I want you to burn it now." The King Commander slowly stood from his seat and leaned against the front of the desk with his arms crossed over his chest.

"That's illegal. You are interfering with the Warlord's decisions regarding his forces," Rúna said. Gil shifted beside her, ready to jump between her and the King Commander if needed.

The King Commander pinned Rúna with his gaze. "The laws are what I make them, girl. Who will stop me if I adjust them as I see fit?" The room was silent, only the crackling of the fire in the fireplace filling the space. The right for the Warlords and Jarls to control their forces independently of the King Commander was one of Drysden's most sacred laws.

And he brushed that away without a thought, content to twist, break, and re-forge the laws to suit his needs. His whims.

To ensure he maintained his power.

"I said to burn the letter, and so you will burn the fucking thing," the King Commander hissed, venom coating every word.

Georg hesitated for a second longer before finally reaching into his pocket and pulling out the letter.

"Wait." Georg froze at the King Commander's order. "I think Jarl Brynja should be the one to burn it. If she believes she is worthy to have *my* warriors pledging support to her, she should also be able to ensure that their attentions don't stray."

I could feel the weight of the others' eyes on me, but I refused to look away from the King Commander. He had said he wanted me to be the villain, but he also wanted me to be a scapegoat. If it came to light that the letter was burned, he could assure them that it wasn't him who did so—it was me.

He was aware of exactly what he was asking me to do; he knew how the country would react if they found out.

The King Commander was as smart as he was conniving and wasn't about to risk being held accountable for his actions. No, he wanted me to be guilty of this treason so that I would be punished should anyone learn what happened.

And with the way he threatened Ma before we left—I didn't want to think about what may happen if I refused him.

My fingers shook, and I tucked them into my pockets to hide them from the King Commander's eyes. My skin met the parchment that already rested there.

A plan slowly pieced itself together in my mind as I stepped forward from my place in line and made my way to Georg. My legs weighed heavily with my fierce desire to be anywhere but here. I took the letter from his hand and approached the fireplace.

Baldur stood closest to it, the light from the flames dancing across his face as he watched me move closer.

There was no way that I could position my body to ensure

that both the King Commander and Baldur didn't see what I had planned. I hoped that Baldur's newfound reasonable behaviour extended to this moment—to uphold his country's laws rather than corrupt them.

I stopped before the fire, tucking the letter in my pocket as I turned to face the King Commander. His face held a sick sense of glee at what he was making me do. "Burn it now, girl," he growled.

I took a deep breath as I turned my back to the King Commander and subtly switched the Warlord's letter to the one that Luka had given me. Baldur's eyes followed my every movement.

After throwing the letter for Luka's sister in the fire, the weight of the Warlord's letter increased as though my every anxiety, my every worry and feeling of anger about the situation had wrapped themselves around the parchment in my pocket.

I turned back to the King Commander. "There." My voice was cold. Emotionless. "It is done."

The King Commander studied me for a long moment before turning to Baldur. "Did she throw the letter in the fire?"

I didn't move my gaze from the King Commander as I kept my shoulders back and my chin high. I didn't reveal a single doubt I had as I waited for Baldur to save or condemn me.

"She threw the letter in the fire," Baldur told his father, casually tucking his hands into his pants pockets. "It is done."

CHAPTER
FOURTEEN
BRYN

We didn't hesitate to leave when the King Commander dismissed us moments later. Baldur followed casually behind us, causing the hairs on the back of my neck to stand on end.

I had seen—I was still seeing—what he did to Rúna when he had learned of something that she had tried to keep hidden. And now he was the only one who knew I deliberately ignored the King Commander's instructions. That I had expressly acted against them.

It was only a matter of time before he also used that against me.

When the doors to our wing closed behind us, I finally let my shoulders sag with an odd mixture of relief and dread as the consequences of what I had just done threatened to overwhelm me.

What I had done didn't just put me at risk. By going against the King Commander's direct orders, I most likely put everyone I cared about in his line of sight.

And he had made it quite clear that he was more than comfortable targeting others to get to people. To get to us.

"Come with me," I told the others and led them to my rooms. The last place I wanted to invite Baldur was to my rooms, but the maids may be around the other rooms, and I wasn't about to invite him into anyone else's space.

When we were safely ensconced and the door tightly shut behind us, I turned towards where Baldur lingered just outside the group. "Why?" I asked him as I unclasped my cloak and threw it across one of the benches.

"It was the right thing to do."

I crossed my arms over my chest. "And what do you want from me? What do you want in exchange for your silence?"

"Nothing," Baldur said, causing me to raise an eyebrow at him. "Honestly, I want nothing. It was the right thing to do."

"Does either of you want to share with the rest of us exactly what you are going on about?" Óskar asked as he flopped on one of the benches. "It's not easy for the rest of us to join your lovely conversation if we have no idea what you are talking about."

I took a deep breath. "I didn't burn the Warlord's letter. I burned Luka's letter for his sister instead. And not only did Baldur see exactly what I did, he lied for me to the King Commander."

"Smart thinking," Aron praised with wide eyes.

"Why did you lie for her?" Rúna asked Baldur, her brows furrowed.

Baldur rolled his eyes. "Like I just told Bryn, it was the right thing to do. One day, everyone in this country will be my responsibility, and the idea of breaking one of our most fundamental laws didn't sit right with me. I may be my father's son, but I know he is walking a thin line between harsh and corrupt. I don't want that to be my legacy."

His words confused me, but I could tell that they shook Rúna to the core. They had shocked everyone else, further destabilizing our view of Baldur as this evil person. There were more layers to him than that, and, not for the first time since he opened up to me on the road, I realized there was more to the situation with Rúna than I had believed.

"Thank you," Gil said, his words gruff as though it pained him to say such a thing to Baldur, but he was unable to ignore exactly what he had done for me. He was well aware of what may have happened if he had not lied to his father.

Baldur acknowledged his thanks with a nod of his head.

"What do I do now?" I asked softly as I pulled the Warlord's letter from my pocket. "About this and about the letter I actually burnt."

"We need to get it to someone we trust within the War Camp," Georg said. "Someone we can trust won't mention a word to the King Commander."

"Jarl Einar." I took a deep breath. He had clarified that his loyalty was to me, not the King Commander. But he had left us to die only a short time ago because we hadn't earned his support yet. It was hard to forget something like that.

But this was an opportunity for us to test whether he was truly with us. It was an opportunity for him to prove that his loyalty did lie with us, not the King Commander.

Baldur stepped forward, his face worried. "You can't summon him directly here. My father will have eyes on you shortly if he doesn't already."

"Then we do it through the grapevine," Aron pivoted easily. "It's not unusual for us to be seen with Sofie, Luck, or Fannar. Use one of them."

"Or better yet, use them all. Host a dinner, invite all three, and have Luck bring along Jarl Einar. It'll be easy enough to have him leave here with the letter when he's done," Rúna added, flicking her blonde hair over her shoulder mindlessly.

I nodded; that sounded easy enough. "And about the other letter?"

"Write a note explaining what happened," Gil suggested, his eyes on me as though he could see my guilt for burning the letter weighing on me. "I am sure Luck would be willing to deliver it for you. If the sister is anything like Luka, she will understand."

With a plan in mind, Baldur was the first to move for the door, clearly uncomfortable with the situation. He had just rested his hand on the door handle when I spoke up. "Thank you."

He froze, looking back over his shoulder at me. Baldur finally nodded, acknowledging my gratitude, and slipped out the door.

Leaving me with no choice but to trust his word that he would do the right thing.

Sofie and Fannar arrived shortly before dinner with Jarl Einar and Luck in tow.

I was happy to see Luck, and while I didn't feel the same way about Jarl Einar, I felt a sense of relief after his arrival. He had made it quite clear before what he thought about bad orders, and I was beginning to sense that his thoughts about the King Commander were similarly aligned with mine.

But there was a risk of revealing my actions to more people.

I knew I could trust Luck—he had done everything he could to help me when he was ordered not to.

But Jarl Einar was a gamble. I had to believe that we had read him and his intentions correctly.

Whether Luck and Jarl Einar picked up on the tension running through us, I don't know. But dinner progressed as it normally would, with the addition of Sofie, Fannar, Luck and Jarl Einar.

The conversation was lively, the laughter ringing, as we all took the moment to decompress. As we took the moment just to be ourselves, not one of the many roles we had to play.

"You haven't left the walls recently, Rúna," Óskar said as he tossed some meat to Yugar. "Lost the travel bug, have you?"

Rúna raised an eyebrow. "We just returned from a trip, you doofus. What are you on about?"

"You used to take solo trips all the time, arriving just in time for training covered for dust from the road."

"We're on the road enough lately without me adding to it." Rúna sighed, shifting in her seat before she turned to Sofie and Fannar's conversation.

Everything she said was true—we were on the road a lot lately. It would only be a matter of time before my legs permanently moulded themselves in the shape of my saddle.

But she had stopped her trips long before our departures began. Rúna had only taken one such trip while I was at the fortress, shortly before she and Baldur had gotten together. I guessed that Baldur limited her access out of the fortress to ensure he maintained control, but that didn't align with my view of the man.

Perhaps she didn't want to admit that her stopping her trips had been completely out of her control.

Enough of her life had suddenly become controlled by

someone else, and maybe it hurt to admit that one more thing had been pulled from her grasp.

As dinner was wrapping up, I knew I finally had to make my move. And with the servants in and out of the room with our food, I had to get them up to my rooms.

"Sofie, Luck, Jarl Einar, I don't believe that you have been given the grand tour of the Verndari wing yet," I said as I stood from my chair. "I would love to show you around."

Fannar's eyebrows furrowed. He was well aware of what there was to see in our wing and that there was nothing fancy to share besides the common rooms and the training room. We all valued our personal spaces quite highly, especially with how the King Commander showed us off like we were his favourite toys.

Aron gave Luck a barely distinguishable nod, a motion only picked up by the closest comrades.

"We would love to," Luck smiled. "Lead the way."

We led them through the first-floor room by room, keeping up the facade before guiding them upstairs. We finally let the act drop when we were enclosed within my room with the door shut tight.

"What's going on?" Fannar asked. "There's no way that you sent us to get Jarl Einar and Luck to join you for dinner simply to give them a tour of the wing."

"Maybe we wanted to show off a bit?" Óskar joked, no doubt trying to alleviate the tension that had seeped into the room.

Fannar didn't say a word as he crossed his arms over his chest, his gaze drifting between Aron and I. Trusting his family to tell him what was happening.

"The King Commander ordered me to break the law this afternoon," I said, causing the others to turn to me in shock. "I defied him, but Baldur knows what I did. He advised that I have you help me."

"I don't know where to start with that. With you disobeying the King Commander or the fact that Baldur is helping you do it." Fannar's eyes were worried.

"We will start at the beginning," Gil said before nodding for me to take over.

I started from the moment Jarl Einar and his forces arrived at the fortress and walked them through every moment, every interaction that mattered, to get them caught up to where we are now.

"The King Commander is treading a dangerous line, and I will not help him slip onto the wrong side." My voice was quiet. "He will have eyes on me, on all of the Verndari, and to a lesser extent, our families. But I need to get the Warlord's letter to his forces and a notice to Luka's sister about the letter I burned."

"That's where Luck and I come in," Jarl Einar realized. "He likely won't be watching us as closely, and if he is, then we won't raise the same level of suspicion walking through the War Camp that you would."

I nodded. "Exactly. But only if you are both willing to do so. If you do this, you will be complicit in what I did. Not to the same extent, but you could get caught up in his wrath if it is discovered."

"I fought to prove that I deserved to fight by your side in what comes next. I am yours, not his," Luck said, stepping forward with his hand extended. "Tell me what to do, and I will make sure that it gets done."

I handed him the note I had written. "Please make sure that Luka's sister gets this."

Jarl Einar stepped forward next, appraising us before

focusing on me. "I swore my support to you, not to him. Your actions only prove to me that I made the right decision." He took the letter from my hand. "I will get this where it needs to go."

"We are going to have to have a discussion—we and those we know are loyal to us—about what to do should his concerning behaviour continue," Georg said, carefully wording his statement, but its meaning was crystal clear.

There would come a time when we would need to discuss what we would do about the King Commander.

And who we could trust to do so.

"I would not be surprised if that conversation happens sooner rather than later." Gil's face was grim. "I will not let him target those that I care about."

CHAPTER

FIFTEEN

GIL

I left Bryn curled up under the furs and dressed for the day. We were all tired, borderline exhausted, but today, Rúna would need all the support that she could get. She would be leaving the fortress shortly, as she did every year, but I always made a point to see her before she left and be there for her when she got back.

Rúna was always in a rush to leave the fortress; the building was filled with so many ghosts and memories for her. Especially today.

On Heimir's birthday.

Her dead brother's birthday.

My boots clicked against the floor as I made my way to Rúna's rooms. I knocked, and it didn't take very long for her to let me know to come in.

I expected her to be already dressed for the journey with her saddlebags packed. But I was wrong. She sat on the couch, staring into the fire with some furs wrapped around her shoulders. Rúna still wore her night clothes, her hair tangled.

"Rú?" I asked softly as I closed the door behind me. "I was expecting to catch you on your way out the door."

She sniffed, not looking away from the fire. "I know that you noticed that I haven't been leaving the fortress lately."

"I thought that you would make an exception for today, for what it means." I took a seat on the couch beside her. Rúna's face was a perfect etching of heartbreak, a complete display of despair. Her eyes swam with tears, her face red from the ones she had already spilt. She fidgeted, picking at the skin around her fingernails until it bled.

"It's not worth the risk," she whispered as her shoulders slumped.

"I will go with you," I offered. "Tell me what to do to help, and I will do it."

Rúna finally turned her attention towards me, a sad smile on her face. "There is nothing you can do to change what happened so long ago."

There was nothing I could do to change the fact that she had lost her mother and her little brother in a fire that burnt down their cottage.

But there had to be something I could do to ease some of her pain.

"Where do you go every year? What do you do?" I finally asked.

She studied me for a long moment. "Why do you ask?"

"If it is as big of a risk as you say it is, then maybe I can recreate some part of it here. But in order to do that, I need to know what part of the trip brings you comfort."

Rúna turned back to the fire as she considered my words. She had always been quite secretive about her trips, never sharing more details than how long she would be away. I never pushed her for more than that, allowing her to keep one part of our very public lives for herself.

But to see her like this now, crumpling under her pain and grief, I had to at least try and bring her some form of comfort.

She took a deep breath before releasing it slowly. "You can't recreate it because it is not a thing. I visit with someone." Her words were barely loud enough for me to hear.

"Who is it? I can bring them—"

"No!" She cut me off harshly before gathering herself. "No. They can never come here."

It was my turn to consider her words, to study the pure panic in her eyes at my offer. "Does this have something to do with what Baldur has over you?"

A tear slipped down her cheek. She brushed it away with the back of her hand.

"This is—" she cleared her throat. "This is *everything*. I can't risk it. Not now, not ever."

"Okay." I pulled a fur over my lap and settled more comfortably onto the couch. "Okay. Then I will be here for whatever you need."

We didn't say a word as we sat there, the fire crackling in front of us. We didn't say a word as the sun rose outside her window or as the fortress came to life for the day. I waited as Rúna disappeared into her bedroom to get ready, only rising to stand when she re-entered the room to put the fire out.

"I have to spend the day with Baldur," she told me. I bit back every retort on my tongue, hid every flicker of anger her words caused. To take away her choices was bad enough, but to force her to spend the day with him on her dead brother's birthday was despicable. "Will you walk me to his office?"

"Of course," I stood and reached out to give her shoulder a squeeze. "I am here for anything you need."

113

She gave me her first true smile of the day. "I know, Gil."

We walked through the fortress silently, trying our best to avoid drawing any attention to ourselves. Yet we still drew stares as people caught sight of us, causing Rúna to withdraw further into herself with each set of eyes that landed on us. When we finally made it to Baldur's office, the door was slightly ajar, allowing the voices inside to drift into the hallway.

Hákon and Baldur.

Rúna's hand wrapped around my wrist, freezing me in place. We crept closer to the doorway until we could make out what they were saying.

"And whose fault is that? Who put me in this position?" Baldur growled.

"I didn't mean to—you have to know that," Hákon's voice was threaded with pain.

"Regardless of that, you have left me no other options, *brother*," Baldur spat, causing Rúna to turn to me with wide eyes. The brothers had never gotten along as far as I could remember. But looking back, Baldur had always avoided anything to do with his brother while Hákon was always staring after the Commanding Son. "You should go. Rúna will be here any moment."

Hákon scoffed. "You're forcing her to spend her day with you on today of all days?" he snapped. "You've already taken away her every choice, any options that she had."

A sound like a chair scratching against the floor rang through the space. "You have done the same—you have stolen my choices and my options just the same."

Rúna's brows furrowed as she stared towards the door with confusion. Unless Hákon was blackmailing Baldur, I don't think there is anything that Hákon could have done to

Baldur that would compare to the pain that he has put her through.

"I don't know how to apologize for that, how to make that up to you. I was just a child," Hákon pleaded, his voice barely loud enough for us to hear.

Something in the room crashed, causing Rúna to jump. "So was I, but everyone seems to forget that part, don't they?" Baldur yelled before there was another crash.

"I don't. I can't—won't—forget a moment of that day," Hákon told his brother.

It was silent for a moment. "I'm not making Rúna do anything today; by having her here with me, it prevents her from being paraded about," Baldur finally admitted. Rúna went rigid beside me. "You've seen what Father has been like lately. He would make her hold audiences or some shit today just to manipulate her grief."

There was a shocked breath. "You're protecting her," Hákon breathed.

Rúna shook her head as though to clear it, and when no further words came from the room, she pushed open the door and strode in. I followed her lead, taking in the way that Baldur stood behind his desk, his hands braced on the surface, only his head turning towards where we were. His chair was tipped over behind him, and books and items from his desk were scattered on the ground.

Hákon turned fully towards the door from where he stood across from his brother. His face was pale as he tucked his gloved hands into his pockets to hide their shaking.

Hákon cleared his throat. "Rúna, Gil. If you'll excuse me, I have training to get to."

He eased his way to the door, carefully avoiding touching us on his way. He paused at the threshold and looked back towards Baldur. "Brother," Hákon said softly with a nod before disappearing down the hallway.

"I wasn't expecting you here today," Baldur told me as he began to straighten up his office.

"He offered to walk me here." Rúna gave my hand a squeeze. "Go—I will be fine."

CHAPTER
SIXTEEN
BRYN

Georg had given us the morning off. He didn't specify the reason, but we all knew there were multiple.

To heal, to destress, to recover, to grieve. To feel like we were more than the commanders on a battlefield, more than pieces to be moved on the map spread out across the War Chamber table.

I happily jumped on the opportunity to visit Ma, practically inhaling the breakfast in front of me in my excitement to get to her. Óskar and Yugar joined me a second later, a small smirk on his face as he took in my behaviour.

"Excited to get somewhere?" he asked me, helping himself to a plate of food.

"I'm going to see Ma. I haven't seen her since the departure."

Since the King Commander had very clearly displayed her weaknesses to a highly divided court and painted a large target on her back.

117

"Mind if I join you? I've been working on something that I think she will like."

I tilted my head to the side, curious about what he may be referring to, but if he wanted to tell me, he would. I trusted him only to have her best interests at heart.

After all, Gil, Óskar, and Aron were all regular visitors to Ma's rooms with me. I think she enjoyed seeing who would accompany me on any given day.

"Of course," I told him with a smile. "I hoped to go as soon as we are done here."

Óskar nodded and started to shovel food into his mouth quickly. "I just need to grab something from my rooms; then I'll be ready," he spoke around a mouthful of partially chewed food.

I wrinkled my nose, shoving him good-naturedly. "We have enough time for you to chew *and swallow* your food before you talk to me, you heathen."

Óskar laughed and slowed down just enough for his table manners to show through before he prepared a breakfast plate for Yugar and disappeared to his room for whatever he needed.

He met me at the entrance to our wing with a large basket tucked under his arm. Yugar, who had been lounging by my feet, jumped to all fours, his tail wagging in excitement.

When I opened the doors, Yugar was quick to take the lead, never more than a few steps ahead, as he practically pranced through the halls of the fortress.

The tension in the halls was thick, weighing on my shoulders. Only the servants travelled alone; everyone else had at least one person as they walked through the passageways. Everyone was armed, their hands kept too close to their hilts to be a coincidence. Ottó and Emília lounged in one of the sitting areas they passed, their weapons within easy reach. Their eyes seared my skin as they followed us until we were out of sight.

I breathed a sigh of relief when we finally reached the door to Ma's rooms. I knocked as Óskar took up a position at my back, guarding me as he would in the field.

Ma opened the door just enough to reveal one of her eyes. When she realized it was me, she swung it open wide enough for us to slip through before closing it tightly behind us.

She hugged me tight before resting her hand on my shoulder and surveying me as though she were searching for injuries. Once she had deemed me healthy, she followed the same routine on Óskar before turning her attention to Yugar.

The dog didn't hesitate to roll onto his back, all four legs in the air, as he begged for a belly rub.

Ma eventually guided us to the sitting area and prepared tea. She handed Óskar and me each a steaming tankard before sitting in her chair by the window.

"How were things while we were gone?" I asked, blowing on my tea before taking a careful sip. "You didn't have any trouble, did you?"

Ma gave me a small smile before shaking her head. Her answer eased some of the worries that had knotted themselves in my stomach since the King Commander's display in the courtyard, but not all of it.

She gestured between Óskar and me with her remaining hand, asking her own silent question.

Did we run into trouble?

"Nothing we couldn't handle," I reassured her.

"There is very little that I can't handle, Mama Cora," Óskar joked as he leaned back, getting comfortable. I rolled my eyes at the nickname that Óskar had started. It had spread easily to

Aron, the two of them drawing a beaming smile from Ma when they used it.

I watched Ma carefully as I asked the next question. "Did anyone give you a hard time?" Ma frowned as she tilted her head to the side. I asked her a more specific question. "Did the King Commander or Ottó seek you out?"

Ma took a deep breath, swallowing nervously. She opened and closed her mouth as though she were trying to find the right words, and the ability, to answer. She finally sighed and shook her head as though frustrated with herself.

"It's okay, Ma," I told her quietly, equally nervous and excited that she had tried to speak to me. I thought I would never hear her voice again, and her attempt gave me hope that I might someday. But for my question to prompt that kind of reaction told me everything that I needed to know.

The King Commander or Ottó, or both, had worried Ma enough that she finally felt the need to speak again.

I exchanged a worried look with Óskar before refocusing my attention on Ma. "You don't need to speak. We've gotten quite good at understanding you just as you are." I told her with a small smile.

Ma tapped her finger on her temple. I took a moment to consider her gesture before saying, "Be smart."

Ma nodded before miming something by her waist. My eyebrows furrowed, confused by what she was trying to tell me. She did the same motion again, pointing to me first this time.

"She wants you to make sure you're armed," Óskar said grimly before Ma pointed to him. "Me too. All of us, if I had to guess."

Ma nodded, her shoulders relaxing as Óskar decoded what she was trying to say.

"We'll be careful, but Ma, you must be careful too. And you'll be here all alone when we get sent into the field." My fingers fidgeted with my tankard as my nerves doubled in my stomach.

"I might be able to help with that," Óskar said as he set aside his tankard and reached for the basket. He pulled out a large cat and cradled its long grey body. It had plenty of fur with a puffy tail, hair extending from its ears, and something that resembled a mane by its neck.

"Who's this?" I asked, startled by the feline addition.

"She doesn't have a name yet; I wanted to leave that honour for Mama Cora." Óskar turned his attention to Ma. "I started looking for a companion for you after the first time I met you. It took me a while to find this girl and even longer to train her how I wanted." His cheeks reddened. "My bloodrite may be with animals, but training animals like I did with Yugar, and this girl here is hard if you don't start when they are young. So, it took me a while."

Ma joined Óskar on the couch, her fingers brushing the cat's fur. Her purr was loud enough for me to hear.

"She will be a good companion to you, but she also knows how to defend you. Her claws are quite sharp, let me tell you. She can also get help or deliver a message. She has verbal command words for each thing, but I also trained her to respond to hand motions so you could communicate with her now. That took us the longest—I struggled with that for a while."

"Óskar, that's incredible," I told him, my voice thick with tears.

He shrugged self-consciously. "If I had been better, I would have been able to give her to Mama Cora before, but at least you have her now."

"I've told you before that your bloodrite is harder to master than almost any other one because the animals have their own free will. The fact that you did this for Ma and put in all this work for her means more than you can know."

"At least with this, when it didn't work, no one was in danger from my mistake." Óskar's voice was thick with frustration.

Ma wrapped her arm around Óskar before gently patting his cheek. She gestured to the cat, and Óskar gently set her on Ma's lap.

Her face was brighter than I had seen it for a while. Perhaps even since Ebonwell—before Da had died.

"What will you name her?" Óskar asked quietly.

I grabbed a piece of parchment and a stick of charcoal that had been nearby — Ma seemed to have gotten into sketching — and passed them to Ma.

She carefully wrote on it before passing it to Óskar.

He read it before smiling at her. "I think Grida is perfect."

It was quite similar to the name of the god of protection and guidance, and I could think of nothing better to name Ma's companion as Óskar began to walk her through the various hand signs that he had taught Grida.

Ottó was exactly where he was when we left for Ma's rooms, one of the many young warriors that Emilía had been cozying up to by his side. His daughter was gone, but Ottó still sat comfortably—regally as though he were holding court.

I felt his eyes as soon as we entered his eyeline, as though he were watching, waiting, for us to return.

"Jarl Brynja," he said, his voice easily carrying through the uncommonly quiet hallway. The uncertainty that had been rampant since the Skolli attacked the fortress had only worsened. "A moment of your time."

I exchanged a glance with Óskar before straightening my shoulders and approaching the seating area where Ottó and the young warrior lounged. Óskar easily fell into place by my side, Yugar alert at his feet.

"I've never heard you speak so politely to us, Ottó," Óskar pointed out, casually tucking his hands into his pockets. "I didn't know that you were capable of it."

"I don't recall inviting you over, boy," Ottó leaned forward in his seat, bracing his forearms on his thighs, his nose scrunched as though he smelt something bad.

"There's that lovely attitude of yours." Óskar sat in one of the chairs, but he didn't relax. He looked ready to move at a moment's notice, and from the way that Yugar sat by his feet, I knew that he had also picked up on the tension. Every muscle of the canine's body was tensed, ready to spring at the slightest need.

I took my own seat across from Ottó. "What do you want?"

"Is that any way to start a conversation when I invited you over so nicely?" Ottó said, his eyes not hinting at the false kindness he had shown before. We were both well aware of what the other believed and where the other stood in the coming conflict, and neither of us was going to waste energy trying to hide it from each other. I hated him for what he put me through; he hated me for representing his daughter's failure.

And nothing was going to change that.

I didn't budge, refusing to play whatever game this was. He called me over for a reason: he would be the one to show his cards first.

"This is riveting," Óskar pointed out as the silence continued, neither Ottó nor I wanting to break first.

The young warrior was the picture of ease by Ottó's side, but by how his eyes darted between us, I knew it was a facade. He knew the people he sat with, what we were capable of, and was waiting for the fallout.

I gave it a moment more, but Ottó stared at me, not saying a word.

I stood from my chair, "Well, whatever you wanted to say to me clearly wasn't that important. I have many other things I should be doing before we get sent out once again." I turned my back on Ottó, trusting Yugar and Óskar to make sure he didn't make a move on me.

"It must be worrisome, the amount of time you spend on the road," Ottó said. I froze but didn't turn back around towards him. "Never knowing what you are riding out to, never knowing what you may be returning to. I'm quite glad that I don't have the same problem."

"You've ensured that considering you have not sworn your support to the King Commander," Óskar pointed out.

"The minute I do that, he will be free to deploy me as he sees fit. But until then, I will stay right here, doing whatever I think is best."

I slowly turned to face him once again. He had been very careful to keep his tone conversational, and I wasn't about to risk igniting this into something more.

Especially not in the middle of the hallway.

So I kept my tone light as I asked, "And what is that?"

"I have ample time to ensure that myself, my daughters, and my warriors keep their skills sharp. There's plenty of opportunities to discuss with the people of the fortress and meet new people." He paused for a moment, casually leaning back. "I hadn't realized that your mother was still struggling. I could spend some time with her, see if I can...help her."

I took a deep breath, keeping my rage locked deep within me. "Her days are fairly booked. It seems there are no opportunities for you to spend time with her."

"What a shame. I'm sure that I could change that if I wanted."

"Let me make one thing quite clear to you, Ottó. I don't give a damn if you train your warriors or make alliances while we are not here. I'd be stupid to think that you weren't after you and your family have made it quite clear where you stand." I stepped closer to him, dropping my voice so no one passing by would hear what I said. "But if you so much as take one step down that hallway towards my mother's rooms, then you won't just incur my wrath. You will have declared war against several of the strongest people in Drysden. And need I remind you what happened last time your family challenged mine?" I leaned closer to him. "You fucking lost. So, stay the hell away from her."

I turned on my heel, immediately stalking away from him. Óskar and Yugar immediately fell into step with me.

"You forget that the Verndari can be deployed at anytime— you won't always be here," Ottó called out to me.

"I wasn't just talking about the Verndari," I called over my shoulder as I continued down the hallway without looking back.

CHAPTER
SEVENTEEN
BRYN

The next morning, I drew back the curtains of my window, allowing the early morning light to fill my room. And, glancing out at the War Camp, I realized it was noticeably smaller.

It seemed Jarl Einar managed to get the letter where it needed to go.

The dread settling in my stomach quickly replaced my relief at our success. It wouldn't take long for the King Commander to realize that his forces had been depleted. And I knew the first person he would blame.

Me.

But I wouldn't allow myself to focus on something that hadn't happened yet or something I couldn't control. I knew that he would react, and I knew that it wasn't going to be good for me. For any of the Verndari. But there was nothing I could do to change that.

It would happen when it happened, and until then, I would try to forget about it.

I had done the right thing. I would not be pressured into doing something unless I had no choice.

I would get on with my duties, continue living my life, and deal with the consequences when they arose.

We didn't speak of Northhold's warriors leaving during breakfast or on our way to the training room, so I had no idea if the others knew it had happened. And I wasn't about to bring it up when there was the potential of ears around us.

When we reached the training hall, I naturally made my way towards my weapons rack, but Georg stopped me before I could arm myself.

"Today is going to be hand-to-hand combat only," he said, causing Óskar to groan. "It's been a while since we dedicated a day to it, and now we know that hand-to-hand combat is a valid option against the Ógn, at least to incapacitate them."

"What are the pairs?" Rúna asked, a wicked smirk on her face. "Please tell me that Óskar's with Gil."

Óskar glared at her. "You are a wicked, nasty woman. I hope you know that," he muttered.

Georg typically paired us up in one of two ways. Either by our pairings or by skill level. Excluding the times when Óskar annoyed him and got paired with Gil, it was the easiest way to do it.

"We're going to change it up a bit today. I want you all to face some new challenges. Gil and Bryn, Aron and Óskar, and Rúna and I will pair up with each other."

"That's not much better," Óskar grumbled, causing me to chuckle.

"Gil and Bryn, you are up first," Georg said, gesturing to the white sparring circle.

I immediately settled into my warm-ups, loosening my

muscles to prepare for the spar. Gil was doing the same thing across from me. When we were both ready, we settled into a fighting crouch across from each other.

"Begin," Georg said.

We began circling each other, both of us trying to evaluate how to play it. I may have sparred against Gil before, but not in hand-to-hand combat since we had gotten together.

After Rúna, I probably knew his strengths and his tells better than anyone. I just had to figure out how to play them to my advantage.

Gil threw the first punch, aiming for my chest. I dodged to the side, his knuckles just grazing me. He didn't pack nearly as much force as he could have.

He didn't want to hurt me.

And that was how I would beat him.

I pivoted, putting my weight in the ball of my foot, and snapped a kick at his stomach.

Gil blocked it with a grunt, his eyes flashing to mine. I hadn't held back. It wouldn't have caused him any damage, but he would have felt the blow.

"Is that how you want to play it, darling?" His lips quirked.

I threw a punch at him. "I don't know what you mean."

His eyes flashed, a playful glint running through them. Gil swept his leg behind my feet, trying to hook me off balance. I jumped backwards, easily avoiding his move. Within moments of landing, I swung another kick at his stomach.

Instead of blocking it as he did before, he caught my leg, his large hands easily wrapping around my leg. "Got you," he taunted before pulling me towards him.

Off balance, my body slammed into his. He dropped my ankle, his arm naturally wrapping around my waist. The other wrapped around my shoulders, pinning me tightly to his body. But I wasn't about to go down that easily.

I pressed a kiss to his throat, his body loosening ever so slightly. My lips travelled his skin to his ear. "Do you?" I breathed before ducking out of his grasp and spinning around to his back.

Kicking the back of his knee to knock him off balance, I pounced on him, taking him to the floor. He turned as we tumbled, taking the brunt of our impact on his back as I pinned him to the wooden floorboards. I straddled his waist, my feet tucked up against his thighs to pin them down as my hands pressed down on his shoulders.

"Nicely done, darling. You are just forgetting one thing," he said, gazing up at me.

"And what is that?"

"You may have discovered how to distract me, but I am not just bigger than you. I am stronger, too."

He surged from the ground, effortlessly rolling us so that he pinned me instead. I struggled against him, but I couldn't get him to budge, and I couldn't get any leverage while on my back. Gil tucked his head into my neck and pressed his lips to my jaw. "I win."

He climbed off me and reached down a hand to help me to my feet.

"Interesting tactics there, Talon. I hadn't tried those before," Óskar teased me.

I snorted. "I think that it's an advantage that only I have over him."

The doors to the training room slammed open as the King Commander stormed inside, the furs on his shoulders flaring behind him as he stormed towards us.

Gil went to step in front of me, but I stopped him with a

gentle hand on his wrist. The King Commander had made his opinions about Gil and his family quite clear, and I wasn't about to let him put himself in the warpath. I knew the consequences of my actions were coming, and I wasn't about to let him bear the brunt of them.

"Does anyone care to tell me why Northhold's forces left the fortress in the middle of the night?" the King Commander seethed.

Georg stepped forward, trying to draw the King Commander's attention. "Their Warlord recalled them."

"The girl burnt the letter, or so she claims. There is no way that they should have known to leave," he hissed, glaring at me. "Unless she lied to me."

"I burnt it. Just like you ordered. Your son saw me do it—ask him if you don't trust me," I said, straightening my shoulders. I would not show an ounce of fear to him.

The King Commander's face darkened with rage. "You dare give me orders, you insolent girl?"

"By the time we left, it was clear that the Warlord doubted us," Aron added, his body the picture of ease, but his jaw clenched. "I wouldn't be surprised if he sent a different communication to his people to be sure that we wouldn't betray him."

"The law is clear—"

"You were leaving his people to die." Rúna cut the King Commander off, causing him to clench his hands into fists. "If you didn't value them enough to protect them, why would he think you would care enough to uphold the law?"

The King Commander glared at her for a moment longer before stalking towards me.

Gil shifted by my side, no doubt desperately wanting to step between us, but that would only make everything worse. I squeezed his wrist, silently begging him to stay put. His body practically vibrated with tension as he forced himself to stand still as the King Commander continued to stalk towards me.

The King Commander didn't stop until he was close enough that his breath caused my curls to blow back from my face.

"If I find out that you had anything to do with this, there will be consequences for your family," he hissed.

I didn't look away, lifting my chin to continue to look him in the eye. "Are you threatening to hurt my family, King Commander?"

"There are so many options before me." He tilted his head like a predator sizing up its prey. "And more than one way to make your family pay. By blood or by grief."

"Ask the Commanding Son if I burned the letter," I said, putting my faith and my family's wellbeing in the unreliable hands of Baldur. "He will tell you that I did, proving I have had nothing to do with this."

"You better hope that he tells the same story as you just did," the King Commander growled before storming out of the hall.

With my spar done, I didn't need to linger by the sparring circle. Typically, we all watched, as there was plenty to learn from watching a fight, but Georg didn't stop me as I made my way to a corner of the room.

I propped a dummy up and wrapped my knuckles with a long strip of cloth. The nervous energy that the King Commander had triggered was running rampant through my body, begging me to release it. Normally, I would take to the grounds and run until I finally felt free of the feeling.

But I didn't think that my running out of the wing after the confrontation would send the right message to the King

Commander, especially when he seemed to be scrambling more than ever for power and control and allowing his rationality to slip.

I settled into my fighting crouch, raising my fists by my chin, focused on the dummy before me.

I tuned out the rest of the room, my heartbeat filling my ears as I threw my first punch.

A flare of pain lanced from my knuckles up my arm, but I ignored it before I punched with my other hand.

Hit after hit, my knuckles became numb, allowing me to pack more force behind each one. With every strike, the ball of nerves that had coiled itself so deeply in my stomach loosened. The anxiety slowly transformed into a rage that made me clench my fists tighter.

I sped up, my knuckles barely landing on the dummy before I was throwing my next punch. Pummelling it.

An arm wrapped around my chest and the tops of my arms, stopping the flurry of blows. It gently pulled me so my back rested against a warm chest. "Enough," Gil breathed in my ear.

I sagged against him, my head hanging. He interlaced our fingers, lifting my hand. A moment later, he released it, placing his hand on my hip. "Let's go," he told me.

Gil guided me out the doors of the training hall and through the wing to my room.

Placing both hands on my hips, he lifted me onto the table before disappearing into my bedroom. He returned moments later with my healing supplies. Gil stepped closer to me, my legs resting on either side of him. He gently unwrapped the bloody cloth from my knuckles, entirely focused on caring for my wounds.

My self-inflicted wounds.

"Why did you do this?" he asked me gently, his fingers light as feathers on my skin as he cared for me.

I swallowed, finally feeling the cuts sting across the back of my knuckles. "Do you think I did the right thing?"

"I would prefer if you did not cause this kind of damage to yourself."

I rolled my eyes. "Not the punching. I meant the letter."

"I do. I know you think so, too. And I would be willing to bet your family would agree with me."

"He's dangerous." I didn't bother to say who I meant; Gil knew exactly who I was talking about. "What do we do?"

"We talk to the others and come up with a plan." He tucked a fiery curl behind my ear. "And we enjoy what we can while we can."

I nodded, tucking my head into the crook of his shoulder and just letting him hold me. Gil's arms wrapped around me effortlessly, one of his hands tracing a line up and down my spine. I kissed his skin, causing his movement to stutter for a moment. Smiling against his throat, I wrapped my legs around his hips, pulling his body flush to mine.

"What are you doing?" he asked as his hands found my hips, not even considering pulling away as he had in the past.

"Enjoying what we can while we can," I repeated as I wrapped my arms around his shoulders, fingers tunnelling into his hair. "If you want to, that is."

Gil groaned, his lips crashing to mine, his hands trying to pull my body impossibly closer to his.

I broke the kiss, pressing a trail of them from the corner of his mouth and down his throat before nipping at his ear. Cursing, Gil's hands found the hem of my loose training shirt, pulling back from me just long enough to lift it over my head and toss it to the side.

It took me a matter of heartbeats to return the favour, my fingers drifting across the bare skin of his chest. His back. His shoulders. Before drifting lower to his stomach.

Gil swept me off the table, causing me to squeak and tighten my legs around him. He chuckled, his one hand sliding beneath me to hold some of my weight, the other tangling itself in my curls. My lips found any patch of skin I could, causing him to groan.

He dropped onto the couch, causing me to bounce against his legs. I settled atop him, my legs straddling his hips as he sat. Gil pulled me back in for a kiss as though we were ravenous for each other. He stripped me of my pants, and I lifted off him long enough for him to do the same to himself.

I hissed as I settled against him again. He took his turn to drift his fingers down my body, finding every spot that made me gasp, every movement that made me moan.

It hadn't taken him long to become familiar with my body, to learn everything that made my toes curl. Gil's fingers did just that, my toes curling and my head thrown back. That feeling coiling tighter and tighter within me exploded, sending tingles through my body.

My hands found his cheeks, kissing him hard as he aligned us and helped me settle against him, linked together as one. We stilled for a moment before I shifted on my knees, pulling back from him before settling flush against him once again.

I did it again; this time, his hips raised to meet mine.

Faster, harder, that feeling once again coiling tightly within me.

It burst, my head finding the crook of his shoulders as I allowed the feeling to run through my body. Moments later, Gil moaned my name before stilling with me.

We stayed that way for several moments—skin to skin, heart to heart.

I finally lifted my head, my eyes locking with his, a small smile curling on my lips. "I love you," I told him softly.

"I love you too, darling." Gil's thumb drifted across my flushed cheek. "We will find a way to get through this."

"Together," I whispered, my fingers interlocking with his free hand.

He smiled softly at me. "Together," he echoed.

CHAPTER

EIGHTEEN

BRYN

I kept my face carefully neutral, without a hint of my thoughts or feelings on display, as I strode through the fortress halls with Aron. I had learned to school my face when we had become a target for rage and hope. But knowing that there were eyes on me, eyes that would report back to Ottó or the King Commander, made it even more important.

The hallways were still tense, the tension weighing heavily upon my shoulders. I doubted the tension would break until we knew who was aligned with whom. No one wanted to make the first move or be the first one to break the ice.

It would take something big to break the fissures spreading through the fortress wide open. And I could feel that it was coming. It was only a matter of time until things were shattered.

Aron was equally stoic by my side, his hands resting too casually by his weapons to be unintentional.

We rounded the corner to find Luck leaning across the wall, his eyes scanning the hallway as Emilía was practically draped over him. His face may not show any of his thoughts, but from the rigidity of his body, it was quite clear that he wanted to be anywhere other than where he was.

"Aron! Bryn!" Luck casually called out to us, inviting us over to join them. I had been more than happy to avoid that conversation, knowing full-well that he could hold his own. He may have even been willing to suffer through Emilía's presence if he thought there was some benefit for him or us on the other side. But he wanted us to interrupt, which meant that there was either something that he wanted us to know or he wanted us to get him out of the situation.

Either way, I would not say no to his plea.

"Hello, Luck. Emilía," Aron greeted calmly, but his weight was evenly distributed, ready to spring at the slightest hint of unrest. "I didn't realize that you knew each other."

Emilía brushed a hand over Luck's bicep as she fluttered her eyelashes at him. "We've been growing quite close since—"

"—I met her today," Luck cut off Emilía, causing her eyes to flash with anger. He was going against her plan, whatever that may be, and I knew how deranged she could become when she thought she was backed into a corner.

I shook my head. "Still up to your nonsense, I see. What is Luck? Your new flavour of the day?"

"More like her new target of the day," Aron added with a snort.

Emilía stepped away from Luck, pushing him back towards the wall, and crossed her hands over her chest. "I don't like what you are insinuating there. You can't speak about me like that. You're just a son of a Warlord. I'm the daughter of a Jarl."

"You forget yourself, Emilía. Your father's title means nothing when you speak to the Verndari," I snarked, resting my hands on my daggers with an eye roll. "And I believe that Aron

137

was implying that Luck was the newest target for your whispers, straight from Ottó's mouth to his ears."

Emilía stepped closer to me. "You have no way of knowing that."

I turned to Luck with a raised brow. He stepped forward, barely sparing Emilía a glance.

"Right in one there, Bryn," he said, shifting to stand by Aron's side. He cocked his head as Emilía gasped. "What? Did you honestly think I would accept your offer to turn against them? You should learn more about who you approach before proposing such a thing."

"You forget that I earned their support by defending their city and being willing to sacrifice myself to protect them," I snarled, tired of her meddling. Tired of her trying to take things from me. Tired of her trying to meddle in a war that she would probably never fight in. "What could you offer them to make them ignore that fact?"

"It's only a matter of time before he realizes how weak and pathetic you are. It won't take him long to join us then," Emilía spat at me, her face finally revealing a hint of the truly ugly soul that lurked beneath her skin.

I stepped up closer to her. "I'm no longer the scared girl you and your father tried to exploit. I've been hardened on the battlefield, bathed in blood enough times that its sight no longer affects me." I stepped forward again so that our toes were almost touching. "I think you'll find I am not the same girl you tricked in the sparring circle. You would not be able to best me this time."

Emilía's lip curled as though she were baring non-existent fangs. "You cannot be everywhere at once—you cannot protect everything at once. It's only a matter of time."

"It's only a matter of time until what?" I cocked my head.

"Until you attack me? Until you attack someone I love? If you do either of those, you will discover that I am willing to kill to protect my friends. My family. You will not walk away from the fight should you face me again. I will not pull my fucking punches."

I spun on my heel, stalking away from her with Luck and Aron flanking me. I called back to her, "Back off before I make you."

~

WE HAD FILTERED into the hidden room in the library slowly, over the course of a couple of hours, so that we would avoid attracting unwanted attention.

Óskar and Yugar had gone first, more than happy to curl up for a nap as the rest of us slowly joined them.

Georg was the last one to enter the room, and he pushed the bookcase closed behind him, sealing us off from the others in the fortress. To gain access to the room, someone from the Verndari or the Commanding Family would have to spill a drop of their blood on the stained bookcase that served as the door. With all the Verndari in the room and the Commanding Family largely distracted with other tasks, no one could disturb us.

And if they did find us, we would be alerted to their entrance before they would have a chance to see, or hear, what we were doing.

It was the one safe place for us to talk freely about anything.

Like what to do about the King Commander.

I roused Óskar by shaking his shoulder, giving him a moment to wake up and gather himself before Georg launched into what we were there to discuss.

"We have all witnessed the King Commander's behaviour," Georg said, arms crossed over his chest as he leaned against the wall. "He has always been strict and felt the need to threaten those beneath him, but it has changed. From cornering Gil's sisters to threatening them into awakening a bloodrite they don't even have, breaking our most sacred laws, and trying to make Bryn into a villainous figurehead. The question remains: What will we do about it?"

Aron leaned forward, bracing his forearms on the table. "What worries me is what comes next. He has shown that the fundamental principles of Drysden don't matter to him. How long until he is truly corrupted? How long until this realm deals with a war, lawlessness, and an unpredictable crown?" Aron swallowed before turning towards me. "He has made it clear that he will not allow Bryn to be the people's hero. What happens when he can't paint her as the villain? If you ask me, there is only one other figurehead behind whom the people will rally."

"A martyr," Rúna whispered, her face paling.

"He will not touch her," Gil growled, tensing by my side.

Georg cleared his throat. "I think Aron is on the right track. It will only be a matter of time before he tries such a thing. And if he doesn't go as far as killing her, he will certainly try to get her to do his bidding by targeting who she loves."

"He will do it to all of us," I said softly. "He's already threatened Ma and Gil's sisters. The King Commander has made it quite clear that no one we care about is safe."

"We all have someone to lose or someone that can be threatened to get us to fall in line. The only one relatively safe is Rúna, and only because her family is dead," Óskar said with a wince.

Rúna shifted uncomfortably in her chair, her eyes downcast.

"It wouldn't be the first time he's tried such a thing," Georg muttered.

Silence hung heavy in the room, the consequences of the spiralling King Commander weighing heavily on each of us. We had sworn loyalty to the Commanding Family; we had a duty to do, an oath to fulfill. The exiled commanding family and their monsters needed to be stopped—there was no question. But would happen when we were successful—if we were successful? Would the King Commander return to who he was before they returned?

Or would he continue to get worse?

"What do we do?" Óskar finally asked, his face grim.

"We choose the lesser of two evils." Rúna's voice was tired. "We decide which option we absolutely cannot allow to happen, and then we do everything we have to do to keep it from occurring."

"Is that what you did with Baldur?" Aron asked quietly, his words ringing with sadness.

She gave him a sad smile. "We all have someone we would die to protect."

I exchanged a long look with Gil. It was the most that Rúna had let slip about what Baldur had over her, but it confused me more than I had been before. With her brother and mother dead from the fire and her father dead from sickness, she had no family to threaten. The closest person to her was Gil, and he could hold his own against Baldur if he had to.

"We cannot allow the exiled commanding family to return. That's our non-negotiable," I finally said, drawing the attention from Rúna, who gave me a small nod in thanks.

"We cannot beat them alone. Or even with Jarl Einar and

his forces. We will need the warriors that have sworn their allegiance to the King Commander, Ragna's intel, and Hákon's Royal Regiment," Gil pointed out.

Georg sighed. "You're right. As concerning as the King Commander's behaviour has been so far, he still stands against the exiled commanding family."

"Then we play along for now. We do our assignments, and we prepare for war. It's our only choice," Aron agreed. "And we start making plans—ensure we do what is best."

Gil pressed his leg to mine, stilling my anxious bouncing. "We cannot do that alone. We need to know who we can trust to stand alongside us for this."

"Then we bring in people we know are with us through whatever we have to face," I said, already running through options in my head. "Jarl Einar, Sofie and Luck. Fannar, Lúdvík, and Hákon." I sent a look to Rúna before hesitantly adding, "Baldur."

Rúna tensed for a moment before nodding her agreement. Baldur had made it quite clear who he stood with over the past few days, and while I couldn't tell if it was with us or what was best for Drysden, it was quite clear that it wasn't his father.

"What do we do afterwards? If we win?" Rúna asked softly.

Óscar ran his hand over his locks. "I guess that determines the way the King Commander falls. Whether he is still as unhinged as he is now."

"Either we continue to support him, or we go about replacing him," Georg said grimly.

CHAPTER
NINETEEN
BRYN

We gathered in the hidden room again the next day, but it was much more crowded.

We had all provided access to the others—the ones we knew we could trust regardless of what stood before us—the additional bodies quickly crowding the space. It was riskier to gather like this, especially if someone from the Commanding Family were to find us.

A gathering of Verndari in the hidden room would be strange but understandable. The collection of people that we had in the room now?

That would be suspicious.

We had discussed long into the night who we could bring to this and how many people would be too many. Eventually, we settled on those in the room with us now, knowing that we would likely need some less knowledgeable people down the road.

But treason was delicate, and moving too quickly or having too large of a group was an easy way to ruin this before it even started.

And that would spell all our deaths.

We had settled on the people we knew were with us regardless of what stood in our path.

Fannar stood with his arms braced on the back of Sofie's chair, both laughing with Rúna.

Luck and Aron leaned against the wall beside each other, Óskar's arms gesturing wildly as he spoke with Yugar by his feet.

Georg and Ísak sat side by side, the old tutor still moving slowly as he favoured his injuries. I had no idea what had happened to Ísak to cause the fading bruises on his face and the tenderness in his ribs and chest when he moved. He wasn't a warrior; he didn't get sent out to attacks or take watches on the walls.

Which meant that the injuries didn't come from a battle.

I approached the table, pulling the chair across from Ísak. Up close, his injuries looked even worse, the bruises an awful mix of yellow and green hues, showing just how bad they had been. His lip looked like it may have been split, but it was almost fully healed. Ísak kept an arm wrapped around his middle as though he was holding himself together.

"Gods," I breathed, taking in the scale of his injuries. "What happened to you?"

He gave me a small smile. "I've just been treated to the fortress' hospitality."

"This happened to you here?" I tilted my head, my eyes wide in shock. Why hadn't I heard what had happened? Why hadn't we been informed of the state of the tutor? "How?"

"The King Commander was not impressed that I had not informed him of the true history," Ísak said, shifting in his seat with a wince. "And he wanted to be sure that there was nothing else that I was keeping from him."

I pursed my lips. I knew that the King Commander was becoming increasingly deranged—unpredictable. But to beat an older man because his own daughter turned out to be a traitor —because the exiled commanding family suddenly challenged him — was despicable.

"When did this happen?" I finally asked.

"Just before the ball. I don't know how long I was down there when Gier finally came across me. I can only assume that he told Ragna about me because it wasn't long until she got me out of that cell."

"And you've been checked? Your injuries healed?" I studied his body carefully. "I can help, or I'm sure Sofie would be happy to heal you."

Ísak shook his head. "We've healed what we can. I can't heal everything, or the King Commander might be suspicious. Trust me, this is much better than it was."

The door to the room opened once more, and Ragna and Gier slid through, shortly followed by Hákon. We all knew that it was a risk to bring the King Commander's children into our discussion, well aware that it would be putting them in a difficult position.

To me, the King Commander was a wolf in sheep's clothing, but to them, he was also their father.

But they had proved time and time again that they cared deeply for their country, cared deeply for doing what was right. Hákon had been ready to die alongside me at Wolfmire; Ragna was working herself to the bone, trying to get ahead of the whispers and information to give us a leg up.

It was a risk to invite them here, but it was more of a risk to exclude them. To exclude the hands of those who had also fought at Wolfmire, who had seen exactly what the King Commander's decisions were doing to Drysden.

I stood from my seat, offering it to Ragna, and made my way back towards Gil and his sisters.

Gil and I stood on either side of his sisters as they surveyed the space around us with wide eyes. Gil had debated whether he should include them long after all the others had gone to bed, his concern whispered across our pillows in the darkness of my room.

His instincts screamed at him to protect them, to keep them far away from whatever this was. But if Gil were to be caught, their heads would be the next ones on the chopping block. Gil eventually decided the devil he knew was better than the one he didn't, choosing to keep them informed as best he could.

Gil couldn't bring himself to allow them on the front lines, in the healing tents, not just yet. But knowledge was power, and he was going to ensure that his sisters were as prepared as they could be for what lay ahead.

Not to mention that their insights into life at the fortress would be invaluable when most of us were likely to be deployed a lot of the time.

"Thank you all for coming," Georg finally said, getting everyone's attention. "I appreciate everyone's discretion in getting here."

"What's with the cloak and dagger?" Luck asked with a quirk of his lip. "What calls for so much secrecy?"

Aron cleared his throat. "The King Commander." Luck's smile vanished, his eyes darting to Ragna and Hákon before returning to his friend.

"He's become unpredictable and dangerous. He is threatening innocents to get us to fall in line," I added, locking eyes with Fannar. "I don't know if you saw the show he put on with Ma before we left, but he's painted a target on her back."

"And he is threatening Bryn. We are worried that if people keep supporting her, he will do everything to turn them against her or remove her from the picture entirely." Gil's voice was rough.

The room was silent.

"His behaviour has become erratic; his decisions are not always informed by intel but by emotion," Gier said bluntly, clearly stating what many of us had seen or experienced.

Ragna sighed, her face drawn, and the circles under her eyes were especially dark. "I've seen it," she said before taking a deep breath. "I have been watching him as much as some of the others in the fortress."

The room fell silent once again.

"What can we do?" Sofie asked quietly. Her eyes darted to each of us. "Why have you gathered us together?"

"Our best bet of defeating the exiled commanding family is through the King Commander. But should that change, or should he become any more deranged, then we will need to devise a plan," Rúna said, leaning back in her chair.

"In other words, you are the people we trust to help us unseat the King Commander should it come to it," Óskar cut in with a brutal grin.

Fannar nodded slowly, clearly digesting the information. "I don't mean to be a downer, but I don't see how the—" he did a quick count of the room "—eleven of us will be enough to throw a coup. Even if we have the support of two of his children."

I rolled my eyes. "We know we can't do it alone, but we needed a solid group of people at the core of whatever we decide to do."

"You want us to overthrow our own father," Ragna said

bluntly, not making any effort to soften her words. "That's more than just treason to us."

"He has made some bad calls, and his actions haven't always been in the best interest of the majority, but does it call for such drastic measures?" Hákon asked softly. He seemed torn as he took in the people in the room. "And do you need to involve his children?"

"His choices may win us the war, but they will destroy this country," Gil pointed out.

Rúna took a step towards Hákon. "He is breaking the fundamental laws of Drysden and abandoning his people to be slaughtered. Hell—he is even abusing the people in this room." She gestured towards me, causing me to nod towards Ísak. Hákon shuddered.

"You see the best and worst of your family, and some part of you will always love them, regardless of how bad it gets," Ragna said as Svanna intertwined their fingers and rested her head on her shoulder. Ragna's eyes fell shut for a moment before turning to her brother. "I know that you have seen what he has done lately, just like I have."

"I have seen exactly what my father has been like, and I will support unseating him if it is best for the country." Hákon pursed his lips. "It is a time for the country to be banding together, not tearing itself apart, and he seems to be the one tearing it apart."

Ragna swallowed thickly. "We will help—just don't make us be the ones to unseat him."

Hákon nodded in agreement.

Luck straightened up. "I'm with Aron, with all of you, whatever you choose."

Everyone agreed.

"What do we do now, then?" Violet asked quietly. "And who do we trust enough for help?"

"For now, we continue as things are, but we are more aware. We see everything, we hear everything, and we share everything with each other," Georg said before running a hand over his bald head. "In terms of who we trust for help, I think that we need a group of people that we trust with part of the picture, but not the full one, until we know how much we can trust them."

Aron nodded. "Lúdvík and Jarl Einar have my vote."

I cleared my throat as I sent a nervous look towards Rúna. "I would like to suggest Baldur." I held up a hand to stop any outbursts I knew were coming. "I know what you are all going to say. Trust me, I have thought the same thing. I am not saying that we give him all the information, at least not anytime soon, but he has lied directly to his father to protect me. I know he is a shitty person with everything that he is doing to Rúna, but just because he is a nasty person doesn't mean that he wouldn't be useful to us."

"Baldur can be difficult. He can be temperamental and unpredictable," Ragna said, her eyes tired as they landed on Rúna. "We have all seen that. But he cares deeply for Drysden, maybe more than anyone in this room. And he is a fierce warrior in his own right. If we can trust him, he will truly benefit us. Especially with how close he is to our father."

"I think I've seen that side of him," I pointed out softly. "The closer we get to the war, the more we see him outside his role in the fortress, the clearer it becomes."

No one said anything for several moments before Gil took a deep breath. "I think that Rúna should have the final decision."

"I don't like him and don't think I ever will," Rúna sighed.

"But Bryn and Ragna are right. I think he would be useful to us. I probably know him better than anyone here, so I will feel him out and see how much we can tell him. Then we go from there."

"Then we go from there," Georg echoed.

TWENTY

BRYN

Baldur was waiting for us when we returned to the Verndari wing, sprawled across one of the benches in the entrance like he owned the place. Which, I supposed, in a way, he did. He acted differently in the fortress than when we were on the road. Here, he reminded me of the person who viciously beat Rúna in the Crepuscule, of the person who was blackmailing her to be in a relationship with him.

But on the road, he was a completely different person. He was a man who loved his country fiercely and would do anything he could to protect it. He seemed caught in a position but didn't know how to make the best of it.

The question was where did the true Baldur fall.

I guessed that it was somewhere between the two.

"I didn't know you were waiting for me," Rúna said, lingering by the door. "You could have sent someone for me."

I desperately hoped that Baldur hadn't done just that because they wouldn't have been able to find us in the hidden room. And if he did, I hoped that Rúna had a believable lie ready.

Baldur brushed away the words. "I haven't been waiting long. I know that you have all been busy."

I shared a look with Gil, surprised by the ease Baldur seemed to be showing. The few times I had seen him like this, we were on the road, never in the fortress.

Maybe he was changing—maybe this was the best time for Rúna to fill him in on what we had just discussed. Maybe he was on our side like we thought.

The doors to our wing burst open, knocking Rúna to the side. She tumbled towards the ground with a cry; Aron caught her as the rest of us spun towards the doors, our hands on our weapons. Baldur immediately made his way toward Aron and Rúna, his brows creased in what I would describe as concern on anyone else.

Baldur's manservant stood in the doorway, his shoulders heaving, his eyes darting around the space until they landed on Baldur.

"Skolli are attacking the homestead," the manservant panted, bending down to rest his hands on his knees. I poured a tankard of water and passed it to him. He whispered his thanks, wiping the sweat from his brow before he took a sip.

Baldur stumbled forward as Rúna's face went ashen. "What?" Baldur breathed, his eyes darting between Rúna and the manservant.

"Skolli are attacking the homestead that we have kept eyes on," the manservant said. "I came as soon as I got the news, but it took me some time to find you."

Baldur closed his eyes for the briefest of moments before reopening them, more centred than before. "What reports do we have on the attack? How big is it? Are there currently any survivors?"

"It's a sizeable attack, but nothing too large. Last I heard, everyone was still alive." The manservant winced. "The fight was described as inexperienced but effective."

Rúna stumbled away from Aron, her hands shaking. "We need to go. We need to go now."

"Rúna, slow down," Georg said, stepping forward to meet her. "Skolli have been attacking homesteads across the country for weeks. I'm sorry to say that if they don't have a bloodrite, they will be dead by the time that we get there, regardless of how effective their fighting is."

"They have a bloodrite," Baldur shared softly. "There is every chance that they are still alive."

"Please," Rúna's voice bordered on begging. "I will be ready to ride in ten minutes. Please come with me." She spun on her heel to look at all of us, her eyes wide and desperate. Her face was deathly pale, her body unable to stay still.

Baldur stepped forward. "I'll go." He turned to his manservant. "Have our horses prepared."

I shared a look with Gil and Óskar, exchanging nods with each other before I joined Rúna's side. I didn't know who lived at that homestead, I didn't know who was currently under attack, but she clearly did. Rúna cared for them, meaning we would do anything she needed. "We're with you, Rúna. We will ride with you."

"Do you know what homestead he is talking about, Rúna?" Aron asked. I could tell from her behaviour that she did, but if he got her to share any information that she knew, it would help us. We would be better prepared when we arrive at the attack.

"I do," Rúna bounced on the balls of her feet as though she had to restrain herself from running from the room.

Gil stepped forward, his hands resting on her shoulders and stopping her nervous movements. "Do you know who lives there, Rú?"

"I do," her voice broke as she focused on Gil. "This is why you need to gather only the people we trust most to join us. Please."

Gil studied her for a moment before he nodded. "Of course. I will go now." He turned to me. "Can you bring my armour, weapons, and supplies to the courtyard? I will meet you there."

Gil waited just long enough for me to agree before he spun on his heel and left the wing. His departure seemed to have been the sign Rúna was waiting for as she immediately tore out of the room at a sprint.

I followed closely behind her to the armoury. Everyone was silent as we pulled on our armour and secured our weapons. I barely had to look at what I was doing; my body was used to the movements now. It knew where every buckle on my armour was, where every one of my daggers lay, regardless of how dark the room or how distracted my mind was.

When I was ready, I turned my focus to what Gil needed. Óskar stuck close to my side, helping me gather Gil's items. I tucked his armour into my cloak, tossing it over my shoulder so it was easier to carry as Óskar grabbed four of his swords.

He led the way to our rooms silently so we could grab our saddlebags, which we had all been keeping packed, ready to go, since the attacks had worsened. I knew the items that Gil kept in his bags as well. I did my own, so I ran a mental inventory of what we had to see if there was anything else I needed to pack to ensure that we were fully prepared.

Without knowing exactly what was waiting for us at the

homestead, we were as prepared as possible. Our saddlebags were predominately composed of various healing items that would come in handy in the aftermath of an attack.

Óskar finally broke the silence as we made our way to the courtyard. "Do you have any idea what we are riding into?" he asked quietly, shifting the items in his arms. "For her to react to an attack on some homestead like this makes me nervous."

"No—I have no idea," my voice was barely above a whisper. "But for both Rúna and Baldur to know? I bet we will learn just what Baldur has over her."

"That's what worries me, Talon," Óskar admitted as he led us to where the stable hands were rapidly preparing our horses. "The secret she has been so desperate to protect is at risk. What happens if it's exposed beyond just us?"

I didn't respond as we reached our horses. I set Gil's items gently to the side and immediately began to secure my saddlebags. Once I was done, I turned my attention to securing Gil's.

He joined us then, Luck and Sofie flanking him. Luck was dressed for battle, much like we were, but Sofie only had the most basic of armour. Instead, her arms overflowed with healing supplies. Having Sofie there eased some of the concern crawling up my throat. Her healing bloodrite would be able to fix almost anything we faced; my healing supplies were merely a backup plan. Rúna swung herself into her saddle as Gil started to strap on his armour.

"It seemed as though the Royal Regiment were in a meeting. I did not risk interrupting them since it seemed as though you wanted to keep this quiet. I found Luck and Sofie instead," Gil explained. I handed him his weapons when he was ready for them.

"Thank you," Rúna smiled sadly before turning to Sofie and Luck. "And thank you for coming."

When we had all mounted up, we naturally formed our lines with Sofie protected in the middle of our train beside Luck.

"Do we need to be dispatched?" Aron asked Baldur quietly. The courtyard was mostly quiet, with only servants crossing the space.

"If anyone asks, I dispatched you. We don't have the time to waste on stupid formalities," Baldur said, nodding to Óskar. "Get us there as fast as you can. I can lead the way."

CHAPTER
TWENTY-ONE

BRYN

Óskar's bloodrite fuelled the horses under us, allowing them to gallop hard across the ground. The land around me was a blur as I allowed my body to settle into the movement, becoming one with the horse rather than trying to fight the surging momentum below me.

"How far are we going?" Óskar yelled over the pounding hoofbeats. "If it's too much further, we have to rest the horses."

"It's not far," Rúna called from behind us. "With your bloodrite, we should be there in a matter of minutes."

I exchanged a look with Óskar. Rúna hadn't been hiding her secret very far from the fortress. If it was treason like she had hinted at, it was important enough to her to risk it being nearby. Taking note of the notice she had given us, I shifted in my saddle. My fingers had a good drip on my reins to keep me from flying off my horse's back, but I was prepared to leap from the saddle the moment that I saw a Skolli.

Baldur eventually turned up a game path, the same game path that we had passed on our way to Wolfmire. The same one that he had used to poke at Óskar. He knew exactly where the path led and had only pointed it out to prove a point.

Óskar cursed just loud enough for me to hear. "What kind of animals use this path, my ass," he grumbled. He had picked up on the same thing that I had. The answer now was becoming clear.

It wasn't wild animals that had travelled that strip enough to wear a path. It had been Rúna, perhaps even Baldur a time or two, that had regularly ridden across it. My mind flashed to her short jaunts from the fortress, the trips where she would arrive just in time for training the next day.

The trips that had ended shortly after her relationship with Baldur had started.

What exactly lay at the end of this path, who lived at the homestead we were racing towards, that mattered enough for Rúna to put herself through everything with Baldur?

And what exactly were we about to be riding into?

I adjusted the reins so that one hand held them, leaving the other free to rest on the hilt of one of my daggers. We had been asking Rúna what Baldur had on her from the moment we knew she was being blackmailed. We had practically begged her to tell us, to let us in, to let us help her.

We were about to discover exactly what treason she had committed.

If there was anything left after the attack.

Screams sounded ahead, a flickering of light cresting the hill before us. Rúna cried out behind us, trying to urge her horse faster. "Óskar!" Her words wavered as though she were on the verge of tears. "Please, give it everything that you have!"

Óskar took a deep breath, rolled his neck from side to side, and closed his eyes. His trust in his horse was absolute, knowing that it would follow Aron's horse wherever we needed.

I felt the moment he funnelled more of his bloodrite into the horses as they surged ahead faster than before. He kept his eyes closed, sweat beading on his temple as he tried to maintain his hold on his power. "The horses can't take much more of this!" he grit out. "We better be close!"

"We're there!" Baldur called out as we crested the hill. Óskar immediately released his bloodrite, the horses slowing before coming to a stop, their sides heaving, glistening with sweat in the moonlight.

Below us, in the valley of another hill, a small home was on fire. The light of the flames illuminated the boy, a handful of years younger than me, standing between a middle-aged woman and a group of Skolli.

The whip in his hand seemed to keep the Skolli at a distance, but one of the monsters decided to ignore the risk, closing the distance between itself and the boy.

A light flickered, spluttering along the length of the whip, just like I had seen Rúna do countless times before. He cracked the whip with absolute precision, catching one of the Skolli in the eye and sending it crashing down to the ground with a roar.

"Heimir!" Rúna screamed, leaping from her horse and charging to the fight in front of us.

"Shit," Gil cursed as he quickly followed her down into the melee, unsheathing his swords as he went.

Luck and Baldur were close behind them, their weapons ready as they moved to engage the Skolli on the outskirts of the group.

"Gods' bones," Óskar muttered with wide eyes as he stared at the fight before us. "That's impossible."

"Fan out," Georg ordered, drawing our attention to him. "Those four should handle those Skolli just fine on their own. You two take the right-hand side. We will take the left before making our way to the others. Sofie, stay close to Aron."

Georg's words seemed to knock Óskar out of the shock that had taken hold of him as we quickly slid from our saddles and readied our weapons. We made our way to the right, scanning the skies and grounds around us for any sign of more Skolli.

I allowed the familiar burning sensation to settle in my eyes as they shifted. Their vision in the darkness was unparalleled, especially with the lack of light that was currently around us.

Some movement to the right caught my attention.

I reached out to Óskar, causing him to pause as I rested a hand on his forearm. I studied the nearby tree line, waiting for any sign of the movement.

There it was again, a Skolli breaking through the tree line.

"The trees!" I called out to Óskar before charging towards the monster. I spun my dagger in my hand as an arrow pierced the Skolli's eye cleanly.

It fell, crashing through the low bushes on the edge of the unkempt forest line to reveal another one in its place.

I leapt at this one, punching my dagger into its throat before viciously ripping it out, leaving a jagged hole behind. We broke through the tree line into the dense darkness of the forest.

"Shit," Óskar spat. "I can't see a thing in here, Talon." He stumbled over a root, knocking into me and almost sending both of us crashing to the ground.

"Grab hold of my shirt, and don't let go," I told him as I locked eyes with another monster deeper in the forest.

Óskar's hand fumbled around my back before finally

finding something he could hold on to. His hand was an added weight I had never had to account for before. As I stepped forward to confront the Skolli in front of me, his movement was delayed as though he were holding me in place.

The Skolli's attention was locked on me; its wings tucked tight to avoid getting caught on anything.

I threw a dagger, but the Skolli shifted, avoiding my blade.

In the time it took me to draw another one, it was on me, its arm viciously backhanding me. I slammed back into Óskar, who cursed and fumbled to steady me. I reached up, wrapping my hands around the back of Óskar's neck as I allowed the burning to settle into my legs.

I leaned back into him, allowing him to take my weight, as I lifted my Skolli-shifted legs and landed a kick with both feet in the centre of the monster's chest. I reached for a dagger with one hand and Óskar with the other before stabbing the monster clean through the eye.

When the Skolli fell to the ground dead, I held still, allowing my eyes to scan the area around us, looking for the next potential threat. After not seeing anything, I turned towards Óskar.

"I think that's it," I said, rolling my shoulders with a wince. "We should check on the others."

A hand wrapped around my mouth, blocking my ability to scream, as something slammed into the back of my head.

CHAPTER
TWENTY-TWO

GIL

I knew the moment that Rúna and Baldur both reacted to this homestead, it meant that this was the secret that Rúna had been hiding. This was the secret that Baldur was blackmailing her with.

But it was not until I heard Rúna scream Heimir's name and charge into the fight that I knew the true monumental nature of the secret. Because I once knew someone named Heimir, someone who Rúna would rush out to save at the hint of them being at risk.

And it was not until the Skolli had all been killed that it had all begun to set in.

Rúna and I had grown up together, learned to fight side by side, and practiced and honed our battlefield abilities. And I had never found it hard to keep track of her on the battlefield until tonight. Every time I turned to find her, to ensure that we were alongside each other, she was not there. Rúna was constantly fighting closer to the boy and the woman.

The boy named Heimir.

The same name as her dead brother.

And now that the Skolli had been defeated and I could focus on what was happening around us, I was struck by just how much the woman looked like Rúna.

Just like her mother had.

What have you done, Rú?

I slowly made my way over to where Rúna was kneeling, hugging both the boy and the woman. She pulled back, searching them for any noticeable injuries. There was some blood that I could see, but nothing serious. They would be fine until Sofie could see to them.

I stepped up to Rúna, Baldur taking a place on the other side. "Rúna? What is going on here?" I asked softly, already starting to draw my own conclusions but not wanting to voice them aloud.

She drew a shaky breath, her eyes darting between the boy and woman, Baldur and me. "This is—" her voice broke. Rúna turned to Baldur, who gave her a soft look I had never seen before as though he were prompting her to speak. "This is *everything.*"

The same words that she had used just a few days ago.

"Who is Heimir?" Luck asked, joining us.

"Heimir was her brother. She lost both her brother and her mother in a fire when she was younger," I said before turning towards Rúna. "Or that is what we have all thought until now."

"He's alive. They are both alive. This is my family," Rúna said, her eyes full of tears and her words barely above a whisper.

The boy—her brother—brushed by Baldur, taking his place by her side. "Hi, Gil," he said softly, his voice so much deeper than when I had last seen him when he was just six years old. Eleven years later, he was almost a man standing before me.

163

He was taller than his sister, and he had the same rich brown eyes and golden-brown hair curled around his ears. His face was splattered with blood, his hands and clothes too, but that was Heimir. I remembered him as a boy, and now he stood before me, back from the dead, a man who had seen battle.

"It is good to see you, Heimir." I was quiet for a moment, my eyes darting between the siblings. "How did this happen?"

"Heimir had only awoken his bloodrite the year before the fire, but he was already showing signs of being stronger than me. I saw it, Georg saw it, the King Commander saw it," Rúna said. I just nodded. I remembered exactly what she was talking about; rumours had run rampant through the fortress that Heimir would be the one to claim their family's spot on the Verndari rather than his older sister. "But he was a soft person, Gil. He would cry over a butterfly that couldn't fly and get heartbroken by a person struggling to walk. Being on the Verndari and doing what is required of us would have broken him. He would have survived whatever fight he walked into, but my brother would not have walked away the same person."

I took a deep breath, clearly seeing where this was going, and my heart broke over what Rúna had put herself through. "You were quite similar to that, too, Rú. You were not meant to be covered in blood on a battlefield either."

"But I could cope with it, especially if it meant my little brother would not have to. So, my mother and I staged the fire along with their deaths, and I visited whenever I could." Rúna's words were soft.

Her trips from the fortress that she looked forward to every time, returning just seconds before being late for training as though she was spending every last minute she could wherever she was.

As though she was spending every moment she could here. With her family.

My broken heart shattered for the woman in front of me, for the girl who had grown to be another sister to me, for the weight that had been put upon her shoulders at such a young age. The fact that she had sacrificed herself, had exposed herself to the horrors that came with being a Verndari to protect her brother.

It was treason—she had put herself at indescribable risk to keep him from destroying himself in the role we all played. To ensure that sweet little boy, who was filled with so much laughter and so much love, did not lose himself on blood-stained battlefields.

I remembered her first sight of blood, the first time she killed someone in a fight. How she had vomited until nothing remained, leaving her gagging against the base of a tree. How she hardened herself, trained herself, to face that again. To lead others into those battles, knowing they won't all walk away.

Rúna still smiled, laughed and joked, but she wasn't the same as when she was a kid. None of us were. But she could have avoided all that had she let Heimir take his rightful place among the Verndari.

But her love for her brother was much stronger than any desire for happiness.

She had borne this alone for all those years. When someone finally learned her secret, and those screens were finally pulled back, he took advantage of her isolation.

I did not doubt that this was exactly what Baldur had on Rúna. It did not surprise me in the least that she had been willing to sacrifice her happiness and her well-being to protect her brother.

"I wish you would have told me, Rú. I would have tried to help if I could," I told her softly.

She gave me a sad smile. "I know you would have, Gil. But I couldn't risk it. I couldn't risk them."

"Is that where you would go when you left the fortress?" Georg asked as he joined us. Aron and Sofie were only seconds behind him. I glanced around for Bryn and Óskar but couldn't see them. They must have been further than Georg and Aron had been and hadn't made their way back.

I would give them a couple more minutes, and if they hadn't joined us by then, I would look for them.

"She visited whenever she could," Heimir said. He was taller than his sister now, but their similarities were striking.

Since Bryn hadn't joined us, I made my way around by Sofie's side as she tended to everyone's injuries. Heimir and Rúna's mother were the worst, but they didn't have any serious injuries. It was a testament to how strong and capable Heimir was that he could hold off the Skolli as long as he did.

When Bryn and Óskar still had not returned by the time I was finished, a ball of nerves settled in my stomach.

Georg was worried as well, his eyes scanning the forest around us.

"How far did you send them?" I asked him, drawing Luck and Aron's attention.

"No further than Aron and me. They circled to the right; we circled to the left. Both should have been back by now unless they have run into serious trouble," Georg said as he ran his hand over his head.

"We need to go after them," I was already heading for the trees, my hands on the hilts of my swords.

Footsteps joined me, and I glanced over to find Luck beside

me, his face grim. "We can't leave the others unprotected, but I'm with you."

It didn't take us long to find the dead body of a Skolli. My chest tightened with the proof that they had faced the monsters, but there was no sign that they had struggled.

From there, it was easy to follow their path into the forest, but once we were within the trees, it was harder to follow in the dark. Eventually, we found the body of another Skolli, but that was it—there were no others to find, and there was no more trail to follow.

"Gil!" Luck's yell startled me. I spun towards him, preparing my swords for whatever monster was approaching.

But there was none.

I tightened my fingers on the hilts of my swords, anxious for the threat to reveal itself.

"Look what I found," Luck said, his voice wavering as he held up Bryn's weapon belt and Óskar's quiver and bow. "I don't think they would have left these behind willingly."

"We need the others." Seconds later, we crashed through the trees and back towards the others. "Georg!" I roared.

Everyone spun towards us, ready for a fight, as we tore across the ground towards them.

"What—"

"They're gone," Luck cut off Georg, holding out Bryn and Óskar's weapons. "We just found these, and there are no other signs of what happened or where they may be now."

"We need to look for them," I demanded as hoofbeats thundered towards us.

Five horses galloped down the hill towards us, and in the very front, his eyes surveying the scene around him in some sort of sick and twisted glee, was the King Commander.

"What do we have here?" he asked as he drew his horse to a

stop right before us. Four of his most trusted warriors had accompanied him doing the same.

I tried to subtly shift my body to block his view of Heimir and his mother, Luck and Aron doing the same beside me as Georg turned his attention to him. "We heard reports of a homestead being attacked and came to see if we can help."

"How strange the entirety of the Verndari, as well as my heir and a renowned warrior and healer, came all this way just for a single homestead?"

Baldur cleared his throat. "It wasn't far, and we could come to try to stop the damage."

"You want to know what's strange?" The King Commander's words were like ice. "The fact that the map, the one that tracks Verndari's powers, lit up an extra time this evening. Right here."

My body tensed. He knew. He knew something was significant when he left the fortress to meet us.

And from the gleam in his eye, the King Commander knew just how he wanted to spin this situation to his benefit.

"We will all return to the fortress, including our two friends you so graciously rescued," the King Commander said.

"Bryn and Óskar are missing, King Commander," Georg said, hiding his surprise well from everyone who didn't know him as we did. He must have seen the King Commander scan us when he arrived and knew that he had dismissed the absence of Bryn and Óskar. "They need our help."

"Then I hope they appear soon because you are all returning to the fortress." The King Commander's eyes rested on Heimir and Rúna for a moment to make it clear that they were included in his statement. "Immediately."

TWENTY-THREE

BRYN

The area around us was dark, the ground hard like stone beneath my back. I blinked and tried to survey our surroundings, my body smarting at the movement.

It stung and ached, but the pain was dull enough that I knew that I wasn't in any danger from whatever injuries I had. Or so I hoped.

The moonlight streamed through the space, cut in lines by something. I twisted, searching for what was casting the strange shadow to find an opening in what appeared to be a wall divided by bars.

Like a dungeon.

Cursing, I pushed myself up from the ground, the stone flooring beneath me, to discover we truly were in a dungeon. I searched for Óskar, for any of the others, and found a body slumped over in the corner of the room. It only took me a matter of steps to reach the body.

To reach Óskar.

I immediately dropped to my knees, my fingers finding his

neck, searching for his pulse. Thankfully, it was there, and not only was it there, it was strong. He was okay, unconscious, but in no serious danger.

Well—no immediate medical danger, at least. I was sure that anyone who awakened in a dungeon would be considered in some sort of danger.

I tried not to think too hard about that fact as I focused my attention on any injuries that Óskar had.

The familiar burning settled in my eyes as I shifted to the eyes of a Skolli so that I could properly assess him in the darkness surrounding us. I scanned him methodically, without him awake to tell me where he might be injured. I started at his head and worked my way down his body. A bump stood out against the back of his skull—that must be what caused him to lose consciousness.

Finding nothing else of note, I continued down to his arm. A long cut stretched along the length of his forearm, but it wasn't deep enough to be concerned about blood loss or damage. But considering where we found ourselves, I was worried about infection.

"Talon?" Óskar croaked as he shifted on the hard ground beneath him. "Gods' bones, my head hurts."

"That's what a bump the size of a coin will do to you," I teased him gently.

He allowed me to finish the inspection of his injuries before he sat up, taking note of the wall behind him and leaning back against it. "I take it we're not in the forest anymore."

"No. I'm afraid not," I told him, shifting to rest against the wall beside him. "Seems like a dungeon to me."

"I was thinking the same thing but hoping your creepy monster eyes would see something that I didn't to prove me wrong."

I sighed. "No luck there."

Óskar was quiet for a moment. "Whose is it?"

"That's the question, isn't it?" It was. Whose dungeon were we in? If we were in the dungeons at the fortress, that meant that the King Commander no longer found us useful or found us complicit in whatever Rúna was involved in and decided to punish us. If we were in someone else's dungeon, there was no saying how this would play out for us or why we were there. "I haven't found anything to show where we are."

"What a lovely surprise that will be then," Óskar quipped before leaning further into my shoulder, no doubt trying to reassure me with his presence. "How hurt are you?"

"Bumps and bruises. Maybe a scratch or two. Nothing serious," I reassured him as a door creaked open down the hall.

Óskar and I carefully climbed to our feet, facing the door with the wall to our backs. I subtly shifted slightly in front of Óskar, knowing that with my Skolli eyes, I had an advantage that he didn't. And from his grumble, I could tell he knew exactly what I was doing. Because he wasn't fighting me on it; he knew as well as I did that it was our best chance.

There was a grating sound of metal on metal, and a slot in the door opened at head height, revealing the face of a man around our age. His eyes darted nervously on either side of the door around him before turning his attention to us.

"Are you both alright?" His voice was just loud enough to reach us only a handful of steps away from him.

"As fine as we can be given the situation," Óskar said before hesitantly stepping closer to the door. I followed his lead, sticking close to him. "Where are we?"

The man winced. "I wasn't alone when I stumbled across you and had a role to play. Unfortunately, that meant that you ended up here."

"Who was with you? Who are you?" I asked.

He cleared his throat. "I can show you."

"What do you—" I was cut off as a scene played out in my mind before me, like a dream or a memory.

The dark forest surrounded us as the distant sounds of a fight drifted through the trees to reach us. It had been meant to be a simple night. There had been rumours that whoever lived in the homestead was skilled and isolated. The perfect recruit for us.

We had waited for the cover of darkness to approach, sending the Skolli first to subdue them. And should they not be willing to hear us out, kill them and harvest their souls for Mother.

But the boy and the woman that lived there had not been easy to subdue. Instead, they had some of the best defence that I had seen against the Skolli. It was too risky for us to show ourselves before they were properly contained, especially with how they reacted to Mother's pets.

Before long, the hoofbeats of reinforcements arrived, not enough to be a true concern for us but enough that it was clear that we would not be able to accomplish our mission for the night. But we lingered in the woods, safe in the shroud of darkness.

It didn't take long for two people to breach our sanctuary. They easily dispatched the Skolli nearer to us, the darkness not affecting their abilities. But then we heard their voices, causing Pétur to freeze beside me, his body rigid.

"What is it?" My words were barely louder than a whisper of wind.

"That is Bryn and Óskar, two of the Verndari," he told me.

The orders from my parents had been clear. Clear anyone who denied or defied us—except for the illustrious Verndari. No, they were meant to be captured and returned to our mountaintop fortress if possible. And with the darkness that cloaked us, there were no better conditions or odds of a successful capture than now.

And as much as I didn't want to cooperate, I could not risk exposing myself. Not without proper planning, and I had nothing in place for tonight.

So, I was forced to follow Pétur's lead as he unsheathed his weapon and crept through the forest.

And as he landed the blow to the back of the girl's—Bryn's— head, I did the same to the boy—Óskar.

I came out of the memory, much like waking from a dream, blinking as I reoriented to the dungeon.

"What was that?" Óskar's voice was gruff.

"My memory of what happened when I had to capture you," the man said. "I thought it would be the easiest way not just to answer your questions but also to show you that I had no other choice."

I clenched my fingers in a fist to hide their shaking. "Ísak told me about the rare bloodrite that allowed someone to show someone their memories—real or fake. It was so rare that we only knew one person with such a bloodrite. The son of the exiled commanding family, Leifur."

"I had hoped I would cross paths with the Verndari in better circumstances," Leifur said.

"How do we know what you showed us is the truth?" Óskar asked.

Leifur's eyes darted around the space outside the door. "It was the truth, but you aren't likely to trust me just yet. But I will prove to you that you can trust me. We're each other's only chance. I will be back when I can," he said as he slid the grate on the door shut once again.

"Do you believe him?" Óskar asked me, his voice full of confusion.

"I don't know, but that memory he showed us answered our questions." I sighed, turning to the window as though I could see back to the others, Gil and Fannar. "We are in the mountain fortress and are prisoners of the exiled commanding family."

Óskar slumped down the wall, sitting and tipping his head back. "*Shit.*"

TWENTY-FOUR

GIL

W e had not been allowed to leave our wing for a week. No one in and no one out.

Our wing, our refuge, had been turned into our prison. We did not know where Heimir and Rúna's mother had been taken; we had not heard any updates about Bryn or Óskar. I could only assume that they had not yet been found, considering they were not imprisoned with us.

My mind ran rampant with possibilities—were they injured? Were they lost? Were they imprisoned somewhere else, or had they seen what had happened with the King Commander and were working to fix it?

I had shared my fears with Georg and Aron, but we had all kept them from Rúna. She was nearly inconsolable. Not only had Heimir been thrust into the King Commander's orbit, but her treason had as well. And we all knew how unpredictable he had become.

No one knew what to expect as the fallout of her secret.

But as Baldur arrived at our wing, his face ashen and his muscles tense, I knew we were all about to find out.

"You've all been summoned to the Gathering Hall," he told me.

We followed him with no fuss. Even though he had shown up alone, not a warrior in sight, we all knew that wasn't truly the case. The King Commander's paranoia had no bounds anymore, and there were surely countless eyes on us as we travelled the familiar path from the entrance of our wing to the Gathering Hall.

Rúna's body was rigid beside mine, her jaw clenched. She knew just as well as I did that we were walking to whatever punishment awaited her.

Two warriors stood at the doors to the Gathering Hall, pushing them open as soon as we were in sight and closing them immediately behind us. Two more warriors took up a post at the back of the hall, in front of the closed doors, blocking our exit.

Giving us no option but to follow Baldur towards where the King Commander sat on his throne on the raised platform.

The only other people in the room were Heimir and Rúna's mother, who were flanked by two more warriors. Rúna's steps faltered, prompting me to drift closer to her side. I didn't dare to reach out to comfort her in any visible way; I could not risk her showing any weakness to the King Commander. Not right now.

We stopped in front of the raised platform and sank into low bows, none of us so much as daring to fidget as we waited for permission to stand.

A few minutes had passed when the King Commander finally said, "Rise."

I straightened, shifting so my feet were shoulder width apart and my hands were clasped behind my back. Showing no threat but ready should the need arise.

"As we approached war, I expected there to be acts of treason. I did not expect them to come from my own Verndari." The King Commander's voice was quiet, almost a hiss across the empty room. "Enemies are breathing down our fucking neck, and you decided to hide a boy, who should have been a Verndari, from me?"

No one spoke. No one even dared to move.

I barely dared to breathe.

"However treasonous your actions are, they have brought me another warrior with the bloodrite of a Verndari as we head into war. So instead of making you pay with your head, you will pay for your treason with blood."

Six warriors came through a door in the back of the hall, near where the King Commander sat. Two went to Rúna's mother, while another two went to Rúna. Each of them grabbed one of her arms and marched her to the open space in front of the platform where the King Commander sat, her mother joining her a moment later.

The two remaining warriors uncoiled whips from their hips and stepped behind each woman.

The warrior snapped a kick to the back of Rúna's legs, sending her crashing to the wooden floor. He ripped her cloak from her body, throwing it to the side and leaving her in just her loose shirt.

I stepped forward, but Georg stopped me with a hand on my shoulder. "Don't risk making it worse for her," he breathed, his words barely loud enough for me to hear as Aron took a place on my other side.

"One lashing for each year of your deception will be a good place to start."

The warriors standing near Heimir grabbed onto him, forcing him to watch as the men behind his family cracked their whips once against the floor before landing a lash against the backs of his sister and mother.

Rúna's back arched in pain, but she didn't make a sound. Her eyes were alight with anger as though she could kill the King Commander with her gaze.

The same couldn't be said about her mother, who screamed and shut her eyes tight. As the second lash landed, the sound echoing through the room, I tightened my hands into fists by my side. The third had me clenching my jaw so hard my teeth creaked to keep myself from shouting at the King Commander. The fourth had Aron's hand resting on my other shoulder, his and Georg's fingers digging into my skin as though tethering me in my spot.

As the fifth lash landed, Rúna screamed, blood starting to soak her white shirt. And that sound was enough to shatter what little willpower was holding Georg, Aron, and me in place. All three of us stepped forward, catching the attention of the King Commander immediately.

"I wouldn't do that if I were you," was all the King Commander said before the door by him opened once again. Two warriors led through Fannar, who surveyed the scene before him quickly before turning to Aron and me with wide eyes. Behind him, another warrior led through Bryn's mother, her face paling immediately at the sight of Rúna on her knees. The last person forced through the door was Violet, who seemed so small and delicate beside the brute holding her.

Aron, Georg and I froze as we watched our loved ones be lined up next to Heimir.

"If you interfere, then your family will take the punishment by Rúna's side," the King Commander said, his words turning to ice in my veins.

My body vibrated, torn between the need to protect Rúna

and to protect the innocents who awaited that same fate if I interfered.

"It's okay," Rúna rasped, my head whipping to her to find her tear-filled eyes already on me. "I can take it."

"Rú—"

"—I can take it, Gil," she cut me off. "Only six more to go," her voice broke.

The final six lashings were fast, raining down upon their backs. Their screams mixed with the crack that echoed through the room.

The guards released Rúna's mother, allowing her to slump to the ground as the warrior behind him ran his hand down the whip, gathering the blood that stained it and flicking it to the ground by his feet.

Heimir was finally released, and immediately ran for his mother.

"The other issue, besides your treason, is that you put your loyalty to your family over the oath that you swore to me, Rúna," the King Commander said, unfazed by the scene before him. He didn't so much as blink an eye at the pools of blood, didn't flinch at the sound of her mother's sobbing.

Rúna bit her lip, not letting another sound escape as tears slid down her face.

I tensed, realizing that while Rúna's mother had been unceremoniously released by the warriors who had been holding her, the same could not be said about Rúna. She still knelt, panting and glaring up to the King Commander, each of her arms held by a warrior.

"I think the best way to avoid that happening again is to make my family your family. You will marry Baldur."

"No," Rúna panted. While her voice was soft, breaking from

179

the screams that had ravaged her throat, the strength of her refusal shone through.

The King Commander nodded to the man standing behind her, and another lash landed on her back.

Rúna screamed, her back arching, her brother watching on with wide eyes as he tried to tend to their mother.

"I will let you try that answer again," the King Commander hissed.

"It's still a no."

Another lash landed against her back.

For every refusal that Rúna made, another lash landed against her body.

Two more.

Five more.

Her shirt hung in tatters against the shredded skin of her back, the fabric stained red as the cuts on her skin dripped blood onto the ground around her.

Staining the floorboards red to match.

"Please, Rú," I finally said. I knew that marrying Baldur was the last thing she wanted, but the King Commander showed no signs of backing down.

And an engagement could be undone, especially if we removed the person who ordered it from the throne.

She refused again, and another lash landed against her skin.

"Rúna, please. We can help you," Georg echoed my words, his lips a thin line at the sight of one of his Verndari breaking in front of him.

"End this, Rúna. Your body can't take much more," Aron's words were pained.

I knelt on the ground, locking eyes with Rúna, who now

lacked the strength to lift her head. "We cannot help you until you end this, Rú."

"No," she whispered, and even that seemed like too much for her as she slumped, held aloft by the warriors on her arms as another lashing landed against her skin. Her back arched again, but nothing louder than a squeak sounded as she tried to scream.

"Rúna," my voice broke as I stared at her. Her body was broken, her spirit shattering before my eyes. "It will be okay, Rú. I will make sure it is okay."

She hung there silently for several moments before finally croaking, "Yes."

The King Commander clapped his hands as he grinned. "Fantastic. Welcome to the family, my dear." He stood as the warriors dropped her to the ground like her mother and left the room. The warriors followed behind him.

I rushed over to Rúna, dropping to my knees and gathering her in my arms. Ignoring the feeling of her blood soaking into my clothes. Violet was there a moment later, already assessing Rúna, trying to determine how to help as Fannar promised to bring Sofie to the wing, leaving the room at a run.

I glanced up to Baldur, expecting a smug smile on his face.

Instead, he was pale, his eyes wide, his face drained of colour as though the sight before him was enough to make him want to throw up all over his polished leather boots.

Not the face of victory I expected—it was one of horror instead.

CHAPTER
TWENTY-FIVE
BRYN

The food dumped unceremoniously into our cell was questionable if I was even willing to deem it food. A watery slop with the occasional clump of substance —a vegetable? A piece of meat? I tried not to think too hard about it as Óskar and I split the food between us. At least what hadn't ended up slopping on the ground in the delivery process.

The water was more appetizing, but we were careful to ration it between us, never knowing when the next food and water delivery would be.

They ensured the deliveries remained sporadic, likely trying to mess with our conception of time to keep us uncentered.

I couldn't care less about what time of day it was; the lightening and darkening of the sky outside our tiny window allowed us to keep track of days, and that was enough for now. We had no need for anything more.

Leifur had stopped by our cell a few more times, always at night and always with clean, fresh water and hard bits of stale bread and cheese. He had apologized the first time he had handed us the food, the need for discretion outweighing the possibility of fresh bread.

Until this morning—midday? — when we could hear his voice down the hall.

"A guards meeting is happening now. I would hate for you to miss it," Leifur's voice echoed down the wall, filtering into our cell. Óskar and I exchanged a look at the change in routine. Nerves coiled in the pit of my stomach, feeling in my gut that a change in routine was never a good thing for prisoners. "I will feed them. Go, get to the meeting."

The slit in the door opened to reveal Leifur, his eyes darting up and down the hall. He carefully passed the slop to us, making sure that all of it stayed in the chipped bowl. Óskar took the tray, setting it down near the section of the wall that we tended to sit against.

Then Leifur's hands were through the slot, and a couple of pieces of bread were held out to me. I took it, feeling not just the roughness of the crust but also something wooden and something that felt like folded paper.

"Hang in there," he told us softly. "Trust me."

The slot closed a second later, the risk of him lingering in the daylight, of getting caught with us, was too high. Óskar and I sat against the wall, and I passed him his piece of bread. I rested my piece on my knee before studying what else Leifur had passed to me.

A folded piece of paper and a match.

I unfolded the paper, my body tensing at the words that lay there.

My sister is going to visit you. Prepare yourselves. Stay strong.

"Shit," I muttered as I passed the paper to Óskar. He grimaced as he read it before refolding it and setting it beside him. He sipped the slop in the bowl before passing it to me.

"That sounds ominous," he said softly. "Remind me again what her bloodrite is?"

I swallowed my sip, trying to ignore its slimy texture running down my throat. "Pain."

"Good fun that'll be," Óskar groaned, tipping his head back against the wall behind us as he took a bite of the bread. He chewed briefly before swallowing and directing his attention back to me. "Why risk telling us? There's nothing we can do to prevent her from seeing us."

I was quiet for several moments as we continued to eat. "I'm guessing that she isn't visiting for a nice chat. I'm guessing she'll be using her bloodrite to try and get information out of us. At least with a warning, we can prepare mentally for it. To prepare not just to experience it, but also to witness each other suffer through the pain." I glanced down at the final sip of slop in the bowl in front of me. "He's trying to get us to trust him."

"And do we? Because I am currently undecided."

"I think that without him, we would be much weaker than we currently are. And I think that he is our best bet at surviving this. Undoubtedly, he's putting himself at risk doing all this." I grabbed the match, striking it against the stone of the wall and lighting the paper on fire. I let the ashes crumble into what remained of the slop, mixing it with what remained of the match until I couldn't see any difference to how it usually looked. "I think we have very little to lose by trusting him right now."

THE NEXT DAY, the door to the cell slammed open, sending Óskar and I scrambling to our feet as four warriors stormed into the room. They shackled each of our wrists to the wall, leaving us slumped side by side. I stretched out a leg, my foot resting against Óskar's shin. He tried to smile at me, but he barely managed to tip the corners of his mouth.

We both knew what this meant—we both knew what was coming.

We just had to be strong enough to survive it.

Eventually, a woman strode through the door, allowing the warriors to leave and shut the door behind them. She surveyed us with a sadistic smile. Óskar and I didn't flinch, didn't show a hint of the fear that was clawing at my throat as we stared at her.

"Is that how you greet the Commanding Daughter? The fortress needs to teach its warriors better manners," she said, crossing her arms over her chest.

"You may have been the Commanding Daughter at one point, but you no longer hold the title," I said.

"Which means you do not deserve our respect," Óskar added.

Katrin blinked, frozen for a moment until her smile grew. "Is that so?" She leaned against the wall, crossing her legs at the ankle before her. "Tell me about your so-called Commanding Family, then?"

Óskar and I exchanged a look. When we had considered what she might ask us about the day before, the Commanding Family was not on the list. Not when they had access to both Pétur and Sigrún.

"I would think that you would know all you need to know, considering that you have one of the King Commander's daughters working with you," Óskar said with a roll of his eyes.

"If you haven't asked her whatever questions you have, then you're more useless than I thought."

I winced at the look on her face. I didn't know if he was trying to hide his nerves with bravado or if he was trying to keep her sights on him rather than me, but a comment like that was asking for retaliation.

His body suddenly tensed beside mine, his back arching off the wall, his jaw clenched. Katrin's eyes were locked on his body, alight with anger—or glee. Moments later, he finally sagged back against the stone, panting.

"Let's try this without the attitude, shall we? Sigrún and Pétur have told us plenty, including that Hákon and Ragna are rather close with you, and Baldur is in a relationship with another of the Verndari. So, I'm certain that there are some insights that you can share."

Neither Óskar nor I said a word.

She quirked a brow. "Let me try asking a little more... forcefully."

Her gaze locked on me as pain radiated from my stomach and carried through my body. It focused on my core, thumping and throbbing as though I were being beaten. As though I were being kicked repeatedly.

And as painful as it was, it wasn't my first time feeling like this. I knew I could survive it; I knew that I could weather it. So, I grit my teeth and waited for it to pass.

The pain eventually eased. "Would you like to answer the question now?"

Silence.

Katrin chuckled under her breath as she turned her attention to Óskar. "Your turn."

The phantom pain in me flared as I watched Óskar, hissing through his teeth as he tried to ride out the feeling. We had no options here, no other play. We just had to let the pain run through us and regroup and recover when it was done.

When it finally eased, Óskar slowly turned to look at me. "Felt like I was back home being forced to train hand to hand with Gil."

I chuckled, my ribs flaring as I did.

"Well, it seems like a beating does nothing to faze you." Katrin cocked her head. "What about fire?"

The pain focused on my feet this time, flickering and bubbling as though I were being held above a flame. It slowly travelled up, covering my legs, coating my torso, singeing my fingers as though the flame were climbing my body.

As though I were being burnt alive.

I had promised myself that I wouldn't scream—that I wouldn't put Óskar through that.

But I broke that promise as the phantom fire reached my throat and eyes.

And my screams echoed through the room, bouncing off the walls like a never-ending cacophony of suffering.

THE COOLNESS of the stone against my back was soothing as I lay sprawled on the ground. Even though Katrin had not physically beat or burnt us, the nerves in our bodies were shot and flared as though they had suffered the trauma she had conjured.

Our bodies had suffered a trauma—we had suffered a trauma—just not in the way that our nerves thought we did.

The cold in our cell had been a hardship before, causing us to spend most of our time leaning up against each other, trying to keep each other warm. But now, it was a boon; it helped soothe our nerves as they still flared with pain. It helped soothe our muscles that had been tensed as we were coated in agony.

Footsteps echoed down the hall towards us, but I couldn't bring myself to move. I simply turned my head to the door and awaited whatever arrival was coming.

The grate in the door slid open to reveal a face I hadn't seen in weeks. A face that I hadn't seen since he had abandoned us, betrayed us, and traveled to this mountain fortress.

Pétur.

He winced as he surveyed Óskar and me. "Are you two alright?"

"Doing wonderful," Óskar rasped, his throat ravaged by his screams. "Just my idea of relaxation, this is."

"Don't make a joke of this Óskar. Is there anything I can do to help?" he asked, his brows furrowed.

I licked my cracked lips, a side effect of the limited water we received, even with Leifur's help. "Not betraying us would have been a start. Opening the door to our cell now would also help."

"I didn't have a choice," Pétur said softly.

"And now?" He didn't say a word, his lips pursed. "I see."

Pétur sighed. "Just hear me out. Please."

Óskar rolled his eyes at me before turning back towards the door. "It's not like we have any other choice, is it?"

"I wasn't lying when I said I had no choice. When the barrier exiling them was first erected, my ancestor was angry. Bitter. He didn't like that an assassin, a merchant daughter, and other people he deemed 'below him' were now seen as his equals. Equals in title, in privilege, in abilities. He swore a blood oath that he and his descendants would keep the exiled commanding family alive and that they would help free them from their prison when the time came."

"What's the importance of a blood oath?" I asked Óskar.

He studied Pétur for a long moment. "A blood oath ties your bloodrite, your very being, to whatever promise you swear. It's not symbolic like the oaths that Verndari and the Royal Regiment take. If you break a blood oath, you die. And by him swearing it on behalf of himself and his descendants, Pétur is bound by that same oath." He turned towards me, his eyes pained. "He really didn't have a choice about helping them. With the barrier, at least."

"How did you help them?" I asked Pétur.

"I would lower the barrier just enough for a Skolli or two to slip out. The Skolli would go and gather some souls and return to them behind the barrier so they could make their life-extending elixir. I directed them to small, out of the way areas where the risk of carnage was low. Where the disappearances could be written off as missing persons rather than murders."

Óskar growled. "And did you always make those decisions?" I turned towards Óskar to find him glaring at Pétur. "When they were ready to start breaking the barrier and gaining strength, did you direct them where to attack then, too?"

My eyes widened, my heart dropping to my stomach as I picked up on where Óskar's train of thought had gone. Had Pétur told them to attack the fortress? Was he behind the attack on Hazelpeak or Wolfmire or Fairguard?

Was he the reason that Ebonwell had been destroyed?

He swallowed, his tongue wetting his lips a moment later as he turned to me with sad eyes. "They needed to make a statement, but they needed to do it in a way in which there were no survivors to tell anyone what exactly attacked their village." My blood turned to ice in my veins. "So, I found a little village with very little power and told them they needed to attack during the raiding season when their most seasoned warriors were away. I thought that I had accounted for everything. I didn't account for the lost Verndari and her family living there."

I pushed myself to my feet, pain flaring throughout my body as I stumbled to the door, slamming my fists on the metal dividing us. "You fucking bastard," I hissed.

"What about now?" Óskar asked from behind me. "You have fulfilled the blood oath, but you are still here."

"They've offered me a position within their forces. I'll be the commander of their armies. They value me here. And Sigrún is here."

"We valued you too," I said, pushing off the door and returning towards Óskar. "But now you better hope that I don't face you on the battlefield because I am not afraid to kill you for what you did to my family."

TWENTY-SIX

GIL

I had never seen Rúna as physically weak, as mentally and emotionally defeated, as she was after the King Commander whipped her into submission. Everything that she had risked, everything that she had sacrificed to protect her brother, ended up being for nothing, as he ended up in the King Commander's sights anyway.

And she ended up betrothed to Baldur as a result.

While we were allowed to leave our rooms now, we still spent most of our time safely behind the doors to our wing. We were confined to the fortress, unable to ride out and search for Bryn and Óskar as I desperately wished to. Instead, Georg, Aron and I trained in the morning before settling into Rúna's rooms, keeping her company and trying to raise her spirits.

A knock sounded on her door. Georg opened it to reveal Baldur. His clothes were wrinkled, his hair messy. "Can I come in?" he asked hesitantly. It was one of the only if not the first, times I had ever seen him ask for something instead of just taking what he wanted.

Georg stepped back, leaving a space for Baldur to walk by him and into the room.

"Did you know?" My voice was harsh.

"I had no idea of what he planned to do. I swear. I didn't want things to play out this way." Baldur's words made me scoff. He swallowed, rolling his shoulders, his gaze drifting to the ceiling. Baldur took a deep breath before turning back towards where I sat beside Rúna. "I'm the Commanding Son— I could have my pick of companions; I could have countless women putting their name forward to marry me. So, have you ever stopped to ask yourself why I would put Rúna and myself through this?"

"I have," Rúna said softly. "I have wondered since the first time you approached me."

Baldur moved to the chair in front of us, beside Aron, as Georg took up a position against the wall. "Can I sit?" Baldur asked softly. At Rúna's nod, he sat, bracing his forearms on his knees, his head hanging. He sighed before looking up at Rúna. "The story, the secret, I am about to tell is not just my own, and I hope you will keep it between us. Because as much as I hate him at times, he is still my family." Baldur took a deep breath, closing his eyes for a moment. "When I was five years old, I showed my first signs of my bloodrite. One of the young children I played with fell and skinned their knee. Upset by their tears, I reached out to them and their knee was healed as my fingers touched their skin. Not completely, but it looked like an old wound on the verge of being fully healed rather than a fresh one."

"You do not have a bloodrite," I pointed out. It was a topic of conversation—the Commanding Son, the future leader of Drysden, with no bloodrite to speak of.

"You're right. I don't. Not anymore."

Rúna sat up straighter. "The only way to lose a bloodrite is tthe Hunger. Someone would have to take it from you, and I am sure that such a thing happening to the Commanding Son would be public knowledge. That the King Commander would publicly condemn, or punish, the person that did it to you."

"That probably would have been the case if the person with the Hunger hadn't been a part of the Commanding Family as well."

"Gods' bones," I breathed, realizing exactly where Baldur was going with his story. I knew just as well as everyone in Drysden, the renowned healer of the Commanding Family who, now that I thought of it, had been incredibly careful never to touch another person without gloves on.

"Hákon took my bloodrite from me. And you know what that means for the throne. There is nothing more valued in Drysden than power. And should someone believe that they are more powerful than the King Commander, the throne could be challenged." Baldur gave a humourless chuckle. "A healing bloodrite, while not useful in a fight, is incredibly useful in the aftermath. I would have value and power to back me as the King Commander."

Rúna's hands were knotted in her blanket. "And you lost it. You had nothing left."

"I had nothing left," Baldur echoed. "Nothing to offer, no power to prove my worth to the people of Drysden. From then on, my father kept me close to his side. Taught me how to be feared and exert what power I had so that no one would ever guess that I was weak. That the crown was vulnerable. I mastered my weapons, but that was nothing compared to the potential that I once had. And I worried that it didn't just put me at risk—that it would put my whole family at risk." His voice broke, and he cleared his throat, pausing momentarily before continuing. "There was only one other way to add more power to my image."

"Through your partner," Rúna whispered.

"I needed to find a powerful partner. In connections, in money, in bloodrite, in weapons—they had to be powerful in some form. And when I learned your secret, I saw my chance. Because you are strong in all four, Rúna, and you were desperate enough to keep your secret to do whatever I wanted." Baldur let his head hang again, talking to his feet, his words just loud enough for us to hear. "And my father had spent years moulding me into the image he wanted. That he believed would show the most strength. He largely isolated me from my family, leaving me to interact only with him or the people he approved of. I learned cruelty at his knee; I learned pain from his hand. I didn't know there was another way to act until I spent more time with you and the other Verndari. Until I could leave the fortress, to get out from under my father's thumb."

No one spoke; only the crackle and the pop of the fire in the fireplace filled the space for several moments.

"This doesn't make how you treated me okay," Rúna said softly, but her words were threaded with steel.

"I know that it doesn't. But it does explain it." Baldur swallowed, his hands clenching to fists. "I care about my country, about my people, and this was the only way I saw to ensure I could lead them. I didn't know what my father had planned, and I would have tried to stop it if I could. But I think that I know how to fix it."

"How?" The question tore from me, desperate to help Rúna.

Baldur turned to me. "It would require the verdict of the King Commander, but it doesn't have to be the current one." His eyes drifted to Rúna. "And I care more about righting this wrong than needing you to be by my side. You get me on the throne, and I will free you from me."

I PUSHED through the doors of the War Chamber, knowing full well that I was interrupting a meeting and finding it hard to care about what the fallout may be. It had been days. Days where Bryn and Óskar could be lost, hurt or worse, and no one gave a damn.

No one was out searching for them or allowing us out to search for them.

They were leaving them to their fate, and I wasn't about to let them be forgotten.

We hadn't been invited to this meeting; the King Commander had begun limiting what we knew, what we were included in. He knew how to control our actions—by threatening the people we cared about—but he didn't know how to control our morals. Our ethics.

Our thoughts.

One way to control our choices was to limit the information we received. To share only what he wanted to, or needed to, to get us to do what he wanted.

His grasp on control was slipping, and he would do everything he could to hold onto it.

Fannar and Luck had wanted to storm the chamber with me, as did Violet and Klara, but I had convinced them to stay out of the King Commander's line of fire by Aron joining me instead. The four of them hadn't been granted admission to the room; they hadn't been named to the War Council. If they were to barge into the room, they would be facing a much worse fate than Aron and me.

As the doors slammed against the chamber's stone walls, drawing everyone's attention, and seeing the shock on some people's faces, I knew that we made the right decision. Or the best decision we could make with our limited options.

"Gil. Aron. What are you doing here?" Hákon asked, his eyes wide. "I heard that you were in the field."

Apparently, the War Council was unaware of why we hadn't been attending the meetings or been seen since we had returned to the fortress with Rúna's family in tow.

Yet another power play for the King Commander.

"We haven't been in the field for days, but unfortunately, Bryn and Óskar are still out there. They were separated from us," Aron said as he crossed his arms over his chest. While he made no move towards his weapons, he was ready should this escalate, with his weight balanced evenly and his feet shoulder-width apart.

I was also ready, but I made no move to maintain neutrality, allowing every aspect of my rage to show across my face.

Gier shook his head minutely as though trying to warn us about something. But I couldn't care less about his warning. We needed to go after Bryn and Óskar. We had to try and find them.

For every moment, every day they were missing, it was more dangerous. More likely that we would never find them.

That meant it was worth whatever risk lay ahead of us.

"Then why aren't you out looking for them? I would have expected that you wouldn't return to the fortress without her, Gil," Hákon asked, starting to stand from his seat.

I growled. "I would be out there if I had not been confined to these walls by the King Commander." Hákon froze, slowly turning to face his father. The King Commander's eyes were fire; they were pure anger, and it was all directed towards Aron and me. "We are here to ask you to search for them or send us out after them."

The Queen looked between us and her husband, her face wiped clean, no hint of her feelings or thoughts showing for us to see. But I could swear I saw something in her eye.

"And if we don't?" an older lady asked, leaning back in her chair. I didn't care for her, never had, but had always been wary of her. She was close friends with the King Commander, and I wouldn't be surprised if he knew everything she heard and saw around the fortress.

"Then I will remember that," I snarled. "And we will return the sentiment should the need ever arise."

Jarl Marik surveyed the room warily, his gaze lingering between Aron and me before drifting back to the King Commander. "We need the Verndari at full strength. Why have we not gone after the others?"

"Because the King Commander would rather keep us under lock and key instead of helping them," Aron spat.

"The Verndari are mine to command as I see fit, and I will use them however I deem best," the King Commander hissed, pushing from his seat. He stalked towards us, no doubt hoping to intimidate us. Neither of us moved a muscle; while he may have the power to make things very difficult for us and our families, we could take him in a fight.

He stood toe-to-toe with me, forcing me to look down to meet his eyes.

"Get out of the War Chamber and return to your wing," he hissed, spit flying from his lips. "You will not be stepping a foot out of the fortress without a royal dispatch. And if you do so, your family will be the ones to face my fury."

TWENTY-SEVEN

"Her bloodrite doesn't leave any lasting damage, but it will take your body some time to fully recover from it," Leifur said as he handed us more bread and cheese. "I've had my fair exposure to it."

The cell was dark, only lit by the moonlight through the small window and the flickering firelight that could be seen through the grate in the door. I remained sat against the wall, letting Óskar get the food from Leifur.

"When did you flip to our side?" Óskar asked as he passed me my portion of the food. "You dove into helping us like you didn't even need to consider whether you would."

"That's because I haven't just flipped to your side. I've been there for centuries." He tapped a finger against his temple. "I can show you."

I hesitated for a moment. Ísak mentioned the powers of the exiled commanding family when he was teaching me the history of Drysden, and I knew that Leifur didn't just have the ability to show us memories and explore our own; he could also make fake memories.

But he had been true to his word so far. The memory from when we were taken in the forest had aligned with what Pétur had said when he had come to our cell and his sister had visited us just as he had warned.

Not to mention the extra food and water he could bring us.

I shared a glance with Óskar, who shrugged—he didn't care which way our decision went.

But we weren't getting out of here on our own. We needed to know if we could trust him, and one way to do that was to understand his past. Understand where he was coming from and why he was doing this.

So, I finally nodded. "Do it."

The memories swirled around us as I closed my eyes, the picture forming clearly as though I had been there.

The gathering hall was full, and a line of people extended from steps before the dais, where my family and I sat all the way out the doors. It had been like this every appearance day for weeks, and the people were becoming increasingly anxious about things in the country.

"Please, King Commander, you need to help us. Our village is isolated and targeted by massive, winged monsters. Any support or supplies you can provide would make all the difference," a young woman pleaded, a small child on her hip. Her face was haggard, drawn and tired.

"We will see what we can do," Father said, not making any promises. It was the first lesson he taught Katrin and me—never agree to anything. If you are always vague, you can't be proven wrong.

She let out a shaky breath. She had probably heard Father use the same line on every person with an audience before her, and he would likely continue to use it for every person behind her. "Do you know what they are? Where have these monsters come from?"

"We are looking into it," Mother said with a lethal smile.

The scene before me shifted, blending and blurring before being replaced with a new one.

A hand wrapped around my elbow, pulling me into an unused room. My hands automatically dropped to the hilts of my weapons, spinning around as I drew. My blade is resting against his throat before I realize who stood before me.

Bayle stayed stock still, his arms raised to show he was unarmed as he waited for me to recognize him.

"Fast reflexes you've got there, Leif. It would have been more impressive if they kicked in before you got pulled into the room, but beggars can't be choosers," Thea joked from the side of the room where she leaned against the wall, her whip coiled at her hip.

"You're not the one with his blade at your throat," Bayle snarked. *"Mind sheathing that, would you?"*

I rolled my eyes as I stepped back and sheathed my weapon before wrapping Thea in a hug and clasping hands with Bayle.

"I know that we try to keep our friendship secret, but pulling me into rooms like this is new," I said as I soaked in the presence of my closest friends.

My parents would approve of my friendship with Bayle, a high-ranking Jarl that would bolster my image. But the same couldn't be said about Thea, a merchant who often travelled to the fortress with her goods. She was among the few willing to journey amidst the monster attacks, but my parents wouldn't see her skill or bravery.

They would see her rank and the fact that it was below mine.

"We had to see you. We have to tell you something, Leifur." His voice was grim.

"What is it? Is everything okay?"

Thea stepped forward and rested her hand on my arm. "People are whispering about your family, Leifur."

I scoffed. "When are they not? Mother and Father have been the subject of their whispers for years as they waited for them to age and pass over the throne to Katrin. And don't get me started on Katrin. She earned her whispers all on her own as she mastered her bloodrite."

"This is different, Leifur." She exchanged a look with Bayle before refocusing on me. "They are saying that your parents control the monsters. That they are behind everything that is happening."

"What?" my voice broke.

The transition from one memory to the next was less disorienting this time, but it still made me slightly dizzy as the new scene became clear.

The darkness blanketed us like a cloak on the edges of the forest near the fortress. When Mother and Father explained their monsters and the elixirs and potions that they made, everything became clear to me.

Why the monsters never targeted the fortress or Goldhelm.

Why the monsters only seemed to focus on the lands of people who opposed my parents.

Thea sat on a fallen log, her legs crossed, and her cloak pulled tight as Bayle leaned against a tree.

"You were right. About everything," I told them.

"I was worried that we would be," Thea said, her voice soft. I made my way to where she sat and joined her. She immediately leaned into my side as I pressed a kiss to her temple.

I took a deep breath. "The question is, what do we do about it? How do we stop it?"

"Thea and I are being called by the people who oppose your family to join them on the battlefield. Our skills have proved to be devastating to the monsters. They need us." Bayle was being humble. Their bloodrites were strong, their skills with their weapons even more so.

And people liked them. People listened to them.

"Let me join you."

"You can, Leif, but—" Thea sighed, leaning back to look at me. "I hate to ask you, but I think we need someone here, someone we trust on the inside."

I swallowed thickly. "You want me to stay here, with them, playing the role of dutiful son? Pretend that I don't hate everything they represent so I can pass you both information?"

"Neither of us wants that." Bayle clasped my shoulder. "But it may just be the people of Drysden's best chance."

The memory swirled again, but instead of taking us into the next one, we returned to the cell. Leifur's eyes were glassy as he watched us. "Now you know. I want to get away from here and end this."

"How do we know that's the truth? How do we know we can trust you?" Óskar asked softly.

"You ask yourself what I have to gain by making false memories like that, which would only spell my death warrant if they got out. My life is in your hands now—I trust you with that. Can you trust me enough to work with me? To get us all out of here for good?"

Leifur didn't have a chance to warn us before his sister visited us again. The door slammed open to admit her, a sadistic smile on her face. If I were on the fence about whether Leifur was different from the rest of his family, that look alone would be enough to convince me.

I had never seen that blatant glee or enjoyment of our suffering on his face. If anything, he was apologetic and horrified about what was happening to us.

That told me more about who he was than anything that

he could say or show us would. His eyes did all the talking when he couldn't and told me exactly who he was.

And that I could trust him.

I just needed to survive the interrogation—the torture—that was coming so that I could tell him, and he could come up with a plan to get us the hell out of this cell.

"How are you two doing? Not too sore from my last visit, are you?" Katrin asked with a chuckle as she watched the warriors shackle us to the walls.

Neither one of us said a word, well aware of the pain that was coming our way. The threat of it had even tempered Óskar's humour-based self-defence, leaving him glaring at Katrin. Whatever relief or satisfaction the quips and snark would bring us would be quickly outweighed by the punishment.

It wasn't worth it.

"Not very talkative today, I see. Let's see if I can change that. Since you won't talk about the Commanding Family, how about you talk about your fellow Verndari." She leaned against the wall across us and propped one leg behind her. "Let's start with the new one. Aron."

Neither one of us spoke.

Katrin waited a few moments, giving us a second to change our mind before cocking her head and focusing on me with a sick smile. "Very well then. Let's try something new today, shall we?"

I took a deep breath, trying to prepare myself for the pain that I knew was coming. I didn't know what form it would take, what feeling it would mimic.

A lancing pain seared down my calf as though a knife were slicing down from the back of my knee to my ankle. A stabbing pain in my hip as though a dagger had been buried to the hilt.

A thumping pain in my hand as though one of my fingers were chopped clean off.

I clenched my teeth, not willing to give Katrin the satisfaction of hearing my screams, not willing to put Óskar through listening to them either. I bit my tongue until it bled, the warm liquid dripping down my chin.

Finally, the pain eased, and I panted, trying to gather myself once again, the room around me fuzzy and unfocused. The sounds muffled.

Eventually, things oriented themselves, and the sounds and smells of the cells were finally distinguishable from each other. Including Óskar thrashing beside me, groaning deep in his throat as Katrin focused her attention on him. Tears threatened in my eyes, my throat tight.

Tears over the situation we were in, over the fact that we were imprisoned so far from the others.

Tears over the amount of pain still coursing through my body, over the torture that Óskar was experiencing.

Tears of frustration and desperation.

But I refused to let them fall—refused to let her see how close I was to breaking.

So, when she turned her attention to me again and screams once again ravaged my throat, I allowed myself to sink into the darkness that had been threatening at the edges of my vision.

Allowing it to embrace me and carry me far from the torture that was slowly destroying me.

I slowly awoke from the darkness, one sense at a time, as my mind gently eased me back into consciousness.

My head was pillowed on Óskar's lap, his fingers gently carding through my matted and knotted curls. I groaned and rolled to my back to look up at him. "How long have I been out?"

"Not too long." His voice was a croak. "Nothing to be concerned about."

"Are you okay?"

He gave me a sad smile. "As okay as we can be, I suppose. We have to hang in there, Talon."

Footsteps sounded in the hall before the grate slid open to reveal Leifur, his lips pursed at the sight of us. He handed through some fresh water.

"I got here as soon as it was safe. It's not much, but it will help soothe your throat."

Óskar gently lifted my head from his leg before he stood and collected the water from Leifur. He turned to look back at me with a raised eyebrow. I nodded before he refocused on Leifur.

"We're in," Óskar breathed. "You get us out of here, and we will help you end this."

TWENTY-EIGHT

GIL

My fear over Bryn's well-being had become a constant ache in my chest, a constant companion in my dreams. I missed her desperately, and I had no idea how or where she was.

Or if I would see her again.

I tried hard to keep my thoughts positive, not about whether I would see her again but *when* I would see her again. But with each day that passed, it became harder, the ache in my chest growing more unbearable.

I walked through the silent halls of the fortress with my sisters by my side. The fortress had become a powder keg as people loudly pronounced their sides or schemed from the sidelines. The whole place was teetering on a sword's edge as everyone held their breath, waiting for the one move, the one choice, that would tip it over.

It was always a dangerous place to be for my family, but it was about to become downright volatile.

I led my sisters through the familiar hallways to Bryn's ma's rooms. I had visited her on my own before, and she always greeted me with a warm smile and a hug. She was content to sit silently with me as I fumbled through my first few tries at healing supplies before she made them with me.

I hadn't mentioned it to Bryn, hadn't mentioned it to anyone, for that matter. It felt like a special time that we shared. There was a comfort there, almost like what I would imagine spending time with a mother would be like. It made me grateful that Bryn had had such a different relationship with her mother than I had, and it was hard to describe what it meant to me that her ma had reached out to me in that way. That she would be willing to bond with me in such a way.

I wasn't sure if I was seeking her out to feel closer to Bryn or chasing the motherly comfort she shared with me, but I was excited to spend time with her. To introduce my sisters to her.

Bryn wasn't here to make the call, but when I explained my plan to Fannar, he was completely on board. It was impossible to deny how unstable the King Commander was and how dangerous the fortress was becoming. To have two people who I trusted implicitly looking out for her when we were called away made me rest a little easier.

I knocked on the door, and it only took a few moments for her to open it.

"Hello," I said softly. "Do you mind if we come in?"

She stepped back with a smile, letting us in without a moment of hesitation.

"Can I introduce my sisters to you? This is Klara, and that is Violet." I gestured to each of them in turn. "Klara is a warrior, but Violet is like you and Bryn. She is a healer."

She smiled and tapped her hand on my chest as though reminding me that I healed too, before wrapping my sisters each in their own one-armed hug.

"There has been no news on Bryn or Óskar yet," I told her,

causing her shoulders to tense. I knew that Fannar had filled her in on what little we knew and wanted her to know that Bryn was on my mind just as much as she was likely on hers.

"I love the healing supplies that you make," Violet jumped in, her eyes bright. "Would you be willing to show me how to make them? My brother has been quite cagey, saying it isn't his recipe to share."

"That is because it is not mine to share," I told her, echoing a familiar conversation.

Violet rolled her eyes before turning back to Bryn's ma. "Please?"

Bryn's ma smiled softly at Violet, her eyes bright and amused, before she nodded. I helped her pull the supplies and set them up on the tall table.

Klara rolled her eyes playfully at me as she watched Violet bounce on the balls of her feet, beyond excited at the prospect of learning more about healing. Klara, who couldn't care less for healing, happily settled onto one of the couches and pulled out her whetstone and one of her blades. More than content to keep us company, Bryn's ma and I walked Violet through some of the most useful medical ointments and salves she may need.

I quickly lost myself to the peaceful rhythm of cutting and grinding herbs. I allowed Bryn's ma to show my sister how they were combined as I systematically worked through the items that needed to be prepped for them.

The comfort that came with having my sisters with me in Bryn's ma's rooms was something that I hadn't expected. I knew that being around her brought me peace and hoped it would make me feel closer to Bryn. But having the four of us here together?

It was almost what I could imagine my family would have been like if my mother had controlled her darkness.

If she hadn't been turned into a monster.

I allowed myself the rare opportunity to fully zone out, focusing only on the herbs and plants before me. The steady chopping of my knife, the rhythmic swirling and crunching of the mortar and pestle. The scent of the freshly crushed items.

A hand on my shoulder startled me out of my peaceful almost-trance. I turned to find Klara by my side, her eyes soft. "It's gotten late. I'm going to get us some food from the gathering hall. I'll bring it back here."

"I can go with you," I offered, immediately setting aside my knife and giving her my full attention.

"Don't be ridiculous," she told me, brushing away my words with one of her hands. "I can handle myself just fine without my big brother protecting me."

"Alright. But I will look for you if you are not back in fifteen minutes."

Klara rolled her eyes. "I'll be careful."

She double-checked that all her weapons were in place before slipping out the door with a wave. Even though I knew perfectly well that my sister knew how to protect herself, that she was a damn good fighter, I couldn't return my focus to my work. Not while she was out in the viper-invested fortress. Alone.

I stepped back from the table and sat on the couch, my body facing to see both the door and my sister and Bryn's ma. There was an unsettled feeling that had taken root in my stomach since the moment that Bryn and Óskar had gone missing, and it was just getting stronger the longer I sat here waiting for her to return.

The door flew open, and Klara tore through it, slamming it behind her and barring it shut. Her eyes immediately found mine. "Armed warriors are heading this way," she panted.

"Everyone is armed in the hallways now," I told her, joining her by the door.

"These ones were being led by Ottó," Klara said before her gaze drifted towards Bryn's ma. "I had a bad feeling."

I cursed. "Me too." I spun on my heel to find Violet and Bryn's ma staring at us with wide eyes. "What room has the smallest windows?" Bryn's ma pointed to Fannar's old room. "You and Violet will go into that room and put your backs to the wall. Stay as far from the windows as you can and stay low."

They both hesitated as though considering to stay in the main room with us, but eventually made their way into the room. Violet paused in the doorway. "I don't want to have to patch either of you back up."

"We'll do our best, Vi," Klara told her before Violet disappeared into the room.

I took a deep breath before turning to Klara. "What are my chances of getting you to join them?"

"Non-existent, brother," Klara said as she drew two blades. A sword in her right hand and a dagger in her left—a weapon she had picked up from Bryn. There wasn't enough room in this space for both of us to be using two swords. "We're facing this together side by side. Maybe this will prove I'm ready to fight on the front lines."

I nodded to her and took my place by her side, both of our backs to the door to Fannar's old room. No one would get by us. We would not allow anyone to reach the people that were hidden there. I drew my swords as thundering footsteps could be heard.

"You want to join us on the battlefield? Now is your chance to earn it," I told her.

Klara smirked at me as something crashed against the door.

"Looks like you were right," I muttered.

"You know this is one of those times I would have preferred being wrong." Klara's words were muffled by another crash against the door. The wood split, but the bar securing it held firm.

But it wouldn't for long.

A third strike shattered it, the bar snapping into pieces and wood splinters flew in all directions.

Warriors streamed into the room. They wore no distinguishable family crests or colours, but I could still recognize some. Most were members of Ottó's forces, but some were warriors that Emilía had approached, swayed to their side by her venomous whispers in their ears.

Klara dropped one with a well-placed dagger throw and quickly palmed another before the first warriors were upon us.

A yowling, feline war cry rang from the direction of the windows, a scrambling of paws on the hardwood followed before the cat leapt at the face of another man with an angry yowl, sinking its claws deep into his skin.

I blocked the warrior's axe, knocking it to the side before slamming his temple with the pommel of my sword. He dropped, unconscious, as I turned to face the next one. The cat leapt at the face of another man with an angry yowl, sinking its claws deep into his skin and allowing me to focus on the next warrior.

Her smaller hand axes were a blur, but I could deflect them. I snapped a quick kick from her stomach, causing her back to slam into the corner of the tall wooden table. Another kick to the side of her knee crippled her.

With each warrior that I faced, each warrior that I dropped,

I was careful not to kill any of them. My family could not risk any potential murderous claims about us. The King Commander was unstable enough that I wouldn't put it past him to lock us all up in the dungeon even though Violet and Klara didn't have the darkness bloodrite.

But as the warriors continued to pour into the room, we quickly ran out of options. We had both taken our fair share of blows—Klara was bleeding from the temple, her lip swollen. My grip on my sword was slipping, my blood causing my fingers to lose purchase on the leather.

I was down to the one thing I had promised myself I would never do.

Using my darkness in front of my sisters.

"Eyes up, Klara," I barked as I sheathed my swords. It was what I told her from the moment I started training her when I needed her to be extra aware. When I needed her to be extra vigilant.

And then I tapped into my darkness.

It started at my feet, spreading thin and wide as it rapidly covered the ground. I forced it to spear across the room to the door, carrying up the wall and completely blocking the entrance to the room.

Once I had sealed the room, I turned my attention back to the warriors in front of us. Clenching my fists, I broke tendrils from the carpet of shadows, sending them spiralling up the warriors, locking them in place. I panted as I forced them to their knees.

"Klara," I growled between my clenched teeth, but I hadn't needed to. She was already moving through the room, knocking them out and binding their hands with whatever she could find.

The monster inside me pounded at the bars of the cage I kept it in, begging to be let out. Threatening to break free.

I shoved it down and reinforced the cage with everything I had, not willing to risk it being unleashed. Refusing to let it gain control in front of my sisters.

In front of Bryn's ma.

When the final warrior was secured, I immediately released my hold on my bloodrite, allowing the darkness to recede into me. I turned away from Klara as the monster roiled and lashed out from its prison, not wanting her to watch me struggle to remain myself.

I breathed deeply, interlacing my hands behind my back. "Are there any others?" I asked, not turning around.

"No one," Klara said softly.

I closed my eyes in relief as the monster calmed with a final grumble. A hand rested on my shoulder, causing my eyes to shut for a moment before turning to face my sister.

But it wasn't Klara who stood beside me; it was Bryn's ma.

She swallowed as her hand rested over my heart. "You are a good man." Her words were raspy and broken from months of disuse, but they still wrapped around my heart like a vice.

I blinked, clearing my heart. "Thank you. I am sorry that you had to see that."

"We didn't see anything," Violet said from the doorway.

"I did," Klara said before throwing herself at me. Her arms wrapped tightly around my shoulders. "Thank you."

"I put you at risk," I told her.

She pulled back to shake her head, her eyes sparkling with fury. "No. You *saved* us."

I nodded, no words coming to mind as I stared at my sister. Nothing on her face showed an ounce of fear. There was some fatigue and a good amount of relief. But there was also something that almost looked like awe.

Klara stepped back and joined Violet and Bryn's ma. "Go. Stop them," she said, nodding towards the door. "I'll stay here with them."

"All of you should go to the Verndari wing when it is safe," I told them, moving towards the door the moment Klara said she would stay with them. I paused in the doorway, turning to look back at my sister. "You earned it," I told her before entering the hallway.

The hallways were eerily quiet, with no one to be seen as I charged through the various turns.

If I had made such a blatant move, I wouldn't stick around after it didn't work out. I would be fleeing.

I sprinted through the hallways towards the courtyard, hoping to make it to the gates before Ottó and Emilía did.

But when I finally reached the front doors to the fortress, they were already open. The gates hung off their hinges as though they had been broken open from the inside.

And Ottó and Emilía were nowhere to be seen.

CHAPTER
TWENTY-NINE

BRYN

We lay near our wall, as I had taken to calling it, our names cut into the stone by Skolli claw one day when I succumbed to boredom. Proof that we had been there—proof that we had survived it, if we ever got out.

We lay, our feet against opposite walls, our heads resting on each other's shoulders as we stared at the ceiling above us. Sometimes, our nerves were too shot to handle touch, thanks to Katrín, but other times, it was a silent reminder that we were together.

That we were both still alive and that we were both still fighting.

"What is the first thing you will do when we get out of here?" Óskar asked, his voice sounding oddly deep as my ear rested against the side of his face.

"Bathe," I answered with a wistful sigh. So much dirt and grime covered my body and clothes that I was pretty sure it was engrained in my skin. Add in a topping of blood and sweat, and I was sure that I made a frightful sight.

I probably smelled quite foul as well, but I'm pretty sure that Óskar and I were nose blind to the scents inside our cell at this point.

Óskar chuckled. "You're laying here dreaming about what is sure to be countless baths to get you clean again, and I've been here practically drooling about the food in our wing. What does that say about us?"

"That you think with your stomach just like Yugar does," I teased with a smile.

He was quiet for a moment. "But outside of the bath, the change of clothes, the food that we both know we need—what else?"

I blinked, my eyes going blurry. "I want to see Gil." My voice broke. "I want to see the others too, of course, and my family, but I need to see Gil."

"Do you think that they are safe?" Óskar's voice was soft.

"I like to believe that they are. If they were in another cell beside us, I think we would have heard their screams by now." With every day that passed, it was harder to remind myself that I believed that they were okay, that they were safe from the horrors that Óskar and I were facing.

And as much as I wanted them to be able to rescue us from here, I also wanted them to be as far from this hell as they could be.

Hopefully, we will soon be far away from here as well.

"What about you?" I asked Óskar, readjusting myself on the hard stone floor. "Besides the food and soft beds, what are you looking forward to?"

He was quiet for a moment. "My dog—Yugar. I can't wait to see him, to hold him close." Óskar let out a humourless chuckle. "That was the last time that I don't bring him to a fight. He wouldn't have allowed them to get the drop on us. Yugar's the best thing that I have done."

"He's a good dog; you two have a special bond."

"Yugar is also the only time I've gotten it right. The only time that my bloodrite was enough—that I was enough," his voice broke.

I sat up so that I could look Óskar in the eye. "He's not the only thing that you got right. You have saved us with your bloodrite before, and you have trained other animals like your eagle. It is enough. You are enough."

"But it has also failed me when we needed it. It could have led to one of us being killed."

"But none of us have died. It comes with your bloodrite, Óskar. The animals have their wills. They can choose to ignore you. But that does not mean you are at fault if anything happens to us." I gestured to the cell around us. "You may not be able to save us with your bloodrite right now, but you are helping me keep going. You help me recover from Katrin's sessions. You are enough."

Óskar closed his eyes with a sigh. "We'll see, won't we?"

My head lolled against Óskar's shoulder as sleep threatened behind my eyes. His fingers lazily tried to work out the tangles and clumps in my hair in an attempt to braid it, but he wasn't having much luck with my curls. They were hard enough to manage at the best of times, let alone when we had been locked in a dungeon for who knows how many days without the ability to care for it.

The door swung open to reveal Leifur, who shut the metal door behind him, leaving it open with just a crack.

I pulled myself to my feet, Óskar doing the same beside me. Because not only was this the first time he had joined us in our cell, but he also held weapons in his hands.

A belt of daggers.

A bow and quiver.

"We've got to go now," he told us urgently, passing us the weapons. Now that I had taken longer to study him, I realized that he was dressed in leather armour and his own arms. "I could grab weapons, but we don't have large enough armour stores where I could pull from it and not draw attention. The best I could do was cloaks and warmer layers."

He tossed us the clothes, and I happily pulled them on, savouring the extra warmth that started to flood through me.

"What's the plan?" Óskar asked as he slung the quiver of arrows around his hips so that the cloak around his shoulders didn't hide it.

"Pétur and Katrín are out leading training with our warriors. They should be gone for at least a night. All that's left here are my parents and Sigrún, who have already retired for the night, and a skeleton crew of guards. It's our best chance."

I nodded, brushing my hands over the hilts of each dagger, familiarizing myself with where they were on the weapons belt. "Do we have horses?"

"No," Leifur shook his head grimly. "We will have to get to the nearest stronghold on foot, but I will do my best to keep us hidden from my parents' monsters."

"We need to get to Newtide. We know for a fact that they are with us," I told him, pulling my matted hair back with a leather tie Leifur passed me.

He nodded. "We must get word to the other Verndari to meet us there. I would not put it past my sister to track us and recapture you—us—by any means necessary."

"Get me some parchment and something to write with, and I will take care of it," Óskar said. His eyes scanned me as though he was checking if I was ready for this before accepting the writing items that Leifur passed him. He ripped the parchment into four pieces and scribbled a message on each before carefully tucking them into his pocket.

"I've done what I can to clear our path but I can't guarantee that we won't have to fight our way out. We must be quick and leave no one who can rat us out behind. I modify their memories, or we kill them. Clear?"

I nodded. "Clear. We're with you."

"Stay right on my tail." Leifur poked his head out the door, glancing both ways before opening it wider. "Let's go."

We slipped out the door behind him, Óskar pulling it shut behind us. It wouldn't be hard for them to open the door and see if we were there, but every moment we could delay and deceive them increased our chances of getting to Newtide alive.

And we all knew how low those chances were.

But it was our only choice.

Leifur led us at a light jog down the hallway, our steps almost silent against the stone floors. Reminding me that not just Óskar and I were trained for the battlefield, trained to be lethal; Leifur had been, too.

Had he been honing those skills in the hundreds of years he had been isolated here?

Leifur held up a hand as we reached a doorway at the end of the hall, the flickering light of a fire easy to spot. He gestured for Óskar and me to stay close to the hall as he stepped in.

A few moments later, he waved us through; a single guard was slumped in his chair, his eyes unfocused. "I modified his memories; he believes that he fed you both and settled in for the night. That should give us twelve to fifteen hours before anyone thinks to look for you both." He started towards the stairs. "Here's where it gets risky. Stay close."

We crept up the stairs and quickly ducked into a servants' passage. Leifur led us through twists and turns before stopping at a wooden door. "This leads outside. We are going to stick to the shadows as much as possible and make a break for the tree line," he whispered. "Can you run?"

"It'll be sore, but we will make sure to keep up," Óskar said before nodding to me. "Talon might even outrun you."

Leifur nodded. "Good. On three."

He opened the door, and we slipped out into a shadowed alcove near the door. We lingered just long enough to shut the door behind us before taking off towards the tall stones in the distance. The same tall stones we watched Pétur disappear behind a few months ago.

The marker of a barrier that no longer stood.

We sprinted, careful to keep to the shadows, charging towards those same stones.

It wasn't until we were closer that we noticed the three guards lounging at the base of one of the stones. Leifur pulled us into one of the last shadowed areas before the large open space between the stones and the tree line. "I can't modify all their memories at once. I'm out of practice."

"Are you saying that being locked away from the rest of the world limited the amount of people you could practice on?" Óskar teased.

Leifur narrowed his brows at him before turning to me and quirking one. "Ignore him. We can take care of them," I said, pulling a dagger from my belt and nodding at Óskar.

Óskar nodded in return, drawing an arrow as I took off towards the guards.

The arrow pierced clean through the first guard's eye, and before the others could realize what was happening, another arrow found the second guard.

Leaving the third for me. I leapt, slicing clean through her neck.

By the time Leifur and Óskar reached me, I had pulled the arrows and cleaned them the best I could. We hid the bodies and disappeared into the treeline.

We ran, settling into a pace we could maintain for longer. When we finally had to stop, we slowed to a walk. None of us was willing to stop completely, but no one could run forever.

Especially through a forest only lit by the moon.

We needed to be smart just as much as we needed to be fast.

The light flapping of wings drew my attention as four birds landed on Óskar. A pair of hawks, a falcon, and an owl. He pulled the scraps of parchment from his pocket and gave them to each bird.

"Take these to the Verndari," he told them. Leifur turned to watch Óskar with wide eyes as the birds seemed to be watching him intently. "Find us help. Take these to the Verndari."

The birds took off with a flap of wings, disappearing into the night.

THIRTY

GIL

We gathered in the King Commander's office, his summons having arrived at our wing only moments before. We stood shoulder to shoulder, Aron and I keeping Rúna as sheltered as we could between us as we waited for him to speak. The King Commander finished whatever he was writing on a piece of parchment before setting it aside and turning his attention to us.

He leaned forward, his elbows resting on the desk, his eyes dark and hard as steel. I kept my own hands tucked behind my back, my fingers clenching and unclenching as I awaited whatever he had to say.

We were still forbidden from leaving the fortress without being officially dispatched by a member of the Commanding Family, and with every day—every hour—that went by, the knot of anxiety and worry for Bryn and Óskar grew.

I knew the odds of him calling us here today to permit us to go after them were incredibly slim, but I had to have hope.

But I was quickly running out of it.

"As you know, Ottó and several of his lackeys have decided

to depart for the exiled commanding family. I must reinforce my forces and have determined that you alone are insufficient." The King Commander's voice was gruff, his eyes cold.

"What would you have us do, King Commander?" Georg asked, his face carefully blank.

The King Commander wasn't wrong; the six of us would not be enough to shoulder the burden of the rapidly approaching war. We would need support. But the way he worded it made me nervous.

"Recall your family members. I would like them in reserve in the fortress."

Rúna gasped quietly by my side. When Verndari retired and passed their oaths and obligations to their children, they were free from military and political obligations. Anything they participated in from then on was completely optional, and the King Commander had decided to rescind that freedom.

"I expect them to be at the fortress within two weeks," the King Commander continued.

Rúna nodded her head, her face pale.

"My mother is already here, King Commander," I pointed out. "What do you want to do with her?"

"Nothing. Yet. But I will unleash her if I need to."

He would release her, knowing that she was consumed by her darkness, completely controlled by the monster within. She wouldn't know a friend from a foe; she wouldn't spare anyone. She would tear through both sides of the battlefield, and the King Commander would willingly let her do it.

"Let's hope it doesn't get to that point," Georg said softly.

"He has other family in the fortress that I will turn to first."

The knot of anxiety in me became a tangle, coiling through my stomach, through my chest and up my throat.

My sisters.

Two days later, the falcon found me in the courtyard; my head tipped back against the stone wall to study the darkening sky above me. I had to get out of the Verndari wing, or I would go crazy. The walls were starting to feel like a cell, trapping me.

The bird swooped down rapidly, a piece of parchment clasped in its talons.

I reached forward with trembling fingers, reminded of Óskar. I unrolled the crumbled parchment.

We're fleeing the mountain fortress with an unexpected friend to Newtide.

We need help. Please find us.

Óskar and Talon

My heart pounded in my chest. All this time, they had been with the exiled commanding family and locked away with the enemy.

I swallowed the bile that was threatening to erupt from my throat as I surged to my feet.

I burst into the Verndari wing, barely waiting for the door to shut behind me before bellowing, "Georg!" He and Aron stumbled into the room, a similar piece of parchment in their hands. "We need to go after them."

"I agree. This gives us something to go off of. The War Council can't deny us now," Aron pointed out, his eyes pained.

"Unexpected friend?" Georg asked quietly. "Are they bringing Pétur back?"

"I do not care who is with them if it means they can survive. We need to go find them now," I told him, breathing deeply.

Rúna slipped into the room with Baldur and Ragna by her

side, her eyes wide and a piece of parchment clasped in her hands.

I turned to Ragna. "Call the War Council. *Please.*"

"No," Baldur said, shaking his head.

"We know where they are," Aron hissed. "Where they *were*. We need to go."

"If you call the War Council, all you are doing is giving them the chance to prevent you from going."

Ragna sighed, her eyes tired. "He's right. Father has carefully curated the War Council since the others were barred from the chamber. Most of them are in his pocket, and will vote how he wants them to. If you go to the War Council and my father doesn't want you to go, they will not give you permission."

I cursed, my fist crumpling the parchment.

"What are our options then?" Georg asked, his lips pursed. "We can't ignore this." He held up the parchment. "This is a call for help."

"If we leave the fortress without permission, we will make everything worse," Aron pointed out, sounding almost pained by what he was saying.

Baldur studied Rúna for a long moment before turning to the rest of us. "Then you leave with permission," he said.

"There is no way Father will grant them permission to leave regardless of those missives," Ragna shook her head bitterly.

"They don't need the King Commander's permission to leave. They need to be dispatched by a member of the Commanding Family." Baldur took a deep breath before locking eyes with me. "I will do it. I will dispatch you."

THIRTY-ONE

BRYN

I had run all my life with Da. I had honed my endurance and stamina into one of my greatest strengths.

But even I was struggling with our desperate charge towards Newtide.

We had long since given up on talking during our brief walking respites; the slower pace was no longer long enough to fully allow us to catch our breath and provide any relief to the stitches in our sides. Óskar was struggling; running had never been his favourite, and he was actively searching for horses that we could use, but we couldn't risk losing time going off-track to find them.

They had to cross our path, or it wouldn't be worth us losing the time. Not when we couldn't guarantee that we would find any.

My legs had been sore this morning, but now they were nothing more than mush. With every step I took, they were heavier, threatening to give out.

The sky finally began to darken, triggering contradictory emotions within me.

Relief that we could finally stop moving for the day and rest before doing it again the next day.

But also dread because the monsters would be free to hunt us down.

When the sun finally set, Leifur led us to a small cave, lingering at the entrance momentarily before leading the way in. The mountainous terrain we were desperately fleeing had plenty of caves the Leifur seemed well aware of.

But caves were as risky as they were safe. They offered us some shelter and shielded us from sight, but they did the same thing for the monsters when the sun hung high in the sky.

The cave Leifur led us into wasn't large, but it was big enough for our purposes. I paced the small space, my body screaming at me to flop against the ground like Óskar was, but I knew that I would be in worse shape if I didn't at least try to work through the pain.

I could practically hear Da's voice in my ear telling me to work through it unless I wanted cramps.

Leifur pulled some dried pieces of meat from the bag that was slung across his back, along with some waterskins. He distributed it amongst us before joining me in pacing.

Óskar peered up at him. "How did you know the monsters wouldn't occupy this cave?"

"I didn't." Leifur pressed his lips together before biting his food. "Large groups of Skolli and Ógn, like what I believe will be in hot pursuit of us, prefer to stay together, making it less likely that they would use a small cave like this as their shelter from the sun." He stopped pacing and sat near Óskar, leaning back against the stone wall of the cave. "I also waited until darkness had fully set to enter. My parents' monsters have been trained to leave their shelter as soon as they can; by lingering that little bit longer, we made it less likely that there would be any unwanted surprises in here."

Finally feeling something other than pain in my legs, I joined the others on the ground as I sipped from my waterskin. "Will they check the caves?"

"They may."

Óskar grimaced, glancing at the mouth of the cave. "That's reassuring."

"I did my best to limit the risk. I chose a cave with a smaller entrance, which would limit the number of Skolli that could enter at once. And we won't light a fire. If we are quiet, there shouldn't be any reason why they will seek us here. We will still need to keep watch throughout the night to be safe."

I nodded in complete agreement with what he said. We were quiet for a few moments as we finished our meagre rations. I passed the waterskin to Leifur before settling into a position where it was easy to see the mouth of the cave. "I can take the first watch," I offered.

"I will take the second watch. You two need the uninterrupted rest more than I do. As uninterrupted as you can manage, at least," Leifur said.

Óskar sighed with relief. "Thank you. For that and for getting us out of that hellhole."

"You don't need to thank me. It allowed me to escape as well." Leifur was silent for a few moments. "Do you think that your message will reach the Verndari?"

"I do. I sent one to each of them. It is bound to reach at least one of them."

"And—" Leifur cut himself off, hesitating. "And you believe that they will come? That they won't think it is a trap?"

Óskar pushed himself up to sit, the weight of his gaze shifting from Leifur to me and back again. "Yes. I believe that they will come. Unless they are dead or dying, they will do everything they can to reach us. We aren't just each other's comrades. We're much more than that. We're each other's family. Sometimes I even think that is too weak a word."

"I had friends like that once," Leifur's voice was quiet, threaded with pain. "But after hundreds of years locked behind the barrier with just my family and recently a pair of traitors, it is hard to remember that feeling."

"I would do *anything* for them. For those I care about," I told Leifur softly, his eyes showing that he understood exactly what I meant by anything.

I would sacrifice myself if it meant that they would walk off of a battlefield. If it gave them a chance of a better tomorrow.

"And I know that they would do the same for me," I finished before turning my attention back to the mouth of the cave.

"You asked how they would know it's not a trap? Only the Verndari, or those closest to us, know that I call Bryn Talon. I used her nickname in the message to show that it was us that were desperate for, *begging for*, their help." They shifted around behind me, no doubt settling in for the night. "Now we just have to hope they can reach us in time."

WE HAD MANAGED to stay ahead of the forces that were pursuing us for a few nights, but all three of us knew that we were no doubt outpaced and outmanned.

And as the wingbeats and pounding hoofbeats started to gain on us as the moon rose, we knew we were in trouble.

"Run!" Óskar hissed as we pushed from our jog into a sprint.

We tore across the ground in front of us, leaping over fallen logs as low-hanging branches whipped at our faces. Thorns from the overgrown bushes and plants around us caught at me and tore at my skin, but I didn't stop running.

As I charged through the overgrowth, I pushed every ounce of willpower, of my remaining strength and stamina, into my legs and arms.

Leifur constantly scanned the area around us as though searching for another option—trying to find anywhere that may help us. Anywhere that may shift the battle breathing down our neck into our favour even the slightest bit.

And as he pushed himself harder and raced faster than before away from the forces behind us, I knew we were out of options.

We broke out of the overgrowth into a small clearing, and Leifur held up a hand, bringing us to a skidding stop.

"They won't expect us to stop and fight. Our only hope is to catch them off guard," he panted, his face grim. "And even that is a long shot."

"A long shot is better than none at all," Óskar said as he nocked an arrow. "I, for one, will take what I can get."

I spun on my heel to face where we came from, crashes closing in on us quickly. Pulling two daggers from my belt, I settled into my fighting crouch. "Then we fight."

The Skolli broke into the clearing first, one after another after another. I cursed as I braced for the first one.

It brought its claws down with incredible force; their impact against my daggers sent tremors throughout my body as I blocked it. I forced the claws out of the way, ducking under the wing it swiped at me. Spinning, I slammed my dagger backwards into the Skolli's throat, the blade piercing one of the few unprotected spots on the monster.

The Skolli fell forward, taking my dagger with it.

Another one knocked me from the side, sending me crashing to the ground. Cursing, I pushed myself to my knees, already pulling another dagger from my belt.

Sliding between the Skolli's legs, I swiped both daggers across the back of its knees, causing it to roar in pain. Dropping my shoulder as I surged to my feet, I drove it to the ground and punched both of my blades through its eyes.

I popped to my feet with a groan as I drew the two remaining daggers from my belt, shoving the worry that caused as far from my mind as possible.

I still had my bloodrite. I wasn't defenceless.

Leaping at the closest Skolli to me, I sliced my dagger across its throat before pushing off its falling corpse towards the next monster.

It tried to shake me off as I shredded its wings before stabbing both my daggers into its back and forcing it to the ground.

I didn't see the Skolli charging at me until it landed a vicious kick on my ribs, sending me tumbling across the ground and into a tree trunk.

"*Fuck*," I muttered, my ribs screaming at me as I allowed the familiar burning to settle into my hands and mouth as I shifted to create more weapons for myself. In my feet and legs, I gave myself more power and more strength as I pushed myself to stand on my Skolli legs.

I snapped a kick at the side of one of the monster's legs, a crack ringing out as I broke the bones, more than happy to rip out its throat as it stumbled.

As I turned, already searching for my next target in the swarm of monsters around me, a loop of chain fell over my head, encircling my body and arms. It cinched tight, attempting to pin my arms. Glancing behind me, I saw a warrior on horseback behind me, the end of the chain in his hands as he stared down at me.

"*Nice try,*" I hissed, surging forward on my Skolli legs, breaking the warrior's grip and causing the chain to loosen.

But another chain landed on me. And then another and another, until four of them cinched tight on my body, throwing off my balance and sending me crashing to my knees.

I screamed in anger. In pain. In fear as the chains started to drag me back into the trees.

"*Bryn!*" Oskar yelled as he took down a monster between us, already trying to fight his way towards me.

But he was across the clearing from me with too many monsters between us.

Burning flared as my body reverted to normal, the pain of my injuries, of the chains around me, radiating through my body.

"Go," I yelled, my voice wobbling.

"No!" Óskar snarled as Leifur fought his way to his side.

"You're our best chance. *Please. Go.*"

Our best chance of getting out of this situation. Our best chance of getting back to the Verndari.

Our best chance of at least one of us surviving this nightmare.

Óskar's face twisted as my words sunk in, and he realized what he had to do. And what he couldn't do.

He turned on his heel, easily taking down two warriors approaching him on horseback. "Mount up," he ordered Leifur as he swung himself up into the saddle.

The warriors dragging me didn't hesitate and didn't attempt to help their comrades. They just continued dragging me from the clearing, the ground already wearing a hole through my pants, my skin surely to receive the same treatment shortly.

Óskar looked back at me once more before he kneed his horse into a gallop and sent their horses surging forward with the help of his bloodrite.

Leaving me to be dragged from the clearing back towards the mountain stronghold we had just escaped.

THIRTY-TWO

GIL

Our journey from the fortress to Newtide was desperate as we pushed our horses to their limits in a charge to reach Óskar and Bryn before the worst could happen.

Before anything else could happen to them.

The gods only know what they had gone through while they were with the exiled commanding family, but my mind was quite active in creating various scenarios that may have happened.

Probably happened.

I tried my best to shove those thoughts out of my head, to stay focused on our push to reach them. But every time we slowed to rest the horses or were forced to stop just long enough to ensure that we didn't fall out of the saddle, those thoughts came rushing right back in.

When we reached Newtide and learned that they hadn't reached the city yet, the thoughts pounded against the walls of the box I tried to shove them into. Threatening to overwhelm me.

We immediately set out for the mountain fortress, trusting that Bryn and Óskar would have been clever enough to travel a straight line between the two spots so that we would have an easier time finding them.

Hoped that was the case.

Our journey became desperate as we took shorter rests, only stopping when we allowed the horses to, willing to risk exhaustion over the alternative.

Over whatever delayed Bryn and Óskar from reaching Newtide.

We pushed on through the night, the full moon's light providing just enough visibility to ensure that we could keep the horses at a gallop.

Georg held up a hand to stop us, the horses slowing, their sides heaving. We were silent for a moment before I heard it. Wingbeats.

Skolli.

"Dismount," Georg ordered. "Secure your horses to the trees and get ready to face the Skolli."

Rúna took the reins of both our horses as Aron did the same for him and Georg.

Georg and I settled into a fighting crouch, our weapons ready, before the others joined us a moment later.

The wingbeats got closer and closer as another sound joined them.

Hoofbeats.

Two horses broke through the tree line ahead of us, one slightly ahead of the other. Óskar was on the first one, panic radiating from every line of his body. As he spotted us, relief was evident on his face, as were the patches of blood on his clothes and the splatters on his skin. His clothes, the same ones he had been wearing when we left the fortress days ago to help

Rúna's family, were dirty and torn, hanging from him in places they hadn't before. A few layers had been added to what he wore, but not enough to protect him in a fight. Barely enough to keep him warm in the cold. And even those seemed too big for him.

As though he hadn't eaten properly in days.

Dark circles had taken up residence under his eyes, a bruise on his temple. Rúna's gasp by my side reinforced just how bad he looked.

The relief at the sight of Óskar was almost painful in my chest as I turned to the other horse, expecting to see Bryn's red curls.

But they weren't there.

A man rode by his side, his clothes dirty and bloody but in better shape than Óskar's, and he also had leather armour on. He looked tired and worn like Óskar, but it didn't appear to be the bone-deep exhaustion that had sunk its claws into him.

And with no Bryn in sight, the relief evaporated as fast as it had appeared.

Where was she?

As fast as Óskar and the other man appeared, so did the Skolli that followed them.

"Get behind us!" Georg roared.

They didn't hesitate or slow as their horses hurtled towards us. If anything, they urged their mounts harder at the support and protection in front of them.

Once they were by us, we didn't wait a moment longer before we charged towards the Skolli. "Rúna, we cannot waste any time."

She spared me a glance before nodding, uncoiling her whip, and taking up her position at my back. I re-sheathed my swords and sunk to a knee. As much as I despised using my bloodrite, I knew that it was the quickest way to end this.

And the absence of Bryn by Óskar's side told me everything I needed to know.

We needed to end this now.

My bloodrite shot from me, the darkness razor sharp as it hurtled towards the Skolli. Never stopping as it skewered one monster and immediately moved on to the next.

One by one, the monsters fell, no match for our bloodrites.

When the final one crashed to the ground, I remained kneeling for a moment. I panted as I ensured I had control before standing and approaching where Óskar and the man were.

The others were close behind me as we quickly closed the ground between us.

Up close, Óskar looked even worse, his eyes tired and weary, his body thin and malnourished.

And at least some of the blood on him was his own.

As Rúna went to Óskar, I turned my attention to the man by his side. "Who are you? Where is Bryn?"

"I'm Leifur, and I—" I didn't hesitate as I drew my sword because I knew that name.

The son of the exiled commanding family.

Óskar didn't hesitate to put himself between us. "No," his voice cracked, but a severity rang through that he often hid. "He is one of us. He is the only reason we got this far."

"I can explain everything—we can tell you everything that happened," Leifur said as he moved out from behind Óskar, earning some respect from me. He didn't hide, didn't use Óskar as a shield. "But we can't waste time."

I watched him momentarily before nodding and turning my attention to Óskar. "Where is Bryn?"

"She's back with them." His mouth tightened, his fingers shaking on the reins. "They caught up to us last night, and during the fight, they bound her with chains, so many that she couldn't even break free even with Skolli strength. We tried to fight our way to her, but she told me to go." His voice broke. "Said it was our best chance. We need to go after her."

"What kind of shape was she in?" Georg asked as Aron and Rúna ran for our horses. "Can she fight?"

Leifur's face was grim. "She was in just as bad shape as Óskar when they got her. By now, she is likely worse." He exchanged a dark look with Óskar that caused my stomach to flip. That look all but confirming some of the treatment that they had faced. "If she is still in those chains, she won't be able to do anything until we free her."

Aron and Rúna joined us, already mounted on their horses and Georg and I didn't hesitate to do the same.

"Can you get us to them? Do you have enough left?" Aron asked Óskar.

Óskar shifted in the saddle with a wince. "Hold on. We will make it."

That was the only warning before our horses were tearing back the way Óskar and Leifur came from. It took my body a moment to settle into the speed, having grown accustomed to the natural speed we had been stuck with without Óskar.

But now the landscape blurred by, our horses covering the ground twice as fast as they charged towards where Bryn was.

Hours later, we came across our first signs of people, a single warrior falling easily to Óskar's marksmanship.

"That's them," Leifur said, pitching his voice just loud enough to be heard over the pounding of our horses' hooves. "We found them."

We didn't bother to be quiet as we galloped into the camp,

Óskar's bloodrite finally releasing the horses back to their natural speed. My attention was immediately drawn toward where Bryn was chained between two trees.

Her body hung limply, her clothes in the same tattered state as Óskar's. While the others stepped forward to face the warriors that opposed them, Rúna and I immediately peeled off towards Bryn.

The closer I got, the more noticeable the injuries became. Her knees were torn and bloody, dirt ground into the wounds as though she had been forced to kneel or was dragged on the ground. Bruises littered her body along with various cuts, and that was all that I could see over her tattered clothing.

Clothing that hung so much more loosely than it had the last time I saw her.

No less than six chains secured her to the trees, and Rúna and I didn't hesitate to release them. When she was finally free, she dropped towards the ground, but I scooped her into my arms before she hit it.

"Bryn? Darling?" I brushed a matted curl out of her face as she blinked open her eyes with a moan of pain.

"Gil?" Her voice was hoarse, crackling and breaking as though it had been pushed to its limit.

As though she had been screaming for a long time.

"You found me," she whispered, her eyes welling with tears before one spilled over. I brushed it away with a thumb.

I scanned her face and her body, noticing every bruise. Every cut, every drop of blood. Far more than what she may have received in a fight. Someone had done this to her. Deliberately. And she couldn't have fought back because she had been chained up.

Rage I had never known was coiled in my stomach, climbing up my throat.

"Who did this to you?" I demanded, even as I ensured my fingers were gentle as they drifted across her back.

Her head turned to the side, scanning the camp. She raised her hand with a wince, pointing out a handful of warriors. I kissed her forehead before gently lowering her to the ground and waving Rúna over to join her.

Her fingers grabbed my sleeve, their grip weaker than normal. "Where are you going?"

"To make sure they never touch you again," I growled as Rúna untangled her fingers from my sleeve.

I turned on my heel, drawing my swords and stalking towards the warriors.

Then I unleashed myself, every ounce of my worry and fury fuelling my movements.

I would make them pay for every mark on her body tenfold.

The first one didn't see me coming as I slashed at the back of their knees, crippling them. They screamed, trying to crawl away from me. I grabbed their ankle, pulling them close, before stabbing them through the heart. I pushed them away and set my sights on the next one.

I didn't want to spend too long away from Bryn—she needed help. She and Óskar both needed healing.

But I didn't have it in me to kill these people quickly. They needed to suffer, if only for a moment, for what they put her through.

I ensured that they all felt that pain, that terror, before they met their end.

And when the final warrior's head bounced off the ground, and the fighting finally settled, I wiped the blood from my blades and turned back towards Bryn.

THIRTY-THREE

BRYN

Gil's hands barely touched my skin as he gently cupped my cheeks, tilting my head to study the injuries that I knew lay there. My eyes fluttered shut as I finally let my body relax, soaking in his hands' warmth and revelling in his scent.

He was here. We were safe.

We had survived.

"Gods, Bryn," he muttered. "What did they do to you?"

I gave him a sad smile, barely twitching my lips, but it was still enough to reopen the cut there. "Enough. They did enough," I rasped, my throat a solid ache. "Where's Óskar?"

"He is here somewhere. He brought us to you," he told me, finally pulling his eyes away from me long enough to scan the area around us. Gil leaned to the side, pointing. "There."

My eyes locked with Óskar's, my own pooling with tears. I pushed myself onto my knees with a groan, struggling to get to my feet.

Gil rested his hands on my waist, gently lifting me and holding most of my weight. "Careful," he murmured, his breath fanning across my skin. "I need to take a look at your injuries."

But I ignored him as Óskar stumbled over to me, Leifur not far from his side. He didn't hesitate to pull me into his arms even though his grip was gentle. Gil kept a hand on my waist even as Óskar allowed me to rest my weight against him as though he couldn't bring himself to let me go.

"Never again, Bryn," Óskar whispered to me, his hands gripping the back of my shirt tightly. "Never ask me to do that again."

"We survived," I breathed. "They found us."

Óskar didn't say anything else for several moments before pulling back to look at me. Gil reached forward, pulling me gently back so I could rest my weight against him. "How bad was it?" Óskar asked me.

I didn't need to ask what he meant.

"Nothing worse than what she put us through," I said softly.

Óskar scoffed. "That, at least, wasn't real. This very much was." He gestured down my body.

Gil's fingers flexed against my waist, listening to what we were saying and trying to understand. Not just because he cared for me and wanted to know why I was hurting but because he was going to have to try and heal whatever had been done to us. Anything he learned about what we went through would make his job easier.

I turned my attention to Leifur. "They knew that you were with us. I don't know if they sent a message back or not. I was in and out of consciousness once they got me here."

"I knew that getting you out would be a very clear state-ment," Leifur said grimly. "Even if they didn't send a message, it would only be a matter of time before they connected my absence to your escape."

"We'll camp here for the rest of the night," Georg said as he joined us. "We have ensured that no one was left to threaten or report on us. It's as good as any other place." He turned towards Óskar and me, his eyes sad. "You two go get some rest." He paused for a moment. "You as well, Leifur. Gil, tend to their wounds and then stay with her. The four of us can handle watch just fine."

Gil led me to one of the warrior's tents and quickly cleared it of any sign of them. He laid his bedroll out on the ground and helped me lay down. I caught his fingers. "Check on Óskar first, then come back for me."

His brows furrowed. "But you are in much worse shape than him."

"I'm not going to want you to leave me alone. If you heal him first, you can return and stay with me for the rest of the night," I whispered.

Gil pressed a kiss to my forehead. "I will be back soon," he told me before disappearing out of the tent.

I dozed as I waited for him; whatever scraps of adrenaline, of the drive to survive, finally working its way out of my body.

I woke to something brushing across my face. I jerked, my eyes wild as they landed on Gil and the cloth in his hand. He froze. "It is just me, darling," he said softly. "It is just me."

The tension slowly eased from my muscles as I calmed down. "Gil," I whimpered.

"I am here, darling." He continued wiping the dirt, grime, blood, tears, and who knew what else from my face. He finally set aside the cloth and reached for the hem of my shirt, on the hem of my pants, his fingers lingering there. "Can I?" he asked.

I nodded, swallowing thickly. I knew that what lay under

my clothes was going to be bad. It was going to be bruised and cut and bloody.

He had seen me bruised at Wolfmire. He had seen me cut and bloody after a number of skirmishes.

But a different type of vulnerability allowed him to see me like this. All those other times I fought, I dealt blows equal, if not stronger than, to the ones I had taken. But not this time.

This time, I had been chained up, locked away, as each hit landed on my body. As each blade cut my skin. As pain had been sent rushing through my body faster than the blood that pumped through my veins.

And I couldn't defend myself—I couldn't prevent it from happening.

And my body was going to reflect every moment of my captivity, of everything that I suffered.

I didn't look at him as he eased my shirt over my head. I stared, my vision blurry from tears, at the ceiling as he gently pulled my pants from my legs.

The cloth gently swept over my skin as he slowly erased the evidence of the past several days from my body. He set aside the cloth and reached for his healing supplies.

"Aren't you going to ask?" my voice broke.

"Ask what?" His voice was soft as he continued his work.

I took a shaky breath. "Ask what happened. What caused the bruises and cuts."

"Darling, no." Gil leaned over me to see my face. I turned away, feeling so raw—so broken—that I couldn't stand that look in his eyes. That pure love. "Please look at me, Bryn." I pressed my lips together to hide the fact that they quivered before looking at him. "I am not going to ask. The injuries you have, the way your ribs are standing out against your skin, tell me enough. And, when you are ready, you can tell me the rest."

"I love you," I whispered, a tear dropping from my eye.

He reached out to me with a sad smile and wiped it away with a thumb. "As I love you, darling."

I didn't look away as he went back to tending my wounds. Bruise paste was rubbed into each patch of brightly covered skin, and every cut was assessed with his careful eye and treated appropriately.

When he finished, he pulled one of his shirts from his saddlebags and a pair of my pants. He locked eyes with me before brushing a kiss against one of my bruises. "You are so strong," he whispered against me.

His lips found every discoloured patch on my body, whispering words of love, of encouragement. As though they may help wipe away the darkness behind the injuries.

Tears streamed down my face when he finally put the clean clothes on my body. He tucked me into the bedroll before laying beside me, a little space between our bodies.

Leaving it up to me whether I wanted to bridge that gap.

I didn't hesitate as I pressed my body close to his and pressed a kiss on his chest right over his heart. Gil curled an arm around my body, surrounding me with his warmth.

Surrounding me with him—his scent, his warmth, him.

My Gil.

My safety.

My home.

CHAPTER

THIRTY-FOUR

BRYN

I blinked open my eyes to find Gil still asleep, his rest heavier than it typically was in the field. It spoke levels to how exhausted he must be. I didn't know what they had faced while we were in the mountain fortress, but whatever it was had taken a toll on him.

While I couldn't sleep any longer because of what I had been through.

I eased out of the bedroll, my whole body smarting, and tucked the edges around him. I ducked out of the tent, limping towards the centre of the camp where Georg and Óskar sat. When he saw me, Georg set aside his tankard, gently wrapping an arm around my waist and helping me join them.

He passed me a steaming tankard before returning to his spot and picking up his drink. "I was just telling Óskar that I wasn't expecting to see either of you up yet."

I gave him a sad smile before sipping my tea. "We haven't slept well for a while."

"I was just telling him the same thing," Óskar grimaced, his black eye gruesome in the early light. "Dungeon floors don't make for a very comfortable rest."

I chuckled. "They certainly do not. I would not recommend it." I took another sip. "The last few nights didn't provide a good rest either. I wouldn't be surprised if Leifur joined us sooner rather than later."

Aron joined us then, ruffling my hair, nodding to Óskar and Georg, and taking a seat. Gil burst out of our tent, his eyes frantic as they scanned the camp before landing on me. His relief was visible as he made his way over to us.

"Alright there, Gil? Seemed a little flustered there," Óskar chirped at him.

Gil gave him a look before turning to me. "I was worried when you were not there when I woke. I thought that you were gone again," he told me softly.

"I couldn't sleep anymore, but I didn't want to wake you."

Gil sighed, sitting down beside me. "Wake me next time. After what I can assume you went through, I would rather be woken than panicked, seeing you gone."

I nodded and rested my head on his shoulder.

Leifur joined us then, silently sitting beside Óskar, one of the two people he knew understood him. That he knew would defend him if the others didn't welcome him with open arms. I sent him a small smile and nudged Aron to hand him a tankard.

Georg cleared his throat. "Speaking of what has happened while we were apart—we need to ensure that we are all on the same page before he returns to the fortress. Our return will be bad enough as it is."

My brows furrowed. "Bad enough as it is?" I echoed, confused.

"It hasn't been good," Aron said as he nodded grimly. "I'll get Rúna—we're only going to want to do this once."

I exchanged a dark look with Óskar and Leifur. None of us were ready to talk about what had happened to us. It was too fresh. We could give generalizations and an idea, but any specifics were out of the question.

Not now.

Rúna's clothes were creased, her blonde hair pulled into a messy ponytail. She shook her head at the offered tankard of tea and sat, her eyes on her hands.

"The fortress is volatile," Georg said.

"It was like that before we left," Óskar quipped.

Aron scoffed. "It's worse. We were ordered back to the fortress, and Rúna and her mother were punished for the treasonous act of hiding her brother away."

"You mean her dead mother and dead brother?" Óskar asked, his brows furrowed.

Rúna pursed her lips. "They were never dead. Just hidden." Óskar whistled lowly. "And the King Commander decided that he needed to be surer of where my loyalties lie, so you are looking at Baldur's betrothed."

"Oh, Rúna, no," I whispered. "Tell me there's a way out of this."

"Not right now, but we're working on it." She glanced up at me. "And Baldur's helping me."

"Ottó and his supporters have left the fortress, but he tried to level a blow to you before he did. He went after your mother," Gil told me. My face blanched, a knot of worry coiling in my stomach. "My sister and I stopped them. She is fine, better than when you left her."

I swallowed thickly, trying to process that the King Commander's actions had led to this. He had shown the whole fortress how vulnerable Ma was. He painted a target on her back, and Ottó went for it.

To get to me.

"Did you look for us?" Óskar rasped.

"We did everything we could but were forbidden from doing so. Kept virtually under lock and key," Georg said grimly. "What happened here?" He gestured between Óskar, Leifur, and I.

"He helped us. Slipped us food and water. He tried to warn us whenever his sister would visit us. He got us out. Kept us alive while we fled," I said.

"Why?" Aron asked, tilting his head as he studied Leifur.

Leifur wet his lips. "When I learned what my parents were doing, I was horrified. Disgusted. My two closest friends, Thea and Bayle, were at the heart of the conflict. They needed someone on the inside, someone they could trust. I had grown up with Bayle. I loved Thea. I was going to do whatever I needed to do, whatever they needed me to do, to end it."

Rúna's head jerked up towards him, causing him to tense, his eyes wide. "They became the Verndari. You helped the Verndari."

Leifur nodded slowly as though he was in shock. "You have her eyes," he whispered. "I've never forgotten them."

"She would have been my many times great grandmother," Rúna said softly, watching him curiously. "What do you plan to do?"

"I plan to finish what we started the first time. I plan to end my parents' reign of terror. For Drysden, but also for them. For *her*."

THIRTY-FIVE

BRYN

T he journey back to the fortress was painful, but it was a feeling that I welcomed. It was a pain showing that I had survived—that I was finally on my way back home.

I would see Fannar and Ma again.

I would be free again.

Or, at least, as free as I could be.

From what Gil and the others had told me, our freedoms and options at the fortress were now more limited than ever. The King Commander was more uncontrolled and unpredictable than ever.

That would be concerning at the best of times, but when we were rapidly approaching a war where my loved ones would be fighting on the front lines, where we would be bearing the brunt of the combat, it was terrifying. Óskar and I had seen what the exiled commanding family could do and had experienced their hospitality firsthand. There was no way we could allow them to win—no way that we could risk them regaining power over Drysden. Their own son stood against them for a reason.

But it was rapidly becoming clear that we couldn't allow the King Commander to win either.

I just didn't know how to ensure that both things were achieved whenever this war was over. Or how we would survive to the war's end when the King Commander seemed perfectly willing to leave Óskar and me to die.

There were limited options ahead of us, and all of them seemed like shit.

It was midday when we reached the fortress. Leifur wore a cloak Georg had given him; the hood pulled over his head to hide his face. Even though he was hidden, we still drew stares. Particularly Óskar and me as the courtyard fell silent, observing the state our bodies were returning in.

The stable hands were the only ones brave enough to approach us, taking our horses without a word. I slid from my horse with a wince, unwilling to show weakness by allowing Gil to help me down. We kept our heads high as we made our way into our wing.

I slumped onto one of the benches with a sigh, finally allowing my body to relax. Barking rang through the space around us as Yugar sprinted towards Óskar, jumping up in joy to be reunited.

Óskar gave a watery chuckle, sinking to his knees to wrap Yugar in a canine hug. "I missed you too," he murmured. "I missed you too."

"I'll go get the others," Aron murmured before slipping back out of our wing.

Gil sat beside me, allowing me to rest my head on his shoulder. Eventually, Óskar was able to separate himself from Yugar long enough to get himself onto the couch; Yugar quickly hopped up to join him, resting his muzzle on Óskar's leg.

The door burst open, and Fannar, Sofie and Luck poured into the room with Hákon and Ragna not far behind them.

And surprisingly, Baldur was the last of the party to join us, carefully shutting the door behind them.

Fannar blanched when he saw me, saw the story that my injuries painted on my body, but when I opened my arms, he gently pulled me into his own. "Gods, Bryn. Never again, you hear?"

"Trust me, I would be happy to never go through that again," I told him, causing Óskar to snort, no doubt in agreement.

The healers immediately approached us, Sofie's hands landing on my arm as Hákon reached for Óskar. Sofie's bloodrite flowed into my body, seeking every bruised, broken, and injured part of me. She cursed under her breath as she found every patch of pain I had, every mark and piece of evidence of what I had been through.

Sofie finally sat back, her eyes watery as she squeezed my hand. "There you go, as good as new."

I swallowed thickly, the feeling of being pain-free foreign. "Thank you," I told her before turning to where Leifur lingered on the edge of the group, his hood still over his head. "Can you take a look at him as well, please? He's the only reason Óskar and I got out."

"You can take your hood off," Rúna told him. "You can trust them."

"All of them?" Leifur asked. He had undoubtedly seen some of these people in Pétur and Sigrún's memories. He knew that three children of the King Commander stood in the room with him—the son of the exiled King Commander.

Rúna took a deep breath, her gaze lingering on Baldur for a moment. "Yes. I believe so."

He hesitated a moment longer before lowering his hood, his body tense. "Pleasure to meet you. My name is Leifur," he introduced himself stiffly.

Ragna gasped as Hákon blanched.

"Gods' bones," Baldur muttered. "I did not expect this."

Fannar tilted his head, approaching Leifur with his hand outstretched. "Based on how the others reacted, I feel like I should know your name, but it does not ring any bells. But anyone who helps my sister is good enough for me. A pleasure to meet you, I'm Fannar."

Leifur shook his hand. "Good tidings. I can provide a bit more context. My father is the exiled King Commander."

"Well, you guys certainly don't do anything small, do you?" Luck joked. "Get captured and taken who knows where and return with the enemy." He paused, studying Leifur for a moment. "Although, given that he helped you and is now standing here with us, I suppose son of the enemy would be more accurate."

Leifur nodded, "I'm with you."

"Then that's enough for me," Sofie said, reaching for his arm, her bloodrite flowing into his skin.

"Father is not going to like this," Baldur cautioned, leaning back against the wall and crossing his arms over his chest. "We will need to keep him relatively hidden until we can break the news to him. And I would do it sooner rather than later."

"It's a shame that you don't have another room in your wing. I would recommend that he stay here," Ragna said, slumping in a chair.

I turned to Gil and cocked a single brow. "We could open up a room for him," I whispered. "If we wanted to."

"If you are comfortable with that, I would be happy to. Yours or mine?" he murmured.

I rolled my eyes at him. "I wouldn't have suggested it if it wasn't okay with me. I prefer to stay in mine if that is alright?"

"It is perfect, darling." He pressed a kiss to my forehead.

"Care to fill the rest of us in on your little whispered conversation there, Talon?" Óskar nudged me with his foot.

"Gil and I will stay in my room, leaving Gil's free for Leifur. He can stay in our wing that way."

I left Gil and Leifur to move Gil's things into my room and get Leifur settled in the wing. Instead, I hurried through the hallways of the fortress on the familiar path to Ma's rooms.

Fannar walked by my side, his hands tucked into his pockets, but his eyes constantly scanned the area around us. Alert to any sign of a threat.

I knocked on Ma's door, bouncing on the balls of my feet. I didn't know if I would ever see her again, and to know that she had been targeted because of me—I needed to see her.

I needed to know that she was okay.

When the door opened, I didn't hesitate to throw myself at her. She froze for a moment, no doubt caught off guard before she wrapped her arm around me.

"Bryn, my girl," she whispered in my ear.

I jerked back in surprise, looking from Ma to Fannar, who was grinning, and back again. "Did you just *speak to me*?" My voice broke.

"I'm sorry it took so long," she said. "I am so proud of you, my girl. Your Da would be, too."

I threw myself back at her with a sob.

I don't know if I ever believed my ma would fully return to me. I was happy with every step she took, content that she was there even if she wasn't herself.

But to have her in front of me, aware and talking, felt like a gift from the gods.

～

GIL WAS READING by the fire when I returned to my—our—rooms later that night. I marked his page with a scrap of leather that he used just for that purpose and set aside his book. I climbed into his lap, straddling his legs and looping my arms around his shoulders.

He raised a brow as his hands landed on my legs, sliding from my hips, down my thighs to my knees and back up again. "Hello, darling."

"Did you know about Ma? When you said she was doing better than expected, did you know she could talk?"

He gave me a soft smile. "I did. She spoke to me after Klara and I stopped the attack on her. But I have learned that healing is not linear, and I did not want to get your hopes up if she still needed some time."

"Thank you again for saving her. I think that if she had to fight again, it truly would have broken her." I kissed him. "What did she say to you?"

His cheeks reddened, his eyes warm. "She said that I am a good man."

"She's right. You are one of the best men I know."

Gil ducked his head in the crook of my neck, dampness gathering there from his tears. "That is all that I have ever wanted to be."

I carded my fingers through his hair for a moment before raising his head so that he could see my eyes. See the honesty in them as I said, "That is what you have always been. How I have always seen you, Gil. How I always make sure people see you."

His lips crashed into mine, intense and driven even as the saltiness of his tears still clung to them. I met him movement for movement as his hands were feverish on my body.

Fully healed thanks to Sofie, no longer needing to be careful about causing me more pain.

He pulled back from me just long enough to tear my shirt over my head, throwing it over his shoulder before his lips landed on mine again.

Gil's hand tangled in my curls, coiling them around his fist as he positioned my head just how he liked it.

I gently pushed him back from me so that I could bare his own torso before pulling him close once again. He lifted me from his lap, pulling my pants down my legs before removing his own.

I climbed back onto his lap as his lips trailed down my throat, over my chest.

He lifted his head to lock eyes with me, a question lingering in their smouldering depths.

I nodded as my hands landed on his cheeks, pulling his lips back to mine as his fingers found me. They played me like an instrument, drawing out every gasp, every moan, as my toes curled and the pleasure within me spun tighter and tighter low in my stomach.

Right before that pleasure could burst, he pulled his fingers away, causing me to cry out.

Gil brushed a curl behind my ear, "I have you, darling," he murmured before joining us quickly.

Bursting that pleasure and driving it higher and higher as he continued to move.

When he finally found his end and stilled, he brushed a

kiss on my temple as he held me close to him for a few moments.

I brushed lazy kisses to any part of his skin I could reach before Gil gathered me in his arms and made his way through our rooms to our bed.

He laid me down on the furs, disappearing briefly before returning with a cloth. After wiping us both clean, he set aside the cloth and climbed into bed with me.

I shuffled towards him, draping a leg over one of his and an arm over his shoulder. I rested my head on Gil's chest, the strong, steady rhythm of his heart thumping under my ear. He coiled one of my curls around his finger before releasing it and doing it again.

"Are there protocols that Verndari must follow if they want to marry?" I asked Gil.

His fingers froze in my hair for a moment before continuing. "Yes. They submit a written request to the King Commander for him to approve. It is a formality, nothing more. I have never heard of it being rejected."

"Would you be willing to submit a letter to him with me?"

Gil gently shifted me so that he could sit up, leaning against the bed's headboard, and pulled me into his lap. "What has brought this up?" he asked softly.

"We responded to an attack on a homestead, and Óskar and I ended up being taken prisoner. We ended up tortured." My voice broke, but I cleared my throat and kept going, the words spilling from my mouth. "Darkness is coming, Gil. War is coming, and we will be right there on the front lines, where the fighting is thickest. We will be sent on the most dangerous missions; we will be the ones in the command tent making impossible decisions. And when we are facing down thousands of monsters and enemy warriors, when we are using our bloodrites so much that we are exhausted, wrung out like a rag, when we are standing on blood-stained fields splattered in a mixture of human and Skolli blood, I want to be able to look forward to the future. I want to walk into this war knowing that we have a future to fight for, that we have us to fight for, and that is waiting for us on the other side of the darkness. I want everyone to know how much we love each other, and I want to fight for it. Fight for a better tomorrow. Fight for a better future. To fight for us and what lies ahead for us." Gil's eyes were filled with love, with adoration. "Would you be willing to submit an official letter with me?"

Gil tucked a curl behind my ear before cupping my face in his hands. "I am not just willing to. I would be honoured beyond words to submit the letter with you. To tell the King Commander, to tell everyone, just how much I love you, darling. Let us get through the war; all I am and have is yours." He wiped away a tear from my eye with his thumb. "But when it comes time to turn this from a promise to a betrothal, I expect to be the one making the speech."

I pressed a kiss to his lips before resting my forehead on his. "You've always been quite careful with your words. Efficient. And you want to make the big fancy proposal?"

"For you, the words are infinite."

THE FIRST THING we did the next morning was summon a servant to deliver our letter to the King Commander. We had sat up together by the fire, furs bundled over our laps and bodies as we wrote the letter together. Each word, every sentence, was carefully selected to convey exactly what we wanted them to.

Luckily, Georg gave Óskar and me the morning off training to allow our bodies to fully heal, so we played fetch with one of Yugar's balls in the training hall while the others worked with Leifur. Now that he had thrown his lot in with ours, we saw him as one of us. He wasn't a Verndari, but he was as close to us as he could get, like Luck or Fannar.

And we needed to ensure he could keep up with us on the battlefield.

I had seen moments of his abilities as we fled, but now he was facing off the best warriors I knew, and he was winning. Against all of them. At once.

While his bloodrite wasn't necessarily designed for combat, his fighting definitely was.

And he had spent hundreds of years honing his skills to make him lethal. After all, what else was there for him to do locked away in that fortress with his family?

He was sandwiched between Georg and Aron as we made our way to lunch, both picking his brain about his various techniques for countless weapons.

One of the King Commander's warriors awaited us in the common rooms. "You all need to come with me," he told us. "Now."

Óskar groaned, "Dammit, I was hungry."

"That's what you're concerned about right now?" Rúna rolled her eyes.

"Trust me, you ate enough of what we did the past several days, and you would be dreaming of food, too."

Leifur winced. "I slipped them what I could, but what they were given was gruesome."

We were silent as we followed the warrior to the King Commander's office. The warrior didn't knock; he simply opened the door, stood aside long enough for us to enter, and shut it behind us. We sank into bows and waited for the King Commander to give us permission to rise.

He took his time.

And when he did, his eyes were full of fire.

"I thought I had made myself quite clear that you should not leave the fortress. My needs outweigh your needs. My ruling outweighs your ruling." He held up a hand as Georg went to speak. "I understand that you were given royal permission to depart—I will deal with that later. What I need to deal with now is who you brought back."

"I can vouch for him, King Commander," I said, my voice strong.

"So can I," Óskar added.

The King Commander's chuckle lacked any sign of humour. "Oh yes, the word of the weakest of the Verndari and the girl seeking to undermine me. I am not about to bend over backwards to believe you."

"I worked against my parents before. I will work against them now as well," Leifur said.

"Forgive me if I don't believe a person who should have died hundreds of years ago, who has been living in the mountain fortress with the enemy and traitors."

Leifur took a deep breath, glancing over at Óskar and me briefly before refocusing on the King Commander. "How can I prove to you where my loyalty lies?"

"I've recently discovered a proven way to ensure people's lives are intertwined with my country. Haven't I, Rúna?" the King Commander said, a sadistic smirk crossing his face.

"You want him to marry Ragna?" she asked, shocked.

The King Commander leaned forward, bracing his arms on the table. "You misunderstand me, girl. I said intertwining him with my country, not my family. He is too much of a gamble to tie him to the Chieftain of the Striking Shadows. But there is another group of people, almost as intrinsic to the operation of this country as my family." My stomach roiled, threatening to rebel. "And considering that you are already betrothed to my son, that leaves us with one option." He turned to me, his eyes alight with a sick gleam in his eyes. "The only way Leifur will be allowed to join us, the only way he will be allowed to live, is if he marries Brynja."

THIRTY-SIX

BRYN

My body went rigid as my mind went blank.

Surely, he hadn't said what I thought he said. Just last night, Gil and I poured our heart out in our letter, and just this morning, we had a maid deliver it.

Maybe he hadn't received it. Maybe he hadn't read it.

"Bryn and I submitted an official request to marry this morning," Gil said, his face tight. "Did you not receive it?"

The King Commander shifted through the parchments on his desk and lifted a folded piece that had been sealed with both our family crests. The seals were broken.

"You mean this?" The King Commander held it up. "I received it. I read it, and I dismissed it."

I swallowed thickly, scrambling for something to say. Something to keep this from happening. "It was my understanding that the letter is nothing more than a formality."

"It still requires my approval, which you will not receive."

I shifted my weight between my feet and locked my hands behind my back to hide their shaking. "I am not a member of your family. I am the head of my household, so you would require my agreement to the betrothal."

The King Commander leaned back in his chair with a grin. "Oh ho, the timid girl has finally grown claws."

I lifted my chin. "I've had claws for far longer than you think."

"And yet, this is the first time you have shown me them." The King Commander tilted his head. "But you forget that I hold all the power here, you stupid, naive girl."

Óskar shifted closer to me, his heat warming my body. In support of whatever was about to play out.

"King Commander?" Georg questioned; whether he was trying to discover the threat he was making or to draw his attention from me, I didn't know, but I appreciated it either way.

"If she does not agree to be betrothed to Leifur, he will die. I cannot trust him otherwise. But I am not an uncaring man. I am willing to make her decision easier. I will remove any potential...distractions."

The King Commander stood from his desk, our letter still in his hand, and prowled towards me until the toes of his boots almost hit mine.

"Let me make it quite clear to you how this will play out. If you continue to be difficult regarding this simple request, I will remove your beau from the picture. Plenty of special rooms are reserved just for his family in the bowels of the fortress, and I will be more than willing to send him where he belongs."

Rúna gasped.

I stiffened, rolling my shoulders back and glaring at the King Commander. "Those cells are for people consumed by darkness. Gil has his under control. He can't be sent there."

"You will find, girl, that there is no limit to what I can and can't do. I will not hesitate to send him to those dungeons if it gets me what I want. And if you continued to refuse me, then I would see Leifur killed."

My chin quivered, so I pressed my lips together to try and hide it from the King Commander. To hide how his threats affected me.

Hide just how well he knew me, how well he knew how to hurt me.

After everything Leifur did for Óskar and me, for getting us out of that hellhole, for fighting with us now, I could not allow him to die. I could not repay his kindness, his courage, and the risks he took by condemning him to an unwarranted execution by a power-hungry tyrant.

And there was no way I was going to allow Gil to be subjected to his nightmares, for him to be locked away in the prison cell that he had seen as his future for too long.

I would sacrifice far more than my happiness to ensure he was never subjected to that fate.

"I'll do it," I bit out, each word fracturing my heart until it was nothing more than pieces in my chest.

The King Commander grinned, showing every one of his teeth. "How wonderful." He stalked back to his desk, leaning against it as he threw our letter at my feet. "Burn it."

I glanced towards the ceiling as though the gods could give me strength before I bent down and picked up the letter. We had been so hopeful and excited as we wrote it last night.

And that happiness was gone, nothing more than a memory, like our letter would be.

I glanced down the line of my friends, my family, to lock eyes with Gil. He took a deep breath and gave me a single nod.

He understood.

He supported what he knew was going to happen.

I took wooden step after wooden step to the fireplace, taking one last look at the letter before closing my eyes and tossing the letter into the flames.

Turning it into nothing more than ash.

~

I DIDN'T HESITATE to flee from the room when we were finally dismissed. As much as I didn't want the King Commander to know that he got to me, that he finally pulled one over on me, I couldn't stand to be in that room a second longer than I had to. I couldn't look that evil man in the eye and play good little Verndari for a moment longer.

My foundation was shaken, my heart broken, and my hopes for the future were nothing but dust in the wind.

I crashed into mine and Gil's rooms, pacing the floor, my fingers tangled in my curls. Pulling, tears falling as I tried to come to terms with what had just happened.

Suddenly, Gil was there, gently pulling me to a stop as his hands landed on my cheeks.

"Darling," he murmured, brushing the tears from my cheeks, but more replaced them. "We will fight it. It is not over yet."

"How?" I sobbed, balling my hands in his shirt. "How will we fight it? He will hold this over our heads as long as he is in power, ready to order us to the altar whenever it suits him. Whenever it hurts us the most."

"Until you and Leifur swear your oaths to each other, there is hope. Baldur is trying to get Rúna out of theirs—the fact that he is trying means that he thinks there is a chance. If there is a chance for them, there is a chance for us."

I tucked my head into his chest and allowed myself to sob

—allowed myself to break—knowing that he was there. He would let me fall apart and help me piece myself back together.

Gil led us to the benches, gathering me in my lap as he whispered soothing noises in my ear, tracing designs on my back with his fingers. Eventually, my sobs eased to sniffles, and Gil pulled back enough that he could wipe away the traces of my despair with a handkerchief.

"One of your greatest strengths is your heart, but when manipulated by someone, it is the easiest way to get you to do what they want. Even if the King Commander doesn't know what Leifer did to help you, he knew the second he threatened me that he could back you into a corner."

"I would never let him lock you away, Gil," I whispered.

"I know. It is one of the reasons that I love you. But the King Commander is not afraid to manipulate us like puppets, and he knows just what string to pull to get you to dance to his tune. If he had threatened you, I would have done the same thing."

I sniffled. "What do we do?"

A hesitant knock sounded before the door cracked open enough for Leifur to poke his head in. "May I come in?"

"Of course," I said with a nod, shifting off of Gil's lap but interlacing my fingers with his.

Leifur sank into a couch in front of us with a sigh. "I'm sorry. I'm so fucking sorry."

"This is not your fault any more than it is hers." Gil's voice was soft. "We all know exactly who to blame for this."

"I should thank you for not letting me die," Leifur joked.

I chuckled wetly. "I'm just returning the favour."

We were silent for a moment, lost in our minds and thoughts. The King Commander's verdict didn't just affect

Leifur and me; it affected all three of us. We should deal with it all together.

"What do we do?" I asked, echoing my question to Gil earlier.

"We try to get out of it," Leifur said softly. "You two don't have to change anything. Keep acting how you normally would. At least until—" he cut himself off.

Gil swallowed. "Until you swear your oaths to each other," he finished for Leifur.

Leifur's lips twisted together. "Yes. We don't just swear those oaths to each other; we also swear them to the gods, and I wouldn't want to break those."

"I understand," I said softly, my heart squeezing painfully. "I respect that. I agree with that."

"Until then, we will do everything we can to find a way out of this."

Gil nodded. "Together."

THIRTY-SEVEN

BRYN

Fannar and I had a long discussion about how much to tell Ma. Neither of us was fully aware of how much she understood, how much she had comprehended, while she wasn't herself. Neither of us was sure if filling her in would set her back if she would revert to not speaking.

Or worse.

Ultimately, we decided that she was an adult—it was her choice. And only she could decide how much she could handle.

The next morning, we set out for her rooms together. When she opened the door and saw us, her eyes lit up.

"Bryn. Fannar. Come in, come in." She grinned, stepping aside to let us in.

I was happy to see that when she shut the door behind us, she ensured it was locked. Someone must have made a point to tell her to be extra safe.

Or, perhaps, she had made the decision herself after being attacked.

"Hi, Ma," Fannar kissed her cheek before sitting on the

couch. I echoed his movements, leaving Ma to sit in her favourite chair by the window.

"What do I owe this surprise to?" Ma asked, pulling a blanket over her lap with her hand.

Fannar and I exchanged a look. "A lot has happened since the attack on Ebonwell, Ma. And a lot more is going to happen. You being attacked was only the first bit." I took a deep breath. "Do you want us to tell you what has happened and what is approaching? Are you strong enough to handle it?"

"I remember bits and pieces of what has happened between now and then, but not enough to understand. And I want to understand. I'm sorry to both of you for having to go through this alone. For not being there when you needed me," she leaned forward, squeezing my hand before patting Fannar on the leg. "I didn't handle the loss of your da well. I needed time to heal. But now that I'm back, I never intend to go anywhere again. And I will be with you through whatever is coming. So please, tell me. I can handle it."

So, we did.

We told her everything.

From learning that I was a Verndari, arriving at the fortress, and competing for my position. From Fannar training with the Royal Regiment to swearing his oaths with them.

The barrier, the traitors, the monsters.

What we faced at Wolfmire, how close it came for us, what Óskar and I faced at the mountain fortress.

Everything.

Every bloody, painful, joyous, love-filled moment between the attack on our village to now. And forward to the war breathing down our necks, the danger we were all in.

Ma was quiet for a long moment when we finished, her

eyes drifting back and forth between us. "You have both been so strong, so brave. Da would have been so proud."

"We have tried to do what we thought was right. What would keep others from suffering how we did," Fannar said as he wrapped an arm around my shoulders.

"And the Verndari? Your brother? Leifur?" she asked.

"I trust them with everything I have," I told her softly.

She gave me a soft smile as she nodded. "Then I will do the same." She leant back in her chair, crossing her legs, her eyes razor sharp. "Now tell me—how can I help?"

When we were done visiting with Ma, I immediately went to find Gil. I found him in the training room by himself, running through sword drills Leifur had shown him. His shirt was soaked with sweat; his hair brushed back from his eyes because of it.

I leaned against the wall, more than happy to watch him move. The pure poetry that came from his body—his swords an extension of himself. He spun, ducked, swung, and blocked with such fluidity, such grace as though it were a dance.

He came to a stop, his chest heaving. "Are you going to stand there and stare at me the whole time, darling?"

"I was enjoying the view," I quipped as I pushed off the wall and approached where he stood in front of the windows.

"I am sure I have looked better than I do now," Gil said as he sheathed his blades.

"It certainly isn't your worst look."

Gil quirked a brow at me but said nothing else as we stared out the window to the thawing grounds beyond, to the spring breaking through the frozen cold.

"How did your mother take it?" he finally asked.

"Better than I expected, but she first asked us how she

could help. How am I supposed to protect her if she is going to insert herself in the centre of it?"

"You cannot." He took a deep breath. "My sisters are going to help, too. Regardless of how far I want to keep them from this conflict, they will be right there with us."

I leaned into his side as he wrapped an arm around me. "How are we supposed to keep them safe?"

"We cannot. They will be just as affected as us if we were to lose. If they want to fight for their futures with us, how are we supposed to stop them?"

I sighed. "You're right. But what if they get hurt? What if they die?"

"Then they get hurt. Then they die." Gil turned to face me. "And it will hurt us too. It will change our lives. But all we can do is give them the best chance at survival. And even though we will be fighting where it is thickest, that best chance lies with us. With our friends."

"And us? Where does our best chance lie?"

"With each other."

THE HIDDEN ROOM in the library was filled wall to wall with our allies.

Ragna and Gier stood side by side, their eyes sharp as they followed the conversation. Hákon and Lúdvík stood together on the opposite side of the room from where Baldur and Leifur chatted with their heads close together. Sofie, Fannar, Luck, Aron, and Jarl Einar stood grouped, Luck and Fannar's heads tossed back in laughter as Aron blushed. I stood with Gil, Óskar, and Rúna as Yugar sprawled at our feet.

Georg finally called us to order from where he sat beside

Ísak. "Thank you all for coming today. Some of you have met Leifur and heard his story. For those of you who have not, what you need to know for this conversation is, Leifur is the son of the exiled King Commander, and that is why Bryn and Óskar are here today. We trust him. And he has information to share."

"My parents have not wasted any time in gaining resources and supporters. The mountain fortress that once held only the four of us, six when Pétur and Sigrún joined us, holds countless warriors and far more monsters. My sister, Pétur and I had been sent out on various expeditions to gain supporters and supplies, and many of my parents' old supporters have realigned themselves with them once again.

"Whole towns and larger settlements have even become secondary headquarters for my parents' cause—one of the most notable being Northhold."

Óskar leaned close to me. "Saw that one coming."

I scoffed. "Writing was on the wall with that one. I wouldn't be surprised if they had sworn their allegiance while we were camped outside their gates." My voice was quiet enough that only those around me heard.

"The war is coming, and it is coming fast. It was brutal and bloody last time, and my parents and sister have nothing they are not willing to do to regain their power. It is going to be dark; it is going to be gruesome, and people are going to die. And you don't have me on the inside feeding you information this time."

"It is going to be another Great War," Ízak said, running his hand down his beard. "Gods save us all."

"There's a large difference between this war and the last," Luck added. "Last time, there was a clear 'good' side. There was evil, and the people who were fighting against it. We have a poisonous viper leading the 'good' team this time, and when we win, we re-cement his grasp on power."

Aron nodded. "That's why we're here. We are all well aware of both sides' threat and must devise a plan to address both issues properly."

"Power has corrupted the King Commander. He is now nothing more than a tyrant, taking joy in abusing his power and playing with his subjects as though they are nothing more than puppets," Jarl Einar spat.

He had never been a fan of the King Commander. There was a reason that he had sworn his allegiance to me instead.

But it was becoming obvious that what he had seen in the fortress since his arrival had done nothing but reinforce his thoughts about the King Commander.

"Not to mention his meddling in our lives to achieve his goals," Rúna added softly. "It started with Baldur and I, followed by Bryn and Leifur. Who's next? What's next?"

Ragna nodded; her lips pursed. "My father has always been a cruel man. He has now become a dangerous man. We need him and the forces he controls to defeat the exiled commanding family, but we cannot allow him to continue to rule like this."

"Then what do we do?" Hákon asked the room.

Baldur stepped forward, his face grim. "We all know exactly what we have to do." He clenched his jaw, his eyes darting between his siblings before refocusing on the others in the room. "We ensure that he cannot continue to rule. We kill the King Commander."

ACKNOWLEDGMENTS

Screams of Shadows has been my escape from the real world, a form of therapy for me as I dealt with the sudden passing of my dog. I have always been able to escape into the pages of a book whenever I needed—this was the first time that I did so while writing.

While writing this book may have been an escape for me, it also turned into everything that I wanted for the next instalment of Bryn's story. My incredible team ensured that it was.

Samantha from Ravens Wing Editing Services has worked with me for every book of the Nightmares of Nightfall series and she has made sure that Screams of Shadows is as strong as it can be. Thank you for your encouragement and support—the reactions you have as you go through my draft always make me smile.

My incredible map maker, Rachael from Cartographybird, transported Drysden from my mind to the page with the most breathtaking map.

The MiblArt team have, as always, created the perfect cover for Screams of Shadows. It is such a joy to have you bring Bryn to live in this way.

To my family and friends, thank you for your never ending support. You theories, and your desperation for the next instalment, makes writing exciting.

To my dog who inspired Yugar, thank you for being my

companion for so many years, for being my silent writing partner when I set out to write my first book. While you may no longer be here with me, you still live on in the pages of these stories—shamelessly begging for food and playing endless games of fetch with Óskar.

And thank you, dear reader, for continuing to read Bryn's story. It has been so fun weaving the story threads together as we explore not just Bryn and Gil's romance, but the war nipping at their heels. We are getting close to the finale and I cannot wait to share the next one with you.

ABOUT THE AUTHOR

Aspen Sherwood is a self-published author from Southwestern Ontario who loves all things fantasy and romance. As a 20-something herself, she loves writing about 20 year olds who are exploring their worlds and discovering themselves just like she is. When Aspen is not writing she can be found cheering on the Toronto Maple Leafs or the Toronto Blue Jays.

Follow Aspen Sherwood on TikTok (@aspen.sherwood), Instagram (@aspensherwood) on Facebook (Aspen Sherwood), or by joining her email list on her website (www.aspensherwood.com).

www.ingramcontent.com/pod-product-compliance
Lightning Source LLC
Chambersburg PA
CBHW060608030726
47498CB00005B/1589